Choosing
Choosing
Choos

OUT OF LINE: WHO DEFINES?

OUT OF LINE: WHO DEFINES?

HALFS, STEPS, IN-LAWS & BELONGING

Heather Tosteson & Charles D. Brockett
Editors

Wising Up Press

Catalogue-in-Publication data is on file with the Library of Congress.
LCCN: 2024939953

Wising Up ISBN: 978-1-7376940-8-3

Wising Up Press
P.O. Box 2122
Decatur, GA 30031-2122
www.universaltable.org

sought
seeking
wanted
haunted

Contents

IV. STEPS

PARENTS

adore
implore
adore
explore
ignore
escape
hope

HEATHER TOSTESON

INTRODUCTION
OUT OF LINE: WHO DEFINES?
THE ORIGINS OF OUR SENSE OF BELONGING

THE LARGER PICTURE: BELONGING

Belonging can be defined as a subjective feeling that one is an integral part of their surrounding systems, including family, friends, school, work environments, communities, cultural groups, and physical places (Hagerty et al., 1992).

We often put out a call to expand our own range of experience around an issue of sustained personal interest. Belonging and families certainly is one of those issues. By the responses to our call, we have found, to our edification and relief, we are by no means alone.

I think about our sense of belonging often. What is it composed of exactly? Where does that feeling state come from? What expands it? Constricts it? Is it constructed—or received? Why is it so important to each of us— whether we consciously acknowledge that or not? Is a sense of belonging an emergent phenomenon—one that can't be explained by the structures that preceded it, indeed is qualitatively different from those structures? Are families so important to us because that is where the experience originates— or where we're told it should?

The question is personally salient to us. Charles and I married in our late forties and early fifties, our children to our minds young adults (although they might debate this). Both of us were divorced. The habits and expectations of our different family systems—both with long histories of loss—didn't mesh smoothly. At all. For more years than I like to recall, the two of us argued intensely and often, in the particular and also in the abstract, about what we owed our young adults. It was amazing how such atavistic energies could rise between us when there was, truly, no one else there but our ghosts and our outdated good intentions. Who were we trying to protect? How? Why? From what? Our adult children were all living on their own, creating their own families, so calling ourselves stepparents felt to all of us inaccurate. We would never live under one roof. There was no need for primal care. On the other hand, all our newly adult children definitely felt they had lost something crucial with our marriage, a grounding, a necessary centrality. All our ideas of family, the habits we had developed in each complicated family system to savor our joys and to temper the pain of great losses, had to shift, willingly or unwillingly.

I think we would now describe ourselves as four distinct family units with strong affection, respect, and commitments to mutual care—with familial myths that often don't mesh but shape our lives deeply all the same. There is a certain primal experience of belonging, however fraught it may have been, that will never return. On the other hand, over the last quarter century, honoring and supporting these separate familial systems has created another sense of cohesion.

However, these early experiences of belonging remain core for each of us. What now supports and defines a sense of belonging is as distinctive as each of the individuals involved. And keeps needing to be refined because these questions are restless. They keep rearing their heads when we least expect them, like prairie dogs. However befuddled, or undermined, we may feel by their incessant reappearance, we do know we are not alone. The many responses to our anthology call prove it.

FAMILY STRUCTURES AND OUR SENSE BELONGING

The phrasing of this invitation—Out of Line: Who Defines?: Halfs, Steps, In-Laws & Belonging—raises the question of what at this point in history defines our societal norms for family. Although we explain relationships in families in implicit reference to biological nuclear family units, these constellations are becoming less common.

Clearly all the ambiguities and complexities of blended families are here to stay. Between 1960 and 2014 the number of children living in nuclear families dropped from 73% to 42%, 15% lived with two parents in remarriage, 26% in single parent families (Pew 2015). In the 2020 Census, one in six children under the age of eighteen were living with a half-sibling; 10.5 million children in the US were living in residential stepfamilies.

Can we, or should we, even with our changing norms, relinquish the biological family unit as our basic referent? Do these implicit references distort other experiences of family—not only for outside observers but for participants as well? Do they imply that the circumstances in which these other families have formed are essentially inferior?

The general social assumption in a biological family (of one or two parents) is that its core purpose is the care and well-being of the children the parent/s have chosen to have. This is also true of adoption. But no other familial constellation has the care and well-being of the children as a socially sanctioned fundamental biological "right" in such a way as a nuclear family.

An important difference between the archetypal biological family (with one or two biological parents) and other forms of family are that the other family forms have at their heart an experience of loss—whether through death, divorce, abandonment.

Adoption is based on an implicit complex of wantedness and unwantedness, especially for the child. Someone brought them into being who would not—or could not—nurture them. This reality of loss becomes part of their experience of wantedness by the adoptive parent or parents. The welcome has an inevitable undertow.

Stepfamilies came into being because of the desires of the couple as a couple. The children of the original family lack choice and also the assurance of "biological" centrality in this new unit. Half-siblings, living in the same household or outside it, also embody this contingent reality. All these other familial constellations deprive the children in them of a certain traction and centrality that sociological assumptions about nuclear families reinforce.

In biologically nuclear families, we are free to have expectations of care from our parents that are societally reinforced. Ones that make us, as children, central. We are the family's raison-d'être. They chose to have us. Which means they chose to have what comes with that decision: our full complexity! There's solid ground that comes with that assumption.

This whole question of who defines "the" family takes on another dimension with in-laws. So often we forget that choosing a partner is not actually an intimate choice done in social isolation. We are also choosing to become, for better or worse, part of another family system that does not have our centrality at its heart. There seems to be a level of indignation or shock in many of our in-law stories and poems—as if people did not see this coming. Certainly, it reactivates questions about belonging—for everyone concerned.

COMPANIONS ON THE JOURNEY

One story from my son's childhood has always stayed with me. It involved his place in my layered family of origin. I was the first child of my father, the second of my mother, who had been married previously. My parents divorced when I was seventeen. The following year my father married his graduate student. Stepmother never seemed an appropriate term given our ten-year-age difference. I married at eighteen and started my own household. The two children of my father's second family and my own son were all born within a twelve-month period. This made for interesting dynamics between those children—especially about what constituted the "real" family. Was it, for my son, the stories told by my three sibs and me? Or the stories the children of my father's second "nuclear" family told each other? At some point my father's children told my son that their father's first marriage to his grandmother had been made under duress, the unhappy result of a reluctant promise their father had made to a dying patient. I believe my son then told them an equally deprecating story, perhaps the story of *his* grandmother discovering *their* mother fondling *his* grandfather in his office. When I asked him why he had shared this, he said, "I'm just so tired of their trying to prove that I have no right to exist."

Growing up, I often might not have wanted to be part of my biological family of origin. The dynamics were exhausting. But I never doubted I had a "right to exist." But this doubt is one that many of the writers in this anthology wrestle with. It is intimately intertwined with their sense of belonging. The costs of a precarious, conditional sense of inclusion—wherever we encounter it—are deep, painful, deforming. Belonging is about feeling wanted, essential, at home, not about sameness. So acknowledging the costs of that ambiguity about belonging and the gift of our own existence and the gifts we may have unexpectedly received from our atypical families as normal is a crucial first step in developing an accurate and resilient sense of belonging.

WHAT WE HAVE HERE

We hope you enjoy the works of the thirty-nine talented authors you find here. We certainly have found the experience of reading and selecting illuminating, poignant, and, above all, hopeful.

We have organized the anthology in a way that concentrates on blended family structures from specific vantage points: halves, adoptions, steps in all roles (parents, grandparents, children), and in-laws. The opening and closing sections emphasize how common—and various—the experiences of blended families now are.

There is a big difference between being an adult agent of change or a child recipient of this change. Accurately describing the emotional reality of our relationships in ways that feel true to our own experience of them is challenging and liberating. If we are agents of change, we start filled with a sense of self-determination and hope. And then the reality hits that we are none of us islands, that our great personal joy may not be shared by those impacted by it, nor are we able to draw on conventional definitions of family or persuade others to justify our choices. All of this requires that we chart new ways to something that feels like genuine belonging, not just for us but for those around us.

The reintroduction of choice is an important dimension in many of these stories. And those choices sometimes involve reconsidering the structure of relations we thought we wanted. For example, discovering a large intensely interactive and networked biological family eager to take us in may not be what we, raised happily in a small, adopted family, are ready for, however attractive the idea in the abstract. In a number of the stories we find here, choice involves giving oneself freedom to refuse more conventional expectations, or take them on by honestly asking: Do I want to be a step-grandmother? Do I want to be both unofficial mother-in-law and grandmother to the young girl my son never married and his child? Do I want to carry on the divisions of the family I married into, or stop ostracizing my father-in-law's second wife? In other stories, accepting how we have been shaped—for better or worse—by the choices of those around us leads to a deeper sense of centrality and grounding.

The opening and closing sections of the anthology, both of which we title Melting Pots, focus on how prevalent non-nuclear families are—and the choices that help us respond to them as the common, but exceedingly complex, reality they are. In both sections, this question of belonging is salient. Do we find belonging where we thought we would? Dare we create it? Claim it where others might not see it?

The next section, Halfs, focuses on half-siblings. These stories felt qualitatively different from the other selections. There was an openness to the mystery of biological connections that may not be reflected in the larger family system. Choosing to connect with a half-sibling who was not part of the family structure put the writers into an agentic position, allowing them to make their own decisions about the nature of the relationships, their own sense of relatedness, family.

The selections in the Adoption section differ between whether one is adopting or being adopted. For adoptive parents, there is a sense of choice, just as there is with biological parents. One is choosing to love and raise this child as your own—and that choice, in its surprise and ambiguities—is very like that of birth parents. The points of view of those adopted are more reactive, coming to terms with choices that were made for them rather than by them.

We separated the selections in the section Steps into parents, grandparents, and children. The accounts by stepparents are valiant and a little shell-shocked by the astonishing will and pushback they receive from their children. What is striking as well is the daunting complexities of bringing different family systems, each with its distinct history of loss, into connection with each other. Having had a positive experience of being step-parented oneself grounds some of the most challenging situations.

The role of step-grandparents is an interesting one, whether it is a choice to some extent imposed on you by circumstances or one that is chosen. Whether that choice is perceived as choice has much to do with the teller of the story, child or grandparent. These two stories span a half-century, so make it clear that the blended family is not in actuality a recent construct, although the reasons for it might be.

The selections concerning stepchildren are appreciative, all told from the distance of adulthood. The most poignant has to do with the very different responses of a loving stepdaughter and an alienated and exploitive biological son to an ailing father.

The section Exes & In-Laws explores, often humorously, how people negotiate the intricacies of finding their own place within different family systems, as a daughter-in-law, an ex-wife. Some also deal with the regret of having refused to engage with extended families, seeing them as threats rather than as potential supports, or the pain of having one's loyalty disregarded.

The photographs I created for this anthology play with all the pattern reversals that go with our changing understandings of family. I chose to work with plants because of the feelings we have in these situations of being uprooted—or seeking solid ground. I used color reversals for similar reasons. The words in the background that appear and reappear in different combinations are ones that felt like some of the floating, fluctuating definitions of stories still in progress.

≽✿≼

We hope you bring your own experiences of family, the ones you were raised in and the ones you have helped create—nuclear, adopted, blended, step, and in-law—to bear as you read. We hope you can also share the book, use it as a way of deepening discussions you may have with family members—near and distant, in all kinds of permutations—about belonging.

Reference
Pew Research Center, "The American Family Today," December 17, 2015. Web.

I
MELTING POTS

DEBORAH BARRETT

THE FIRST MEETING

When we walked toward the door to Jim's birth mother's house for the first time, he turned toward me with prayer hands, his signal to say a prayer for us. His apprehension over meeting his birth mom for the first time had increased on the flight from Houston and the bus ride to the outskirts of New York City. I felt uneasy as well. I knew his mom must be as full of anticipation as I knew Jim to be. Also, I worried about capturing their initial moments together without intruding. Jim wanted me to record it, so I planned to do so but hoped to keep the video camera as much out of view as possible. The stories I had read about a child's first encounter with birth parents depicted some going well and some not so well.

I put this meeting in motion by encouraging Jim to find his birth family, for health reasons, if for no other, since he was in his fifties. Neither of us succeeded in locating his relatives, so we hired Pamela, a specialist in finding adopted children and their parents, recommended by the New York Foundling Hospital, which we had stumbled upon on one of our many rambling walks around New York City. The research took her longer than usual, but she called us in six weeks to tell us she had found his birth mom and contacted her to find out for sure before arranging a call between Jim and his mom, Rennie.

Rennie told me later she was suspicious, but Pamela had her first name and maiden name, the name of her high school, and her nickname, "Rennie." Also, she asked her if she knew a Kitty (Jim's father's sister) and if the name "James Jeffrey" meant anything to her. Pamela knew Rennie had the right person and told her Jim was looking for her but did not want anything but to talk to her. After her conversation with Rennie, Pamela told her to call her back if she wanted to talk to him. Rennie said she hung up and was "an emotional wreck." She wanted to talk to Joe, her husband, but he was asleep, and she knew it was too late to call her daughters, so she tried to sleep but stayed awake all night, thinking and crying.

Rennie was still afraid to be too assured, but she was beginning to believe that whoever this Pamela was, this James Jeffrey was the son she had given up over fifty years ago. Rennie called Pamela back the next morning and asked her to arrange the call. Rennie was scheduled for a medical procedure the day before the call and panicked that something might go wrong, and she would never talk to Jim. She was tortured with the fear he would think she had rejected him again. The day after the procedure, she called, and I recorded the conversation. They were both halting at first, which was unusual for Jim since I had witnessed how easily he talked to strangers. Rennie's voice was so soft that I did not catch all of what she said, but it seemed that soon they were conversing like they already knew each other. She invited us to visit her as soon as possible, and the reunion was set for a month later. Rennie was about to meet her firstborn son.

When we walked in, I stood back recording the two of them as they moved toward each other. A flush moved into Rennie's cheeks, and she took a deep breath as she tried to speak. She stepped closer toward him. "Jim," she said, struggling to get his name past her lips. She moved closer and wrapped her arms around him. He wrapped his arms around her for the first time. They clung to each other as if letting go would mean the other would vanish again. Jim's shoulders shook, his sobs in unison with hers. When they separated, I saw how much they looked alike, both with blue eyes and a flushed, freckled complexion. He had Irish written all over him, as did she, so unlike the German family who had adopted Jim when he was eighteen months old.

Rennie told me later that at that moment, all she could think about was him as her baby, the baby boy she held for such a short time before the nuns at the New York Foundling Hospital took him away. His birth was still vivid in her memory. I imagined her parents, Irish Catholics living in the Bronx at the time, telling her, "You cannot keep him. You are only in high school. What will people say?" She said she had lived her life with this tremendous secret and felt a massive weight of regret and embarrassment over being unmarried and pregnant.

In the fifties, being pregnant before marriage usually meant hiding the mother away from the public eye. As we know today from the stories about homes for unwed Irish Catholic mothers, the custom was to remove the child from the mother right after she gave birth. Rennie told me that when she saw the movie *Philomena*, she felt it was her story. Philomena spent fifty years looking for her son, whom the nuns had removed from her and given up for adoption without her being able to tell him goodbye. Rennie recalled the nuns telling her she had to let her son go. She was too young to care for him, and giving him up for adoption would mean he would have a better home.

After all these years, she still asked herself, why'd she let them make her give him up? She worried Jim would not forgive her for leaving him fifty years ago. She wanted to keep him, but her family was adamant. She was so young and had no means to care for herself, much less a baby. She sneaked back to the hospital days later to see him, planning to steal him away with her. Where they would go, she did not know, but they would be together. The nuns told her he had been moved to a foster home. She went back again, desperate and determined to take him with her, but the nuns told her he had been adopted. They would not tell her by whom. Her baby was gone.

All she had left were memories she had hidden from everyone all these years. She told Joe and told her daughters and one son when they were teenagers about getting pregnant as a teenager but said nothing else to them about Jim. She did not tell her son Larry or her five granddaughters. Rennie had celebrated Jim's birthdays by herself every year since his birth, quietly praying for his health and happiness wherever he was. She had spent many hours wondering what had happened to him.

As a young woman living in New York City, she would stare at groups of children, hoping to see a red-headed boy and hearing someone call out "Jim." She talked to a private detective, but he said he did not do that kind of work. She went to a psychotherapist a few times, but he told her it was best for her not to pursue it anymore. "Just let it go," he said, as if it would be that easy. Later, she used the Internet but found no clue where he was or who had him.

She was embarrassed to tell her family about a baby born out of wedlock when she was a teenager. With him entering her life, she met with each child and grandchild and told them her story. All were understanding and sympathetic, except for Larry, Jim's full brother and her oldest, at least until Jim came along. Larry was not too sure how he felt and told me later that he had no idea he had a full brother and thought he was the oldest of four children. Although Rennie told Larry about his birth father when he was old enough to understand, he said he did not want to meet him and never had anything to do with him, and he didn't know Jim existed. He was skeptical of who Jim was and was not accepting of him at first. Rennie told me later that telling Larry and her granddaughters was some of the most difficult conversations she had to prepare her family to meet Jim.

When all the children met Jim and lined up for their first photo together, Larry and Jim could have been twins. His half-brother Carl and his half-sisters Kim and Tricia resembled each other with brownish hair and green eyes, taller than Rennie, although they all looked like her in their features. Jim and Larry were the same height and had the same coloring, pale skin, thinning reddish-blond hair, and crystal blue eyes, just like Rennie.

Now, Jim had found his mom, and she had him in her arms. She did not ever want to let go but knew she must. She was probably making him uncomfortable. When she broke away from their hug and looked at Jim, she said, "Jim, Jim, I can't believe it's really you. I'd given up on this day ever coming."

Jim turned to me just behind him. "This is my wife, Deborah."

Rennie hugged me and said, "Please, please come in. Can I get you something to drink?"

"Water's fine," I said, not wanting to stop my camera but knowing I must as we moved to sit in the living room. We sat quietly for a minute, me providing Kleenex for Jim and Joe for Rennie. Rennie clutched the Kleenex, looked down at her hands, and then up at Jim. Jim and I sat across from her, unsure what to say or do next.

We were relieved when Joe broke the silence by asking, "Well, how was your trip?" After some back and forth on the flight, Grand Central, and the bus ride out of the city, Rennie stood and moved toward her dining room.

Rennie said, "Here, here, Jim, come with me. Deborah, you, too."

Joe stayed seated on the sofa and said, "Rennie's gallery tour." Jim and I were unsure what that meant but stood and moved toward Rennie.

"I want to show you the photos of your brothers and sisters and their children. All are coming to meet you later," Rennie said. She never uses the terms *half* or *step* when she refers to Jim's family members. As far as she is concerned, her children should not be distinguished from one another in any way. They are fully brothers and sisters, and Joe is their father, with no "step" needed. Like a cake batter, mixed and cohesive, they are thoroughly blended.

We followed Rennie from room to room, looking at walls of photos, in the dining room, the basement, along the stairs, in the halls and bedrooms upstairs. I thought about my own home where I grew up and did not recall any family photos on the walls or anywhere. I had visited the house in which Jim had grown up with his German mother, adopted brother, and Oma, his grandmother, and I did not recall any photos on the walls there either. We looked at each other and shared the same thought. We had entered a different family world. When we returned to the dining room, we were beginning to see even more about how different our growing-up experiences were from what Rennie and her children had experienced. We listened to Rennie tell who was whom in each photo, beaming with love and joy, as she showed us photos covering the years of childhood experiences and accomplishments.

Then, we heard a man's voice come from the kitchen. It said, "It's 3:00. Love you, Mom."

Seeing the puzzled look on our faces, Rennie said, "That's your brother Carl's voice. My clock has the voices of each child and grandchild recorded at each hour, saying the time and a greeting." She moved closer to Jim and gently touched his arm. "When you're ready, I want you to record your voice there too." She had left the 1 o'clock hour with no voice recorded in case she ever found Jim. Each day, as the hands of the clock made their trip around the face, she heard each voice, except one, that of her firstborn. For that hour, only silence. Jim recorded his greeting on the clock later that day: "Hello, Mom, it's 1:00, hope you are having a good day."

Once we had completed our tour and relaxed with drinks, Rennie asked if we would like to watch some family videos she had created. Of course, we were eager to learn as much as we could about the family. It turned out Rennie had created a DVD for each of her children, showing photos of their lives from birth to adulthood. Jim and I shook our heads in disbelief, awed by the time, dedication, and love each video indicated.

When we returned for our second visit with Rennie and Joe at Christmas, Rennie had created a DVD for Jim with photos she had obtained from his adoptive mother, ones she asked for from both of us, and ones she had taken on our first visit. In addition, on the tree, she had placed an ornament with our photo and our names and had sprinkled photos of us in with the others in her dining room. The clock, the photos, and the DVD were just the beginning of our exposure to this new family we had discovered, one we were soon to find was our family as well now. We had neither experienced such expressions of love nor devotion in our family environments.

Jim's adoptive family never expressed emotions. German stoicism prevailed in their home environment. His mother and father divorced when he was eight, and his mother and grandmother left Long Island, where he had spent the first eleven years of his life, and moved to a small town in Florida when he was thirteen. Soon, his mother married a man with whom Jim never connected.

I, too, grew up in a reserved home, with no hugs and no expression of emotions, except for my mother's temper, which emerged often. My mother gave birth to me when she was forty, and my sister married and left home when I was eighteen months old, so I grew up as an only child. My mother worked all the time, including all holidays when she made extra money for overtime. My father took care of me most of the time. I do not remember holidays being treated as special or meeting many relatives. We would sometimes go to my uncle's house for Thanksgiving, and for Christmas, my father would usually buy a tree, and we would decorate it while my mother was at work. My mother was usually not around for either holiday.

Rennie's family gathered several times over the holidays and often celebrated together, not just for holidays but for birthdays, too. For Jim's first birthday after we had found his family, Rennie, Joe, Kim, Tricia, and Carl came to Houston to give Jim a surprise birthday party. In addition, the family talked almost daily, and Rennie often cared for her grandchildren. She was involved in their lives, and they were the center of hers.

Unfortunately, Jim never got to meet his birth father. He died a few years before we found Rennie. As much as Rennie told me about her family and giving Jim up, she never discussed Jim's father or the story of how he was Larry's father, too, but they never married. And Larry, too, was silent on him, apparently seeing Rennie's first husband and his brother Carl and sister Kim, children of this husband, and now Rennie's second husband Joe and his daughter Tricia as his family unit. Rennie divorced her first husband and married Joe when Larry, Carl, and Kim were children, and all of them refer to Joe as their father, never as their "stepfather." Larry described his early childhood as difficult and dangerous, but his focus was on the Bronx neighborhood, not his family. When I asked about his and Jim's father, he said he had no relationship with him. His tone told me he had no desire to know the man. So, that part of Rennie's life remains a mystery to me.

Rennie did arrange for us to meet his aunt Kitty, although they had apparently had nothing to do with each other over the years. It was Pamela who told us she existed, and when we asked Rennie about her, she contacted her for us. We had lunch with her and Rennie at Tavern on the Green during our second visit over the Christmas holidays. We also traveled to Ireland for a writing conference and while there, arranged through Kitty to meet Jim's father's family and visit their original and still current home northwest of Dublin. One of Jim's cousins is a priest and is the family's keeper of memories and photos, one of which was of Jim's father. No one else had a photo of him, so we treasured seeing him for the first time, even if only in an old photo.

It has been thirteen years since we became part of this warm, welcoming, and generous Irish family. It has not always been easy since neither of us is used to having such family closeness. Jim has no children and was a bachelor most of his life until we met twenty-five years ago and married fifteen years ago. I was married before Jim for thirty years and had experience with in-laws; however, I only saw them on holidays. Also, I have a son and a daughter, but by the time Jim and I married, they had their own lives. I see them a few times a year and spend Christmas Day with my daughter and her two children.

So, Rennie's family world is outside of both of our experiences. I wonder if any family could be as close as Rennie's, particularly a blended family, except perhaps for those in the stories on Hallmark. Whatever measure is used, Rennie is an amazing mother and grandmother, which makes her finally reuniting with Jim life-changing for her. Their coming together filled a hole in her life and changed our lives.

We have grown into a comfortable relationship, although we are probably not as present in the everyday of their lives as Rennie would prefer. We have learned we have very different interests and are not used to having such a large family and having them involved in our lives. We may seem somewhat aloof to them at times. We went to New York for the first few Christmases but soon found it was all a little too much for us, and now, we only join them for selected family gatherings, such as Rennie's birthday. When Rennie and Joe moved from New York to Myrtle Beach, South Carolina, and each of Jim's brothers and sisters moved there as well, Jim flew there for Rennie's eighty-fifth birthday last year, and he joined all his family again for the first time in several years. He sends a birthday card to each of his siblings every year, calls Rennie often, and always sends her a Christmas present. He also talks with Rennie's sister, who lives here in Houston, and we have joined her family for holidays on occasion.

Having this extended Irish family of a birth mom, a stepdad, half-sisters, a full brother, a half-brother, half-nieces, and cousins has opened a new world of family dynamics for us. Jim tried at first to stay in touch with all of them through Facebook posts, but he's found it challenging because they have such different life interests and points of view on politics, social issues, and even religion. After viewing their posts, he often comes to me and says, "You know, there is something to be said for interests beyond eating, drinking, and family." I see by how red his face is that reading their posts elevates his blood pressure. I tell him to stop reading them, but he says he feels guilty not trying to keep up with them and to participate somehow. His family expects his posts to be more frequent and supportive, but he struggles with Facebook in general and feels posting photos and "likes" all the time without context is not true to his personality.

To us, their posts and views are repetitive and narrow. They lean right; we lean more toward liberal causes. They are Catholic and not interested in other cultures or religions. We are explorers in culture and in religion. For example, for his family, the ideal vacation is a cruise or staying at a resort, whereas we were disappointed in the one cruise we took since most of the people on board were fellow Americans, and port stops were limited to tourist places. Also, we find resorts limiting and boring. We much prefer spending time with the locals and staying in the small boutique hotels and B&Bs. We are open to all religions and have visited mosques, synagogues, churches, and temples across the globe and follow no one religious denomination.

Rennie and Joe have visited us a few times, and while we welcome spending time with them, we feel we do not provide enough entertainment, such as going out to eat and having family gatherings. The last time Rennie came to Houston, she came with Carl and stayed with her sister instead of staying with us. We were worried that meant we had offended her and created a separation. Jim's aunt's son (one of Jim's new cousins) arranged lots of activities, and the family got together every day she was here. They had a party at Jim's aunt's house on her first night, went out for dinner the next three nights, and gathered again over brunch the day she left. We joined them for three of the gatherings, but we are not used to such a beehive of family togetherness.

Jim is outgoing and enjoys being with people but has a reserved and quiet side. He often wants to stay home and read; sometimes, he doesn't want to talk to anyone, including me. Some of that preference could come from being married to a highly introverted and obsessive reader for so many years, or perhaps the quiet, reserved family with which he spent fifty years of his life has shaped him to a great extent. The debate over whether nature or nurture is more powerful comes to mind, and I wonder about the Irish and German influences in Jim's life and if nurture can overtake nature given enough time. However, when I see how immediately his eyes fill with tears any time we recall the memory of our first meeting with his mom and the hug he shared with her for the first time, I witness the deep emotions living in his Irish heart.

JANIE BRAVERMAN

HOW MANY IS NOT SUPPOSED TO BE A TRICK QUESTION

Do you have brothers and sisters?

At a dinner party, a wedding, the first day of camp, this could be an icebreaker. In grade school, it could be a prelude to drawing a family portrait. At an initial speech pathology evaluation following a serious brain injury, it's supposed to be something else, a yes/no question, to elicit a yes/no response. An entry to analysis not only of the ability to speak, but of cognitive function as well.

Do you have any brothers or sisters?

My son doesn't always answer. He is reserved in his willingness to communicate with people he doesn't know. The damage to his short-term memory means it takes time and repetition for him to know someone. I categorize people for him: *That is someone we don't know.* A constant refrain in hallways and elevators headed to therapy or on an outing to the grocery store, a basketball game, or a movie theater. *Not someone we know. Not someone we know.* When it's someone new to his care team or his medical team it goes like this: *This is [insert name]. [Name] is [insert relationship].* Repeat and repeat.

My son has been asked the screening question about brothers and sisters many times.

By the first speech pathologist, at the University of Iowa Hospitals and Clinics (UIHC), during his first hospitalization. A lovely white-haired woman with dangling earrings and the aura of an interesting past, who connected well with him. She was evaluating how much he could understand, how well he could express himself. He used his eyebrows, as he still does, but that was when he wasn't speaking at all.

By the speech pathologist at On With Life, the first of several rehab facilities, who fed him pancakes to evaluate his ability to swallow. Still not speaking.

By the speech pathologist at the Center for Disabilities and Development at UIHC, where no, he did not want to shoot the little mermaid and her cartoon cronies, using lasers by moving his eyes while staring into a computer monitor. Evaluating him for a speech assistive device as he struggled to speak. He was, however, alert and aware enough to roll those eyes with an edge of snark, not wanting to be treated as a child.

I sat there thinking, *Die, little mermaid, die already!* I wonder, had I said that, if he would have been more willing to use his eyes as lasers, to blast her doe-eyed little icon off the computer grid. Maybe. Maybe not.

He was asked by the speech pathology students at the speech clinic at UIHC: *Do you have any brothers? Or sisters?* What they lacked in experience, they made up for in enthusiasm, in being closer to his age (twenty-two or so to his then thirty-two—young adults who hadn't forgotten how to play), and in their ability to learn from what doesn't work, like the inevitable question that comes after he says yes:

How many brothers do you have? or *How many sisters do you have?*

How many is not supposed to be a trick question.

The answer is supposed to be a number. The question is supposed to be about memory, word finding, aphasia screening, and other things speech pathologists assess. Sometimes my son closes his eyes. Sometimes he averts them. Sometimes he rolls them. But it's a question he never answers.

In speech therapy, it's not useful for the family to answer for the patient. We make an exception for this line of questions.

He has three sisters. Ask them. If you're taking a medical history, he has two. If you're asking about early childhood, he had two. Now he has three.

He has brothers. If you're asking about early childhood, he had one. He lost him for a while, but now mostly remembers that he got him back; if you're taking a medical history, it's his half-brother. If you're taking a history of the heart, that's complicated, too. My oldest daughter's now ex-husband calls my son *little brother.* My son's best friend from middle school and best friend from high school, both brothers. Those are just the ones I know about. He loves them. That makes them his.

How many children do I have? For a medical history, I have three. If you're asking about their early childhood, I had four until I lost one in the divorce. If you're asking about now, I have four. I gained a daughter in my second marriage. My husband gained two daughters and a son. Ask any of the daughters, they'll tell you they have three parents.

It's complicated for speech therapy, but we know who we are.

COURTNEY J. CORNELIUS

ROUNDING UP (AND IN)

Pam hadn't liked me at first.

That wasn't just my impression, the kind you might expect of any girl meeting her boyfriend's mother; she'd eventually confessed as much to my face. But much had changed by then.

Looking back, I can't really blame her. I was sixteen and on a mission to be a Bad Girl; and although deep down I was still sweet and naïve and vulnerable (I think), my behavior demonstrated otherwise. I dressed like a tramp, I cut classes at school, I smoked and drank and had sex with her son—not atypical of a teen with my kind of foundation, but not attractive to any parent.

As far as parents went, I wasn't exactly solid with mine—any of them. I'd been adopted as an infant after a short stint in a maternity home, a fact I learned when I was nine. (My adoptive brother had come three years later, born to another set of bio-parents.) My adoptive parents were already sleeping in separate bedrooms by then, and separate houses shortly thereafter. Soon, Dad met and married my adoptive stepmother, and they had a "natural" son; so, I had an adoptive half-brother.

As if things weren't complicated enough to explain by that point, I tracked down my birth parents when I turned eighteen. My birth mother had married a man not my father, and my birth half-brother was born three years after me. (She had soon divorced and married again, so I also had a birth stepfather.)

It would seem to be almost an excess of family—but that's not how it felt.

Get-togethers with my adoptive relatives subtly revealed the chasm: My cousins had my grandpa's nose, or my aunt's forehead; no such analysis was discussed regarding my brother or me. Our ancestors had written an account of their travels across the United States in a covered wagon—but somewhere inside, I intuitively understood that it wasn't *my* blood, it wasn't stock from which *I'd* descended . . . so it wasn't my source of pride to own, either.

Holidays and reunions with my birth family were a novelty at first, as my nearly-two-decades-later return was celebrated, but soon the factors that separated Me from Them came to the surface. While I resembled certain family members, shared visibly obvious genetic traits and subconscious mannerisms, I'd missed a lifetime of events, stories, history. I wasn't part of the old tropes and shared jokes or "remember-when-they-were-a-little-kid-and . . . " I could only raise my eyebrows in a questioning expression, waiting for someone to realize, and say, "Oh, right . . . " and fill me in.

I didn't have a Family Tree; it was a random collection of totally different species of flora that had somehow ended up on the same land. And I wasn't a branch, or even a leaf, on any of them, but rather an oddly colored bird that flitted *among* them, never building a nest but only perching for a spell until it was time to move along. Every side of the "family" required a qualifier. Legally, I belonged to one (fragmented) group; by blood, I could be attributed to another (also fragmented) . . . but rather than recognizing what made me a member of either, the glaring, unspoken (sometimes) sentiment always seemed to be that I wasn't really *all the way* in.

Such was the scenario when I gave birth, out of wedlock and way too young, to Pam's granddaughter. But while she might not have been thrilled about her son's choice of vessels, she was over-the-moon in love with my child.

Although I had three "mothers"—birth, adoptive, step—none of them were involved; it was Pam who taught me how to make formula and change diapers and figure out why the baby was crying. It was Pam who cared for her while I attended community college, enabling me to get my associate's degree and, subsequently, a decent-paying job. It was Pam who relieved me at least one weekend a month (as much for her enjoyment as my own, but still a huge benefit for me as a single, working, exhausted mom).

We didn't see eye-to-eye on everything. I wasn't happy she gave my daughter soda; I'm sure she wasn't happy that I—well, plenty, probably. But we shared a top priority: the baby.

I came to deeply appreciate her for that; and she, I'm certain, came to recognize my earnest attempts to be a good mother. I couldn't have done it without her, and when I was eventually able, I tried to let her know it. I took care of her after her surgery, I always treated her to lunch on our outings, I called to say "Hello"—because I wanted to, not from any sense of obligation.

The baby was soon a thriving, elementary-aged child. One day, the three of us went shopping to purchase back-to-school clothes and stopped along the way at the grocery store where Pam worked.

She greeted the cashier, a coworker she apparently knew well, and introduced her granddaughter with a beaming smile. Then she gestured to me.

"This is my daughter-in-law," Pam declared.

Technically, I was not—I'd never married her son. In fact, that relationship had ended before my pregnancy did. What was more, Pam had a legit DIL by that time. (I can disclose these facts without causing offense, as both are now deceased.)

But she *claimed* me. She made me feel important with the use of a title higher than I owned. It didn't matter that I, personally, was not of her genetic tissue. It didn't matter that legally we didn't owe one another a thing. It didn't matter that we didn't approve of or care for every quality of the other. We were family.

My daughter was an adult (thankfully) when Pam died. We attended the funeral and the memorial afterward in the surreal fog that customarily accompanies such events. I hadn't seen Pam's sons, including my own ex, in years, but they were still familiar—we traded catch-you-ups and how-ya-beens and laughed as we recalled the events of our wayward youth. It suddenly struck me that I was *included*, I was part of the core of this group, a central member of this story.

I no longer make distinctions, unless it's to upgrade; my assorted brothers are simply my brothers.

It's my mom's legacy.

thought
seeking
wanted

II
HALFS

LENORE BALLIRO

FAMILY SECRETS

"Dad is not my dad," she said. "I mean, he is my dad, but he's not my biological father."

My sister blurted this out one summer night when I was eighteen. She pulled her 1969 VW Beetle onto the side of the road in our small town. We had been visiting my boyfriend, my former high school English teacher. His dad had fixed each of us a gin and tonic. I was heady with expectation and love, en route to my freshman year in college that fall, so happy to be hanging with my sister, who was briefly home from California. We had re-established a close and loving relationship as we entered adulthood, and I cherished it.

"What?" I said.

My reaction was physical—adrenaline rush, vaso-vascular response, increased respiration, a cold sweat. Stored memories clashed into other stored memories, disbelief fighting with her news. I opened the car door, certain I would vomit up the gin and tonic, the fast food that preceded it.

We both lit cigarettes: me, Marlboros; my sister, Tareytons. My fingers were shaking like crazy. The story came out little by little. She answered my questions as I tried to unravel the carefully constructed history my parents had created, down to the altered birth certificate listing my father's name as the biological father.

"Were they really childhood sweethearts?" I asked.

Over the years, we had heard stories of their courtship, how my mother kissed my dad on a dare in the movies. How they hung out at the Arnold Arboretum and Franklin Park in their Jamaica Plain, Boston, neighborhood. We had a dreamy, soft-edged photo of my parents at age fifteen, two beautiful young people leaning their heads in close to each other, a photo my dad's uncle took in his studio. Were these all lies?

"They were childhood sweethearts," she said. "All of that stuff about their courtship is true. "

"Then what happened?" I asked.

Haltingly, my sister revealed the details. My parents dated from the time they were fourteen until they were seventeen. They did live two blocks from each other—my Dad with his Italian immigrant parents and several siblings, my mom, an only child, with her alcoholic single mother.

Then my mother ditched my dad for a navy guy she met at a dance, someone from outside the neighborhood. She ran off with him to Portsmouth, Virginia, and they got married. My dad, heartbroken, joined the army, even though he was underage. He was stationed in Germany, and the day before he was scheduled to return to Boston, he got orders to go to Pusan.

While my dad saw combat in Korea, my mother lived in a Quonset hut on the naval base with her husband. Then she had my sister. The navy guy turned out to be a louse, and my mother had the good sense to leave him. She returned to Boston where her mother took her in. My sister slept in a carefully padded bureau drawer for a couple of months until they could save for a crib.

When my father came back from Korea, he learned of my mother's situation. He wooed her, and eventually, she accepted his marriage proposal. My father adored my mother, and he adored my sister, too. They married, and thirteen months later they had me.

My sister and I were sweetly close when we were children. She taught me things: jump rope songs, how to play jacks, card games, how to memorize the Hail Mary. As we grew up, we suffered the same jealousies and annoyances that any two sisters endured with nearly five years between them. But we became exceptionally close as we got older, a relationship we both cherished.

"I might have lost you," I said, "if things didn't turn out like they did."

"Yes," she said. "That's why I wanted to tell you. I wanted to tell you for a long time."

My mother had revealed this secret to my sister when she was fifteen, a time when she was complaining that my dad was unreasonably strict with her. My mother offered the story as a way to explain my father's protectiveness. "Don't tell the other kids," my mother said. And my obedient sister complied for ten years. My mother never talked about it again. It might not have ever occurred to my mother what a burden my sister was about to carry. According to my mother, the past was the past and there was no need to go digging into it. Her approach was to reinvent one's life, a strategy that might have worked for her, but not for everyone.

Knowing the secret, however dislocating, helped me understand some of my family's peculiar dynamics. I also realized that all my aunts and uncles—my grandparents—knew our history and were complicit in the lie.

I kept the secret. My parents did not know she told me the truth.

Ten years after the night in the VW, my mother received a phone call from a man claiming to be my sister's half-brother. He wanted to get in touch with my sister. My mother was furious. Her carefully tended veneer had been cracked. But to her credit, she gave him the telephone number, knowing the crack would open up.

The man contacted my sister, they met, and he then introduced her to his sister. So my sister had another sister. Soon I met them, and I discovered that they were more like her than I was; they laughed easily and teased each other. I was scared and jealous and thrilled for her all at once. I wanted her to connect with the other siblings, to connect to the truth of her life. I also wanted them to go far away.

The truth came out to our other siblings. My parents never explained any of their choices, and we didn't press.

Fifty years after my sister's revelation, I look back at our lives—our joys and losses, the miles between us, the births and deaths. For years my sister has lived Kauai, Hawaii, far from the small town where we grew up, and I am still on the East Coast. Despite any issues I have had with my mother over the years, I am grateful that she brought her child home, that she reunited with my father, that my sister and I have had a long, close relationship and don't keep family secrets from our own children.

MICHELE MARKARIAN

AN ONLY CHILD

Kate was nervous.

An only child—or so she thought—Kate had recently done an Ancestry DNA test, only to find an email in her Inbox from Ken, a man who claimed to be her brother. Half-brother, actually. It turns out Kate's father had had a baby with a girl he must have dated in high school. Kate was pretty sure her father didn't know about this baby, who was here in the form of an email named Ken. And here she was, driving across the state line to meet him.

Kate was juggling a bundle of feelings, all competing for the spotlight. What was her older brother like? Would they become friends, or, at thirty-five and forty-five, were they meeting too late in life? Would her brother be disappointed in her? The whole thing was a little overwhelming. Kate wished she still smoked pot so she could calm down a little, but she had lost her taste for it after it became legalized.

Ken had requested that they meet at a Panera in Pawtucket, which Kate agreed to. She wondered if he chose Panera because he thought she was broke? But if he did think that, wouldn't he have offered to take her, his newfound little sister, someplace special? Maybe he didn't want to embarrass her by suggesting that she might be broke? Kate, a CPA, wasn't broke, but somehow she had the idea that he was more flush than she, just by virtue of being older. Would he have a good sense of humor? Kate imagined that she would look at Ken and be struck with an instant, familial connection.

She hadn't told her mother what she was up to, although she was dying to. Her mother had been less sure of herself since Kate's father died last year, and there was no reason to believe that she'd known about Ken. It didn't seem fair to bring her into it until Kate was on firmer footing with this brother.

Kate pulled into the Panera parking lot. She ran a brush through her hair, and hastily applied a thin layer of lipstick over the coat she'd applied earlier. She hoped she looked okay.

She went into Panera and looked around. There were two women at a table, obviously friends, and a father and his two kids eating sandwiches in the corner. The father was saying something to make the kids laugh. Ken didn't mention having any children. The father seemed younger than her.

"Kate?" Kate turned around to see a man, about five foot nine, with longish graying brown hair and a mustache. He was wearing a T-shirt that said "Beer, Bongs and Babes," which featured a cartoon buxom woman in cutoffs and bikini top with a water pipe in one hand and a beer bottle in the other, over pressed blue jeans and workman's boots.

"Ken?" Kate squeaked in disbelief. Ken reached out and gave her an awkward hug.

"This is weird, huh?" he said, gesturing towards a table. "You, uh, hungry?"

"Um, yeah. Sure," said Kate.

"What would you like? My treat," Ken said, looking at his boots.

"Oh, no, that's okay, I can't let you—"

Ken looked wounded. "You're my little sister. This is a special day for our family, isn't it? My treat."

Kate realized it would be rude to say no. "Oh. That's very sweet of you. Thank you."

"My pleasure," beamed Ken. "So. What would you like?"

"I—I might be too excited to eat," confessed Kate. Excited? Disappointed? Stunned?

"Let's grab a table," said Ken. He gestured again towards a small table. Kate sat down. Ken sat across from her. "So. We're related."

"Yup." Kate was struggling for the right thing to say. "Do you— we— you—have any more brothers? Or sisters?"

"My mom has two kids with my stepdad. They're younger—twins. A boy and a girl. They're twenty-one, no, twenty-two. Twenty-two."

"Wow." It took Kate a second to realize that the twins were not related to her.

"You?"

"No. Just you." Kate felt shy. "So. Tell me about your life. What do you do? Do you have kids?"

"Sis, I am starving! Let me buy you some grub and then we can talk! What would you like? Anything on the menu! Anything for my little sister!" Ken smiled, but Kate could tell that he was nervous. He had a beaten down look to him that inspired repulsion and pity in her.

"Um . . ." Kate scanned the menu quickly. "Uh, a turkey sandwich. Yeah. Turkey sandwich."

"Okay." Ken sprang up and went to the counter. The clerk said something to him, and he turned and called to Kate, "Chips or fruit?"

"Fruit,' said Kate.

"Fruit," she heard Ken say to the clerk. "It's for my sister. That's her, over there." He fished money out of his pocket and placed it on the counter. Then he came back to the table holding a flat round buzzer, which would go off when the food was ready. He looked at Kate expectantly.

Kate was trying to find something of their father in him. Their father had been confident, almost cocky, a small business owner who always made sure to make everyone in the room feel special. Maybe a little around the eyes? Ken's eyes were kind, and almond-shaped, like their father's, but didn't have the same spark. He was slighter than their father but had the same dark hair.

"What do you do for—"

"What was he like?"

Kate knew who he meant, but she asked anyway. "Our father?"

Ken nodded. "What was he like?"

Kate hesitated. "He—you never met him?" Stupid question, she knew. Of course he hadn't.

"Once or twice. It was a long time ago."

Kate's stomach flipped just as the little buzzer started to vibrate on the table, signifying that their order was ready. "Be right back." Ken sprang from the table and went over to the counter. He came back with Kate's sandwich and apple, as well as a sandwich and chips for himself.

"Thank you." Kate forced a smile. So, her father had known about Ken. Did her mother know? Why didn't anybody tell her? "Did you know about me?"

"No. I met your dad—our dad—when I was little. You weren't born yet." Ken took a bite of his sandwich. "So. Sister! What do you do? What are you into? Are you married? Have a family?"

"No," Kate choked. She tried to take a bite of her sandwich but found she couldn't eat it. How had she not known for all these years that her father had had another child?

"Me either," said Ken. "I like to say it's because I haven't found the right woman, but maybe I'm just a bachelor by nature, you know?"

Kate knew she should be asking Ken some personal questions about his life, but she couldn't help herself. "How did you two meet? You and my dad?"

"Let's see—I was really little. He came by when I was maybe three or four. I don't remember much. I didn't know he was my dad until I did the Ancestry thing. My mom told me he was a friend from work who wanted to say hi."

"But why?" Kate had so many questions, as well as a huge sense of betrayal.

"No clue." Ken shrugged. "My mom is a pretty open person, but she can be tight when she wants to be. My guess is that they were just too young."

"Who did you think your dad was?" Kate was having a hard time with the fact that Ken's mother had kept his paternity a secret. Then it hit her—her dad was the same way.

"I don't know. She told me he died when I was a baby. I didn't think too much about it. She met my stepdad when I was seven, and I just kind of accepted him as my father, so—Ken shrugged and took another bite of his sandwich.

"What did he say to you? When he visited?" Kate's calm voice betrayed the anxiety she felt.

"I don't remember much. Like I said, I was small. I remember he brought me a big red dump truck. I loved that truck." Ken looked wistful.

Kate had an overwhelming urge to go home and confront her mother, shake her, scream, "Did you know? Did you know this whole time?" But what if she didn't? What if baby Ken and his mother were a secret, just like Ken's paternity was a secret to him?

She was jolted out the cyclone in her head by Ken. "What was he like? Our Dad?"

"Umm . . ." Kate wasn't quite sure what to say. He was a good dad? He always had time for her? He was supportive? She could talk about anything with him? It all seemed false. Did she ever really know him? "I don't know if—"

"Oh, I'm sorry," said Ken earnestly. "I know he just died last year, right? This is probably too soon— "

"It's okay," said Kate. The room was spinning, just a little. You're okay. It's okay, she told herself. "He was a good Dad. He, uh—he was well liked."

"What did he do? For work, I mean?" Ken's earnest eyes looked like mud flats.

"He was an accountant. He had an accounting firm." Kate didn't mention that he had wanted her to take over the firm, but she chose instead to work for a larger corporation.

"Wow! So he was good with numbers! That must be where I get it from!" Ken exclaimed. "I am excellent with numbers. I should have gone to college for math or something, but my stepdad is an electrician, so." Ken shrugged.

"Oh. That's cool." Kate wondered if her dad had paid child support, but it seemed tactless to ask. "Did—were—your mom and my—our—Dad childhood sweethearts or something? Do you know their story?"

"I don't know. My mom doesn't talk about it."

"Does she know you're meeting me?" asked Kate.

"I told her I found you an Ancestry." Ken looked uncomfortable. "Does your mom know? About me?"

"Maybe," said Kate bitterly. Her world had just become bottomless. How well do we know our parents? How well do we know anybody, for that matter?

"Sis? Are you okay?" Ken leaned in.

Kate looked at Ken—his eyes, so like her father's, his dark hair, that stupid T-shirt. "Uh, I have to go. I have—an appointment that I totally forgot about."

"You just got here," Ken protested.

"Yeah. Yeah, it's my mom. She has medicine that I forgot to pick up and she really needs it," Kate lied.

"Oh, shoot, Sis. I'm sorry. Moms are important. Here, at least take your sandwich." Ken clumsily wrapped up her uneaten sandwich in a napkin and thrust it at her.

"Thanks. Let me give you some money." Kate fumbled for her wallet and took out a twenty-dollar bill. She wanted to owe him nothing. She wanted to forget they had ever met, put her world back together again.

"No!" Ken protested. "No!"

"But I feel badly about leaving—"

"No! Next time, you can get lunch! How's that?" Ken smiled and wrapped his arms around her awkwardly. "Okay? Now go get your mom those drugs before something happens!"

"Okay." Kate forced herself to smile. She felt badly for taking advantage of his guilelessness, but she had to clear her head.

"I'll message you, okay? On Ancestry!"

"Okay," said Kate. She waved goodbye and strode back to her car quickly. Once inside, she found she couldn't breathe. Stop it, she told herself in a panic. You're okay. It's okay. You're okay. It's okay. It's okay. She put the key in the ignition but couldn't move just yet. So much to unpack. So much she didn't know, and still didn't know, and might never know. Her father was dead. He couldn't know his son, and never would.

Kate pulled out her phone. There was a message on it from Ancestry. Ken. She put the phone back in her purse. Tomorrow, she thought. I'll look at it tomorrow. Then I'll message Ken, and we'll do this again. And again. And again, until this feeling goes away, is replaced with something else, something close to family.

TARRI DRIVER

R. JR.

The school bus dropped me off at the entrance of the neighborhood, and I started the short walk to our house. The house was near the back of the neighborhood, and it was a storybook kind of autumn day, a perfect blue sky, crisp air, and the leaves were beginning to turn orange and yellow and red. I was thinking about nothing and everything as teenagers are apt to do, and I slowed my pace three doors down from the house when I saw an unfamiliar car in the driveway and an unfamiliar man sitting in it. His hair was long, his beard was scraggly. With both hands on the steering wheel, he watched me. With my alarm bells ringing, I defiantly walked into the driveway, averted my eyes, quickly passed the car and entered my house.

The vinegar hit my nose as soon as I walked in the door. I heard my mom in the kitchen with the spray bottle. Brrrt . . . brrrt. Silence. Brrrt . . . brrrt. Silence. I knew she was frantically cleaning. I also knew she was upset, because cleaning was her main coping skill. She was spraying and wiping the crumbs off the countertops when I asked her about the stranger in the car.

"That's your half-brother, and I don't want you talking to him. Stay away from him! Do you hear me?"

My mom told me that he was currently homeless and wanted to stay with us at the house. That he showed up out of nowhere, and that my mom didn't want him in the house without my dad present. So there he sat, in his car, in the driveway, while we all waited for my dad to get home from work.

I went upstairs to my room and peeked out of the blinds where I could get a good look at the mystery figure. I was intrigued. Who was this guy sitting in our driveway? What was he doing? Where had he been all along? I sat by my window and watched him, and he sat in his car with his hands on the steering wheel and stared straight ahead. I sat there and peered out until my feet fell asleep.

When my dad came home from work, he and my mom argued

desperately.

"What do you want me to do?! He's my son!"

"Tell him he can't stay here! He's not safe! He's unstable."

And he was. He was off of his meds, actively hallucinating and paranoid. He had been driving his car up and down the interstate aimlessly for who knows how long.

The night passed slowly as I laid in my bed and worried about my half-brother. I felt bad that he was sleeping in his car and I was in my warm, comfortable bed. What if he had to go to the bathroom? What if he got thirsty? What if he was cold? What if he had a scary hallucination? Who would comfort him and tell him he was safe?

My heart pounded as I walked out the front door the next morning. I felt uneasy as I watched him watching me when I passed his car on my way to the bus stop. His face was partially obscured from the glare on the windshield, and I couldn't get a very good look at him, so I wasn't even completely sure he was watching me or if I was just hoping that he was.

After a couple of days of my parents arguing, my dad gave his son some money and told him he must drive south and return to his mom's house. So he left.

I watched him drive away through my window, and his car shrank as he drove farther and farther down the street. I felt a physical ache from his departure. My shoulders slumped. A pang of deep and panicked thirst dropped into my chest, and I felt betrayed because I had only been given a measly sip to try and quench it. The desire to know and understand my half-brother intensified, and that private, forbidden feeling grew more forlorn over time.

Many years later, I had a thirtieth birthday looming, and I felt an urgency about life. I typed my half-brother's name into my browser's search window. His recognizable name came up immediately in the search results. Links to hundreds of published poems and short stories appeared on my screen. My fingertips buzzed as I clicked on poem after poem, story after story. I drank it all in. His work felt familiar; I already knew it in my bones, even though I'd never seen any of it before. I found his email address on a poetry website, and with clammy hands, I emailed him. Cold turkey.

I received a response the next day: 'Hi Sis, yes it's me and good to hear from you yes thank you hon.' My heart melted.

We exchanged several get-to-know-you emails, excitedly learning that we shared many favorites: music (heavy metal), movies (horror), authors (horror), cars (1979 black-and-gold T-top TransAms). He emailed me photos of his artwork. The haunted faces in his forests and outer space worlds jumped off the pages. Sometimes the faces were attached to winged bodies like angels or demons, and sometimes they were bodiless, floating around, groundless. He emailed me stories and poems, some already published, some not. His work was spooky, dark, rich and romantic, full of earthy decay and magic. I snail-mailed him a drawing of a moth and burned him CDs of my favorite Metallica and Black Sabbath songs.

The time came when he abruptly stopped responding to my emails; maybe it was too hard or just too much. I didn't pressure him to continue communicating with me.

A few years later, my dad received a call from his ex-wife to notify him that their son had died. Heart attack? Suicide? My dad didn't ask, only speculated.

In my art studio, I have a photograph of my half-brother and me. He's in his early twenties, and I'm around three-and-a-half years old. It's from a family gathering, perhaps a birthday. In the photo, we're sitting side by side on the carpeted floor. My half-brother is sitting criss-cross applesauce, and I'm sitting next to him leaning against his right arm.

I'm looking at the camera with a shy smile. My hair is long and brown, and I'm wearing a pale, yellow sweatshirt. His hair is long, shaggy and brown, and he is sporting a mustache and a trimmed, short beard. His shirt is fitted, long-sleeved, brown velour, with a white collar. His chest hair is visible, and he's wearing a silver chain necklace with a wolf pendant. His hands rest palms-down on his knees. He is not smiling, and his eyes bore into the camera.

They are blue, the same blue as mine.

ZOË LOSADA

CARRIE

I wrote this fragment of a poem for my half-sister, Carrie, shortly after her death:

> *Flotsam*
> *You floated from family to family*
> *shore to shore.*
>
> *You found no earth to settle, no spot to grow*
> *Until*
> *Like a mangrove*
> *You spread your roots through the warm air*
> *To the dark earth*
> *In a country*
> *Far from home.*

I had just returned from the trip my brother and I made to Carrie's funeral in a small town in Senegal, where she owned a country home. We had planned the trip hoping we could see her, alive, and maybe even take her back to the U.S. for medical care. In the early morning on August 3, 2019, the day of our departure, as I got up in the dark to get ready for the trip to Senegal, however, I received this email from the man I thought was Carrie's partner:

"Sad news, Carrie suffered a cardiac arrest this morning a little after 7am.

"Sorry first for her then for all of us.

"Good luck."

Overwhelmed by sadness, despair, and guilt, I went anyway. I took a train with my son and husband to Miami, followed by a flight, alone, from Miami, met up with my brother in New York, and flew to Dakar with him on a nine-hour flight. We were met at the airport by a friend of Carrie's, the same one who had contacted me several weeks before, saying that my sister's situation was taking a turn for the worse. As we drove through the endless, dry, dusty land, I noticed groves of Baobab trees, improbably flourishing in an inhospitable land.

After what seemed an interminable journey, we arrived at Carrie's house. It was tall and white, built on a dirt road in a newer part of Dakar, located in front of an unfinished building, fully inhabited by an army of squatters. We were met by her household: her guard, of whom she had often spoken with affection, her maid, her partner, with whom we had been communicating, and another young man, who apparently took care of her other house, located about four hours from Dakar, in a small village called Sokone. This young man had been helping care for Carrie in the clinic where she died.

My first surprise entering Carrie's home was a large photo of her, surrounded by a crucifix, with a huge image of Jesus Christ above her. "Was Carrie a Catholic?" I asked my brother, in a whisper. "Not that I knew," he whispered back, "Wasn't her father Jewish?" Yes, he was, and Carrie had gone with us to the Episcopalian church we grew up in but had never spoken to me about her religious beliefs.

A few minutes later, as we entered Carrie's living room, the young man from Sokone showed us the will that Carrie had deposited with a notary in Dakar. Much of the conversation was in French, and there was no translator around. (This was before Google Translate had reached its current level of proficiency.) I should have been forewarned by his hurry, but I wasn't, just confused. We had just finished a long, overnight plane ride and two-hour drive, and we were tired and had little interest in Carrie's will, only sadness about her death.

The next few days were a blur of activity. Details stand out in my memory: the wrenching trip to the morgue; the ceremony as we left the morgue, when we read prayers; the long trip in an un-air-conditioned jeep to her country home. The entire village appeared for the procession, the funeral in the Catholic church, and then came to her house to share a meal, eating together from the same plates.

Throughout those days, I had many conversations with the people who knew Carrie. One young man, who worked in an NGO in the area, told me that Carrie had changed his life, helping him study, create a resume, and giving him the courage to apply for a job. In Dakar, I met her goddaughter, named Carrie after her. The priest and mayor each gave speeches in the church in Sokone, expressing gratitude for all Carrie had done for their town. I was overwhelmed by the feeling that, in the end, these people were her family. She had created her life here, and had, I thought, chosen to die in Senegal, surrounded by the people who loved her.

Since I was seven, Carrie had appeared infrequently in my life, like a comet. She was my half-sister, and her father was a man I never met but had heard a great deal about. He was tall, had married several times, looked just like Carrie, and was very wealthy. Carrie had gone to live in Europe with her father in high school, during a tumultuous time in my mother's marriage to my father, and she would reappear from time to time, speaking French, cooking exotic dishes like ratatouille, trailing boyfriends.

For a brief period, I believe Carrie returned to live with my mother and me for her first year of college, when I was in sixth grade and our mother was divorcing my father, completing a psychiatric residency, and drinking far too much. As an adult, I would see Carrie briefly, in trips to my father's or mother's homes. She even visited me twice at my home in Venezuela, disappearing once on a long adventure to Eastern Venezuela, alone, and reappearing in a rented car with a very tall young man named Abe, who might have stolen her watch. That visit ended with her having to leave the rented car on the side of the road when it broke down on the way to the airport, and our hailing down a cab for Carrie, Abe, my husband, our two children, me, and Carrie's multiple bags and suitcases. She almost missed the flight.

As we got older, I began to think that Carrie's life was less glamorous than I believed, and lonelier. She left her long-time live-in boyfriend in France and moved to Africa. She started having difficulties with her heart rhythm, probably related to the ventricular septal defect that she had been born with and that was repaired in the Mayo Clinic when she was about ten years old. Before and after her father's death, she entered a long controversy with her stepsister, half-sister, and stepmother about her inheritance, despite the $1,000,000 that she received from her stepmother after his death.

In 2016, three years before her death, Carrie joined my daughter, grandson, husband, and me in Italy, where I lived from 2015-2017. Our visit to Venice went well, when she was staying with a friend. But when she came, alone, with my family to Cinque Terre there was some conflict. Our grandson was only five years old, and most of my attention was on him. Carrie clearly felt left out. She was not feeling well and had a hard time with the numerous hills in Cinque Terre. She was planning for medical checkups in Paris. I visited her there later that year, after a small cancerous lesion in her breast was removed and she went through radiation treatment. She seemed more at ease then and had returned to the generous and kind, if demanding, older sister I knew. I met her current partner, a Senegalese politician, who was taking care of her in the small flat she had rented.

The last time I saw Carrie was in my condo in Palm Beach Gardens, Florida a year later. She had returned precipitously from a visit to the Bahamas, where her father had lived and died and where her stepmother, and stepsister still lived. Apparently, she had a fight with her other half-sister, who was visiting, which resulted in Carrie leaving—or being asked to leave.

❧❦❧

During the last eight months of her life, after two bad falls she had in Dakar, I was in almost daily contact with Carrie regarding her various medical complaints. She went to Paris with her partner for medical care and seemed terrified that he would leave her. My brother visited her twice in Paris during that last year and found her exhausted and fragile. We researched different options for her in the U.S., in Florida, where I live, in New Hampshire, where my brother lives, and in Boston, where she had been treated before. The type of medical care we were looking for changed as the months progressed: first, an orthopedic surgeon for her shoulder, which was in bad shape after a fall in her house, then a gastroenterologist for stomach issues and, finally, a cardiologist at Brigham's in Boston, who had treated Carrie in the past.

❧❦❧

Then, suddenly, in May, I found out that she had left Paris and had returned to Dakar with her partner.

In May and the beginning of June, Carrie's health was clearly declining. I found a nurse who could go get her in Dakar and bring her back to Florida, but she seemed reluctant to go. The last message I received from her was on June 6, 2019, after she was hospitalized. I had begged her to go to the hospital there, and she was vehemently opposed. She finally went, and I believe her phone was taken from her. I then went on a long-awaited trip to Australia to visit my daughter and grandson, hoping that my sister was recovering. My other sister, brother, and I did communicate with her partner and doctors, but, finally, we were contacted by a friend and then by the U.S. Consul with the U.S. Embassy in Dakar regarding her failing health. My brother and I finally, after months of discussing different plans, decided to go see her. It was too late. She died the same day we left. Too late.

During those days in Senegal, part of my sadness was a deep regret that I had not arrived earlier to this place that Carrie called home. I imagined her in her garden, dressed in the long, bright robes she loved to wear, or traveling with us to Sokone, or meeting her endless group of friends, having dinner, swimming together in the ocean. When I saw Carrie in the U.S. or Europe or Venezuela over the years, she was usually alone. I had met her partner briefly once in Paris, and she had mentioned her life in Africa, but I had never imagined it as it was or how beloved she was and how beautiful a life she had created there for herself, and for those around her.

Throughout the trip, I was aware of how little I knew Carrie. I kept on wondering to myself, as I still do, how she ended up in what felt to me a dusty, foreign place, so far from her family. She seemed to have divided her life into distinct spheres. The words from the Norman MacLean's story, "A River Runs Through It," kept repeating in my mind,

> *. . . it is true we can seldom help those closest to us. Either we don't know what part of ourselves to give or, more often than not, the part we have to give is not wanted. And so it is those we live with and should know who elude us. But we can still love them - we can love completely without complete understanding.*

➤❧➤

During the first days that I was in Senegal, I was comforted by the obvious love so many people had for Carrie. There, at last, she seemed to have found a home that she hadn't been able to find in her two families or with the previous partners with whom she had shared her life. Her partner seemed genuinely saddened by her death and clearly had taken care of all the arrangements for her funeral, something I had thought that we would do.

After her funeral, however, as I sat in her room in her house in Sokone, I received an email from one of her friends in Paris, and then from another, and then from at least five. With differing degrees of vehemence, all were very suspicious of Carrie's partner, particularly about his role in her death. They accused him of taking her very suddenly from Paris, where the medical care was better, much better, than in Senegal, of taking her cellphone from her, of not sharing our contact information with them, and even of having a direct role in her death.

The next day, in Dakar, my brother and I received a visit from an ambassador who was a good friend of Carrie's. It was a short conversation. She told us that a person (whose name she did not divulge) had come to the embassy with information that Carrie had been poisoned in the clinic where she died. The ambassador stated clearly that she could not be involved, but that we (my brother and I) should investigate this.

My brother left the next day, so I went to the U.S. Embassy alone. The consul calmed my fears. Apparently, they had heard the same rumors and had even checked Carrie's medical records and blood tests. If Carrie had been poisoned or murdered by another method, she explained, the plot would have included an entire clinic, including several doctors. I left Senegal the next day, exhausted and bewildered.

❈

Looking back, I wonder if Carrie's life truly ended surrounded by people who loved and cared for her. She was a foreigner there, a white American with a Jewish father who ended buried in a Catholic cemetery in a small, dusty, Senegalese village, with a funeral presided over by a Catholic priest. If my brother and I had managed to get her to the United States for medical care in the months before her death, would she still be alive today? At first, I was skeptical of the claims made by Carrie's friends in Paris made, but now I wonder if they had some basis for their suspicions. Her relationship with those friends was another sphere of her life that I knew very little about, yet they had known both Carrie and her partner for years.

Carrie reached out to me many times over the years. For all our adult lives, we lived on different continents, yet she always found a way to visit me wherever I was. I remember her telling me that she often felt excluded by my paternal grandparents but had a wonderful relationship with her paternal grandfather, who I never met. Without any concrete evidence or revelations from her, I can only imagine that she didn't feel part of either her mother's or her father's family and chose to live a life connected with both families only through brief visits. Maybe because of that lack of connection, she did not create a stable, lasting family with her own spouse or lovers. In the end, I am, again, wondering if, during those final days of her life, she truly trusted her partner or the other people who were taking care of her.

I wish desperately that I could have at least been with her during those last days of her life, or even have gotten her medical care that could have saved her life.

Looking back, however, I see with a clarity that I did not have in 2019 that Carrie's choices led her to live in that place, with that partner. Like all of us, she was probably entirely unaware of the ultimate result of her choices or even of the reasons for those choices.

I only know that I loved her. She was my glamorous older sister who lived her life with freedom, courage, and conviction. I loved her even though there is much about her life, and particularly her death, that I don't understand.

PETER SCHMITT

LONELY HEARTS

Back when they were still speaking to my father,
his two sons from his first marriage brought over
one day their bright new copy of *Sgt. Pepper*,

hoping to turn my father and mother on
to Lucy in the Sky and Mr. Kite.
I was eight, three years from my first 45,

but even I could see the futility
in their trying to bridge, as it was called then,
the Generation Gap—however timeless

the music. With college student earnestness
they persevered, my half-brothers, even
setting up the small box record player

they'd also brought, as if my parents' old four-
legged console stereo were suitable
only for Sinatra and Nat King Cole.

But at least they tried, back then, on holidays
from school they still came over, still would call
my father and sometimes my mother too.

In those days, they thought of her as pretty
and smart and a good cook, which their own mother
would not have wanted to hear. Had they been pressed,

they'd have to admit my father was happy.
But in time—and you would think it might work
the other way—it became harder for them

to forgive, to stop blaming my—our—father
for the divorce. Even into their forties,
feet propped all those years on analysts' couches,

they never made peace with it, could never
understand. By then they were older than
my father had been when he'd filed the papers,

and each was recently divorced himself—
which, who knows, they may have also blamed on him.
So by the time his business, finally,

went under, and then the cancer, they were all
but gone from his life. Each certain, in the way
only a child can be, of his own version

of experience—as if hearing only
what would play on the little turntables
of their hearts, now folded and locked away.

FELICIA MITCHELL

MY FATHER'S FIRST WIFE

Her name was Dawn,
and I think his day rose with her
and then set when she left him.
Although he loved my mother,
and would have more children,
my father carried the loss of first wife
and first-born son inside a psychic pocket
like too much loose change.

When I was a small child,
I found nude photographs of her,
as children do, shuffling through boxes,
but did not know who she was then.
At 17, her breasts were like a statue's
in my aunt's art history textbook
or a girly magazine's glossy pages.
Perhaps I led my mother to them,
because one day they were gone,
nothing left in the old box but us
and an empty film canister.
Or maybe my father just threw them away.
Later I would learn Dawn took a train home,
the way women do in country songs.
I would learn my father had another son.
I was told the whole story before I was ten.
When my father told me she had lied—
said he beat her, that she was black and blue,
but not to listen to anybody who said he did it—
I knew that he could have beat her.
People are complicated and complex,

even the father you learn to love.
Much later, Dawn and I met through the mail,
exchanging Christmas cards and notes
between my home and her nursing home.
She had married a quiet man.
She had had a good life on a farm.
She had had many more children
but was glad I connected with my half-brother
in time for me to fulfill my father's dying wish:
to know that his son, this son, was okay.

Family can be as complicated as a fist,
as secretive as a box of nude photos,
as simple as a sweet old woman
accepting her first husband's daughter,
but it is always family—
even when some secrets are scattered
like loose change shaken
from the pocket of a dead man's clothes
before you fold them one last time.

grief
Choos
love
blood
Choosing
grief
love
Chose
Chose
bloo
Chose

III
ADOPTIONS

SHERRYL ENGSTROM

MY EYES ON THE PRIZE

Tik-tock, tick-tock. It starts slowly and softly enough. I am thirty-one years old, thriving in my fulfilling and adventuresome life, except . . . something is missing. The inner beat persists, becoming insistent, demanding. Tick-*tock!* By age thirty-three, while I'm cocooning within the writing of my way-too-long master's thesis, I get it. No more denial or debate; I know full well that I must become a mother.

With M.A. accomplished and a creative writing job I loved, I took action. No man was in sight, so I began the process of adopting a baby girl from India. Then, within months I met Ken, my husband-to-be, leading to the inevitable talk of marriage and family. I was thirty-four and beyond ready. Unfortunately, infertility revealed its scarred face. Fortunately, though, we were both completely comfortable with adoption, so we started the labor-intensive process of networking, choosing an agency and applying. Three years and three foiled trials later, hope rekindled itself; a baby girl was within reach. As we were on our way to meet her, our home phone rang.

"I'm so sorry. The birthmother has changed her mind and does not want to relinquish her baby," said the voice from Hades.

Crestfallen again. After four unfulfilled attempts to become a mother, and having just had my job eliminated, I felt like a motherless child. Drowning in my stewpot of self-pity for weeks, though supported by friends and an infertility counselor, I felt punished by the gods and sure motherhood was not my fate.

The saving grace phone call came—on February 28, 1989, one month shy of my thirty-ninth birthday. We would have a child, a baby boy, just twenty-six days old. We had already picked out our boy name, Anthony, for its meaning alone—precious gift.

My ultimate dream was in my arms. But now what? I worked as an adjunct college instructor and knew other career women who were older or adoptive mothers, ready to encourage and assist. One particularly close friend, who adopted her first child within weeks of mine, wisely stated, "Well, now we've got our beautiful babies along with the hardest job in life—parenting. And it doesn't come with training or licensing!"

We fumbled and bumbled, laughed and vented, realizing that this was indeed the most challenging and unpaid profession, yet the most rewarding job we would ever have. This most marked transition took me from being a largely self-occupied career woman to becoming other-centered. My son's life seemed to be lying tenderly in my arms. And yet some day, this little boy would become a man, truly his own person.

Anthony was an easy baby. Content, focused, able to self-amuse, introverted, joyful and, to my delight, verbally expressive, talking before he walked. His intellectual curiosity seemed endless. When just two years old, and told he would soon be getting a brother or sister, he wondered where the baby was. "Mommy, is the baby in your tummy?"

"No, honey."

"Is it in Boppa's [Grandma's] tummy?"

"No."

So we dove into the mystery of explaining adoption, far before we'd ever thought we would. Anthony was twenty-six months and needed to understand. At three, when I was in the throes of mothering our second child, he felt his loneliness, inventing his friend "Cinquo" to be his companion. At the same age he asked another piercing question. "When will my skin color be the same as yours, Mommy?" This convinced me that I had the most imaginative and wise adopted toddler in the universe.

Anthony continued to demonstrate his curiosity and wit into middle school. In seventh grade, he was entrusted to walk brother Aaron to church when we had to drive there earlier. When they failed to show, we pondered an apropos consequence and gave him a chance to weigh in.

He said, "I will preach a sermon for you." He did just that, Bible in hand, half mocking, half serious so as to be acceptably contrite, conducting his service from his music stand, which he used for piano, guitar and trombone. Another priceless memory of his unique expression came when he was in sixth grade. I was well into my early menopause, sometimes being short-tempered and impatient. I apologetically explained to him what menopause was and that the discomfort was called "hot flashes." He quipped back, "Mom, that sounds a lot more like internal heat waves."

Second child, Aaron, was much more of a handful—high-maintenance was my term. His birthmother had had no prenatal care, not one medical appointment. At birth he showed some delayed neurological issues, so he was observed for a month before being released to us, accompanied by two pages of instructions from a pediatric neurologist. It seemed expanding the family would be a bigger game-changer than expected. At five, Aaron began getting dozens of tests and seeing several health professionals. In his teenage years, I once counted a label or diagnosis for each finger of my hands. In summary, Aaron had multiple learning disabilities that made traditional listening and desk-sitting impossible. He was extremely dyslexic and dysgraphic so he didn't conquer reading until ninth grade. The diagnosis we longed for did not come until high school: Pervasive Development Delays, Not Otherwise Specified. *What? Did some psychiatrist invent this nebulous term when they didn't know what else to declare?* Only a decade later did this get translated into Autism Spectrum Disorder, which piled high on top of everything else, particularly ADHD and anxiety.

Ironically, Aaron was a cheerful, sensitive and happy child, who had a large heart for most everyone, and could get easily hurt due to his trusting nature and naiveté. In fact, all our family and friends loved Aaron, who was so amiable, cheerful and playful that I thought maybe a TV show like Raymond's could be called *Everybody Loves Aaron;* well, everyone except his peers, that is. He was just too different, odd, quirky, immature and boundary-less to be accepted.

And now, it is a known fact that autistic children, even on the mild end, do not have friends and peers to connect with. So, bullying and loneliness were the norm for him in adolescent and teen years. But in Aaron's optimistic soul, there was always room for hope and perseverance. So, he didn't give up or drop out, but stuck it out to the end, through sweat and tears.

The African proverb, "It takes a village to raise a child" has echoed in my mind since my teaching days in the Democratic Republic of the Congo. I witnessed this practice based on genuine community and wanted the same for my sons fifteen years later, so I tried to build a circle of trusted and open-minded friends. With a friend, I created a playgroup for adoptees and we spent as much time as we could with other families of color. Our miniature village soon included a diverse group of warm, wonderful and eclectic people. Yet, best of all, and indispensable, were my parents, who lived a mile away and were ever ready to become a deep and wide part of the boys' lives.

My mother embraced the boys right away, calling them her "joy boys." My more traditional father took a tad longer, but not much. They both relished their role as grandparents, giving their love, attendance at school events, and nature walks and bike rides galore. The best gift was their boundless, loving daycare and sleepovers providing years of fond memories, including Grandpa's Swedish pancakes, especially at holidays and times of intergenerational family feasts.

Crossing the bridge to motherhood was proving to be both fun and rewarding, despite the exhaustion that accompanied the reality that I would never be a Supermom who could do both full-time work and child-rearing well.

The secondary challenge for me was fully accepting the notion that we were now an unusual kind of family—adoptive, biracial, mixed, transracial; people used many different phrases as if to fit us into a prescribed category. Of course Ken and I knew that we lived in a society that was often bigoted, shortsighted and indeed built on a sort of artificially created caste system, often dependent on false realities and peoples' prejudices. And that is partially why we decided to have a second child who was mixed race—a term I loathe because it contradicts one of my core beliefs that there is just one human race. Both boys would likely identify as black as they grew older. So, at least they would have each other as a mirror when society wasn't providing them the reflection they needed.

We took countless Metra trips to Chicago to visit my college friend whose family was also non-white and adoptive. Our field trips included museums, ethnic restaurants and black barbers and churches. When possible, we vacationed in places like Puerto Rico and the Virgin Islands, aligning with like-minded friends and different cultures we wanted our sons to understand and value. The boys' black history study started early with our home library, gospel music, Kwanzaa, Martin Luther King celebrations and a Culture Camp every summer for years to be with other multiethnic adopted children. For better or worse, our sons learned about slavery before they started kindergarten.

I can recite many anecdotes and stories that demonstrate the layers of racism in our society, a few of them remaining unforgettable. Our first son was only four when a friend in preschool shunned him because his father insisted they not play together. At five, he was chased out of a playmate's yard, a tool in the man's hand. Countless times we were asked if they were "real brothers." I generally replied, "Do you mean biological brothers?" (What I wanted to ask was *why do you need to know that?)* The first memory I have of this senseless and privileged line of questioning was when Anthony was a baby. We were in a grocery store line, him in a sling on my chest. The clerk said, "Oh what a cute little guy. Is he a foster child or legit or what?" "Neither. He's my child," I answered, while growling sotto voce, *what a dumb question!*

Another dark incident occurred two years later. We were at my husband's employees' holiday dinner party with all white employees and their spouses. The boss was a wonderful full-hearted woman named Helen, whose husband narrowly escaped suffering in a Nazi camp. One of the sales representatives posed a ludicrously racist riddle. It was during the era when Smurfs, silly little blue cartoon characters, were a sensation. With a smug grin on his face, he asked, "What do you get when you cross a Smurf with a black person?" My pulse rate raced into overdrive and I thought my heart would leap out of my chest onto my plate. I was speechless until inspiration hit during the inevitable awkward pause instigated by the jackass who outed himself as a clueless racist. "Oh, Helen. I forgot to show you our new pictures of Aaron" (who was then six months old). I took the baby pictures from my wallet and passed them along to Helen. She seemed simpatico to my little scheme and passed them around the large table, making sure The Joker would see them. I hoped he learned a life lesson then and there. Judging by the chagrin on his face, I needed to believe that he had; I finished my dinner feeling sanctimonious and satisfied. This episode seemed an epiphany to me. I pledged to myself and to the Sacred Spirit that I would never qualify or describe my children's looks or their ethnic roots before anyone met them. If someone felt inclined to make a judgment, show surprise or utter something out of line, so be it.

Watching my sons become kind, creative, young, black men is truly indescribable. Aaron's strengths became much more visible as he matured. His neurodiversity shone brightly, evolving into passions in weather, history, politics and all things digital. He was clearly very sensitive to and expressive about racism, sharing his experiences openly. For example, after deeply understanding the phenomenon known as Driving-While-Black, particularly in a largely white area, he became a vigilant cop-watcher. "Mom, I need ten bucks. My tail light is out and I don't want to get pulled over!" was an outcry heard more than once.

Anthony, while in college, and watching his beloved grandmother survive a traumatic brain hematoma after five days in a coma, decided on psychology as a college major. He also explained—partly tongue in cheek—that bearing witness to my poor stress management helped him to realize his deep interest in wholistic health and the field of mental health. He was my first teacher of Positive Psychology, having been concerned about me and my below average coping skills when it came to maintaining my peace of mind about the social injustices I disliked so much.

"Mom, you were so stressed out on trying to be a perfect mom, and getting us over our adopted child hurdles, while working two part-time jobs, that you were sometimes a little dysfunctional," he once explained. Well, he wasn't wrong. "Not to mention all the struggles Aaron went through with his disabilities. I know I can put those experiences to good use in my career," he added. Regarding adoption, I had become aware of the concept of the primal wound that adoptees experienced. In retrospect, I realize that perhaps I expended too much energy on that and often projected that anxiety onto them—another of my dysfunctions, I suppose. Despite all my missteps, I have a heart full of gratitude at the love and forgiveness my sons have embraced me with. One way this became evident was when Anthony affectionately named our family The Motley Crew. Misunderstanding the word "motley" I questioned him. He explained the definition as diverse, enlightening me with the notion that the pronounced personality differences within our family of four are the very qualities that could make us successfully co-exist and solidify our unity and interactions. About that same time, in 2012, two big events came about that exemplified each son's autonomy in choosing his own path. Younger Aaron produced a precious daughter and Anthony completed his B.A. degree in psychology.

Half a lifetime has passed since I became the mother I dreamed of being. Well, not exactly. I could never have imagined all the agonies and ecstasies of parenting and how demanding it could be. But now at thirty-three and thirty-five, these men are still joy boys, and can make me laugh and cry like no other humans on earth. The elder thinks he is getting old and plucks out his silver hairs. He's an ambitious social worker on the East Coast, after completing his master's degree at Morgan State University, founded in 1867. My heart bursts with pride and gratitude at the thought that, while raised by white parents, he chose a historically black college. And watching him devote himself to advocacy for ex-offenders, marginalized people and those with disabilities has carried over to The Motley Crew. Since caring for a non-verbal autistic man twice his age, he has become highly knowledgeable about Autism

Spectrum Disorder, which has greatly helped us to accept the complexity of this diagnosis that Aaron navigates every day. Aaron is a devoted father who spends as much time with his daughter as possible. And as a cell phone technician, his self-taught expertise in technology has benefited his baby-boomer parents countless times. His strengths vastly outweigh his limitations as he continues to live from the depth of his heart and his strong Taurus personality, accepting his neurodiversity as an instrumental part of who he is.

So, dear sons, as you've heard before, you are:

Not flesh of my flesh, nor bone of my bone,
but still miraculously my own.
Never forget for a single minute,
you did not grow under my heart, but in it.
—Fleur Conkling Heyliger

TIFFANY WASHINGTON

I SHOULD HAVE KNOWN

The night I became your mother
your 6-year-old self
tried to convince me
your bedtime was 9 p.m.
And since that moment you've
been trying to convince me
to bend me to your will—
"Just a little later,"
"Just a little longer,"
"Just a little . . . more."

It took me years to
unmask the pathology—
the harmful nature of
elaborate stories—
describing, in detail, an
art class—never attended
or a song whose
lyrics you claimed
as your own.

It took me years to
unearth the self-preservation,
the unconscious compulsivity
of hoarding food in
pillow cases and dresser drawers.

It was ages before
we knew that trauma changes
the chemistry of the brain—
and that at 6, yours was burrowing
deep in cranial cavities and
rewiring synapses
that could not be undone.

Yet, I still try.
Here, today,
to see the good I believe
to be inside you—
to believe the lies you
tell when you
say you love me.

I still hold Hope,
(That defiant bitch)—
close to my mother's heart
and anticipate the day
you'll change.

But I know, logically,
it is a fool's belief,
a childish dream
wrapped in orphan fantasies—
shaped in Annie and Daddy Warbucks,
Oliver and Mr. Brownlow.
Adoption stories warped
in happily-ever-afters
and "together at last."

One day, maybe soon,
I'll wake up and realize
what a cruel trick this all has been.
Or maybe, I'll just cling
to my own lies
—the naïve notion that love
could ever be enough,
that a second mother could
ever be loved like a first,
and that all of this
time was worth it.

"PIO, PIO, PIO"

The year I was a mother,
you woke me at 6 a.m.
with the only bits of the children's song
you remembered, "The cheese stands ALONE!"
Your toddler voice bellowing
until at last I comforted you with our
lullaby, replacing "me" with your name
confirming, nightly, who Jesus loves.

Your older brother soundly sleeping,
in the next bed,
the only brother's name you heard daily—
while confusion of your twin brothers
confound weekly visits.
One always running, one always hitting,
both with one name,
the other not remembered.

The pill bottle next to my own bed,
tempting repose from an insomnia
plagued with only one fear—
How quickly our lullaby will fade
like "little Spanish chickens"
from your once bilingual tongue.

MAMA

The night you came to live with
us, I laid on the floor next to your
crib—thinking my big hands could
offer comfort.

But they were still the hands of a stranger,
not yet a mother.
Mother had to be earned—
with persistent dedication,
with repeated patting my chest, saying "Mama."

You still called every woman
you met "Mommy"
because in your short life,
you had already known too many mothers—
One, too young and unprepared,
One, an aunt, doing her best, but not enough.
Another, and maybe even another
before they brought you to our door.

We sent the boys to school
to let you enter our house,
less chaotic.
You toddled to the toys
we'd cultivated from friends
and bins we'd hidden in
the basement after the
boys outgrew them—hoping
we'd get a second chance.

They said you liked animals
and were busy. That between
the two of you, you only knew
a handful of words.
But you knew "mommy"
and "milk" and maybe even "puppy."

So we fought hard to
become your mothers—
the ones that would wake each night with you,
for years of nightmares,
the ones who would learn
how to cornrow and box braid
with clumsy white fingers,
the ones who would stuff stockings
and light birthday candles,
the ones who would hold your hand
for stitches, so many stitches.

But that first morning,
too exhausted from the
idea of raising four children—
we did not hear you wake.

Instead, we found your new
brother, sitting by your bed
reassuring you of your safety
in our family.

And we've tried, to keep your safe,
because that's what I thought mothers
are supposed to do.

And I swear, I tried.

But the world is
unpredictable
and violent.

So, instead I can teach you how to
struggle through, overcome, move forward.

So now, when I hold your hand,
a mother's hand, I'll do my best—
to help you push through
the pain, the uncertainty.

KATIE KENT

FATHER AND SON

"Your son needs an operation on his leg. He'll also have to have a blood transfusion." Dr. Anand did his best to speak gently as tired eyes peered out from behind blue-rimmed spectacles.

"What?! No." I felt my knees begin to shake and my chest tighten. I lowered my head and squeezed my eyes shut, trying to pretend this wasn't happening.

"Please don't worry, Mr. Collins. It was a serious accident, but after the surgery Jamie should make a full recovery."

I felt the pain start to ease as I let out a breath. I had feared the worst when my neighbor Sadie had come running to me in the garden this morning to say that Jamie had been hurt. I'd sat with my son while I waited for the ambulance to come, stroking his head gently. There had been so much blood. Sadie's boy Mike had been inconsolable, wailing loudly while snot dripped out of his nose. A pile of vomit lay in the street next to him; I could only imagine the shock he would have had at seeing his best friend come off his bike, his leg impaled on a wire fence. Curtains twitched around the neighborhood, and some kids watched from their gardens, their eyes wide.

Jamie was my life. Ever since Debbie passed away, he was what I was living for. I couldn't lose him too.

When Debbie succumbed to cancer three years ago, leaving me with a four-year-old to look after, I thought it would be too much for me. She had been the one who had really wanted a baby. I loved him, of course, but she was the one who had doted on Jamie, cared for him while I worked long hours in my job as a barrister. What did I know about being a single parent? But my son had been my salvation. Without him, I think I would have fallen apart. He forced me to keep on living, showed me that I still had a purpose.

I thought back to that first day after she had passed away. I was at the kitchen table, my eyes red from lack of sleep and crying, when Jamie came bounding down the stairs in his robot pajamas, his hair tousled.

As I poured the cereal into his bowl he looked at me with wide eyes and said, "Where's Mummy?"

I swallowed a lump in my throat. "I'm afraid Mummy's gone." My voice cracked.

He scrunched up his eyes. "Gone where? When's she coming back?"

I poured milk on top of his cereal. "She's not. I'm sorry, son. Mummy's gone to heaven."

He looked at me curiously. "Okay." He picked up his spoon, stirred the milk into the cereal and then put a large spoonful of it into his mouth, chomping noisily. Then he suddenly sneezed, and milk shot out of his nose. It was such a comical scene I couldn't help but laugh, even though laughing felt so wrong.

"What's a matter, Daddy?" he asked me, as my laugh turned into sobs.

"Daddy's just a bit sad that Mummy has gone."

He beamed at me. "Don't be sad, Daddy. Mummy will be back from heaven soon."

I put my arms around him and buried my face into his blonde hair as I cried, breathing in his scent. It was comforting; not everything had changed.

≥✿≤

"Do you know Jamie's blood type?" Dr. Anand asked me, interrupting my trip down memory lane.

I shook my head. "No, but I'm A positive, and I'm pretty sure that Debbie was O negative."

He nodded briefly. "Okay, well we'll test him to be sure, but in that case he will be either A or O. I'll make sure the blood is on its way as soon as possible. Then we'll patch up your son." He smiled reassuringly.

≥✿≤

"Mr. Collins?"

I looked up at Dr. Anand from the travel magazine I had picked up off the table. I had been reading an article about Rome. It was somewhere Debbie had always wanted to go—it was on her bucket list. Unfortunately though, she got sick so quickly that we weren't able to cross it off her list. Reading the article, I thought about taking Jamie there. He'd love it—his class was doing the Romans at school, and pizza and ice cream were his favorite foods.

I imagined us walking hand in hand around the Colosseum, him throwing a coin into the Trevi Fountain, me eating a mountain of pasta and polishing off a slice of tiramisu with a glass of wine in the evening.

"Please come into my office for a moment."

"Okay . . . " My heart started to race. "I thought you said that everything would be fine?"

"Yes, it will be. We're just prepping Jamie for the surgery," he said, as I followed him into his office. He shut the door behind me, pulled out his chair and sat behind his desk, then took off his glasses and put them carefully on the desk.

"So what's the problem?" I asked. "You look like you're about to give me bad news."

"We tested Jamie," Dr. Anand continued. He paused, taking a deep breath. "His blood type is B."

"Oh, okay. Well, maybe I got Debbie's wrong. It's been a few years. I could well have remembered it wrongly."

"No, you were right. I checked back through her records to be sure." He looked into my eyes and spoke gently. "Is it at all possible you got yours wrong?"

"No." I looked at him, my brow creasing. "I know my blood type—I gave blood just the other week. So what does this mean?"

"I'm really sorry to tell you this, Mr. Collins, but Jamie isn't your son." He fiddled with the arms of his glasses.

I gripped onto the edge of the table tightly as the blood rushed to my ears. "There's got to be some mistake."

He shook his head slowly, trying to avoid looking me in the eye. "I'm afraid there's no mistake. I ran the tests a couple of times. You and Jamie are not blood relatives."

I stayed silent, barely even daring to breathe. I felt my stomach tighten, and gasped.

"Mr. Collins? Mr. Collins, can you hear me?"

I was vaguely aware of the words, but they sounded so far away. I felt like I couldn't get enough oxygen and that the world was spinning around me.

"Deep breaths now. Come on, breathe with me."

I looked over to Dr. Anand and copied him as he breathed in and out slowly. Eventually I started to feel like I was back in the room.

"Are you okay?" he asked me. "Maybe I should call the nurse." He moved his right hand towards the telephone.

"No." I stood up abruptly. "I just need to get some air." I turned and opened the door, slamming it behind me.

➤❀⟵

"John?"

I jumped as I felt a hand on my arm, and looked up into the face of my brother, Kevin.

"Thank goodness you're here," I said, as tears began to fill my eyes.

He looked alarmed as he sat down on the bench next to me, resting his bottle of Coke on the seat next to him. "You sounded so scared on the phone. I left work immediately. What's wrong, is it Jamie? I thought you said he was going to be fine."

At the mention of his name, a sob escaped my throat.

"John?" Kevin handed me a tissue from his pocket. "It's clean," he assured me, and I took it and blew my nose noisily. "What is it?"

I took a deep breath, struggling to reign in my anger as I started to relive the conversation. "They told me . . . " I didn't want to say the words again. They made it more real. "Jamie isn't related to me."

"What?! What on earth do you mean? Jamie is your son." Realization must have suddenly dawned upon him, as his eyes widened and he said, "Oh."

I laughed bitterly. "Yeah, 'oh' is about right."

"I'm really sorry." Kevin scooted closer to me and put his arm around me, which made me start to cry again. "Did you have any idea?"

I shook my head. "I thought what Debbie and I had was real."

"Of course it was! She loved you as much as you loved her, anyone could see that."

"Then why did she cheat on me?" I dabbed at my eyes with the fingers on my right hand, feeling suddenly wiped out. "She didn't even come clean at the end."

He sighed. "Well, I guess we'll never know exactly what happened. Maybe you're right, maybe she cheated on you. But it could have been something else."

I felt my breath catch in my throat as the meaning of his words dawned on me. "You think she could have been raped? Oh God!" I didn't know what was worse. The thought that my wife may have cheated on me, or the thought that she could have been attacked and kept it to herself.

"My point is that we don't know." He gave me a sympathetic smile. "And we'll probably never know. The important thing now is to deal with it and move on."

I leaned back against the bench and looked off into the distance. "He'll have to go and live with his grandparents."

"No, John! The boy needs his father."

I couldn't meet his eyes. "But I'm not his father."

"Not biologically, no. But you are in every other way."

I coughed. My throat felt scratchy. "You think they'll let me keep Jamie when they find out I'm not actually related to him?"

"You've cared for him for the past three years, alone. Anyone can see what a fine job you've done. He's a credit to you." He passed me his bottle of Coke and I took a swig. "Please, don't let this change how you feel about him. And you made a promise to Debbie to look after him. There's a boy in there that needs his dad. He needs *you*."

I nodded as I looked at my watch. "I should go back in. The operation will be over soon."

"You should probably tell him, at some point," Kevin said. "It's not fair to keep secrets from him."

I stood up. "I know. And I will one day, I promise. Just not yet."

❧❦❧

I sat in a chair next to Jamie's bedside as he slept. Dr. Anand had told me that the operation had gone well. Jamie looked so small and vulnerable. I bent forward and pushed a lock of blonde hair out of his face.

He stirred and opened his eyes, looking around the room. "Dad?" he asked, sleepily.

I had tears in my eyes as I squeezed his hand. "I'm here, son."

DIANE KENDIG

THE GUARDIAN

My sister's daughter asked, "What if
I want to live with Aunt Diane instead?"
And my sister, surprised, said, "Oh honey,
you will see her all the time like we do now,
and stay with her at her beach every summer."
Like Spaulding Gray behind his water pitcher,
my sister the actor told the story
from behind her bed tray, on her back,
all that excruciating week.
What else to call the week
you're told you have very few to live
and you must prepare your kindergartner.

For years the guardian
refused to let the child visit me, no,
no reason in particular.
It's just that their life is too busy.
They hate to make plans.
She said she never heard the promise,
and if it had been important,
it would have been in writing.
I'm putting it in writing now.

CUSTODY AND VISITATION

i. Custody

Dad of 4-year-old patient denies Disney trip.
*   —NBC 4 Toledo*

Custody means "protective care," and, contrarily,
"imprisonment." In four-year-old
McKenna's case, her father manages, warily,
to aim for both in his YouTube video, scolds
and tries to talk his way through:
"The 'Make a Wish' should go to sicker kids,"
not his daughter, on chemo since age two.
Then he slips in his taping,
saying, "It ticked me off," waiting
for his visitation. Revenge then
is how he's arrived here, when
he's finally able to withhold consent.

ii. Visitation

No legal right to see the children you helped to raise.
    —Brinkman and Associates

Visitation means less and less,
and in Ohio law I've checked means zero,
for uncles, aunts, or godparents
who have no rights, although
they helped to rear. The custodial
parent keeps the care or prison key.
I am an aunt without visitation
who stood on the porch—my sister dead
five years—and the guardian said
to me, "I don't like you." No reason more,
turned her back and shut the door.

BRIAN DALDORPH

CUT GRASS

The air smells sweet with cut grass. He'd mowed the lawn late afternoon then had supper with his parents. They didn't have much to say to him. They weren't talkers. His mother felt guilty about what had happened to him, that it was somehow her fault. Had she taken less of an interest in him because he was adopted? No, no, she'd treated him just like he was one of their children.

He'd like to tell them what happened to him inside the walls, but he knows they don't want to hear it. He'd gotten lucky: his cellie Kyle had looked out for him and didn't ask him to pay. He'd been like a father to him. Lucky.

He'd gone to church a lot in prison, not because he believed in anything like that but because church attracted the guys who wanted to make the most of their lives, who refused to give in to despair. Joined photography class and running club: yes, the running club guys ran round and round the prison yard and ended up exactly where they'd started.

He can't talk to his parents about his crimes. What did they know about the hunger he'd been feeling? A hunger that had to be satisfied, because what else mattered? The hunger of growing up without his family: he'd been given up for adoption when he was a baby. Anyhow, his criminal life was all behind him. He reckoned that in prison he'd slain a few demons.

His mother's beef stew.
He eats it because he can't bear to tell her that he's a vegetarian now. The meat they served in prison was like ground bones. It's just like the way he goes to church with them though he's gotten into Buddhism. Spends at least an hour a day meditating.

"Thank you for cutting the grass," his dad says. "That's a big help."

He'd like to start at Juco after Christmas, training as a nurse or medic. He's working as a delivery driver for a pharmacy, and though that's like putting a thief in charge of a bank, he hasn't gotten into the neatly packaged chemicals in the back of his truck.

The smell of cut grass. How else to thank them for everything they've given him?

COFFEE AND DONUTS

Long drive home, a *lot* of not talking, then we stop at a gas station for coffee and donuts. My father says: "Didn't they feed you in there, Jimmy?"

"They kept us hungry. Food was like a chain round our necks. You do good then you eat."

My father picked me up at the gate. He wouldn't look at me, though I knew what he thought: I'd disgraced his family's good name. What a way to pay him back for adopting me when I was seven and I'd already been in more homes than I could remember. Maybe I'd turned to crime just to get at him?

Hard to believe after all I'd seen inside, a *lot* of blood, that I'm in line with my father peering into a glass-fronted cabinet full of fresh donuts in rows. I pick out one with chocolate and sprinkles, another like a cream-filled shell.

We take our small plastic trays to our table and then I'm sitting opposite my father who's angry with his no-good son who was always trying to get out of hard work, always looking for a quick deal.

My father's drinking black coffee, won't touch anything frivolous as a donut.

At last he stares straight at me and says: "What the hell are you going to do now, Jimmy?"

Wouldn't we both like to know.

LOUIS FABER

MOTHER'S DAY

This is the day I am supposed
to honor my mother
but I am torn as to which mother
I should pay tribute, or is it
both or possibly neither.
One carried me, bore me
into life and departed,
for my good, for hers, and
the grave has sworn her to silence.
Is it the woman who
adopted me, I her only
until her new husband
gave her two of her own
and I was the extra, the spare,
the five percent according
to her last will, just an almost.
I will ponder this until
at midnight the clock will
resolve the issue for me.

BACK WALKING

Walking back through my life
I can now begin to see when and where
things changed, where I changed, where
the place I thought of as my home
became alien, altered, as though
the weathering of time wore away
what I now know were carefully applied
veneers, real enough seeming to me
and to others who stopped to visit.
And when the music changed one day
I was the one with no real partner,
sitting along the wall on a folding chair
imagining myself still on the familial dancefloor,
but knowing my place was gone
and I had become more acquaintance
than family, moved out of the core,
invited back when something was needed,
with cards and wishes on holidays.
But that home has crumbled to rubble,
and I know my leaving saved me
from having to pick up the pieces
of what could never be reassembled.

DEPARTINGS

He had a feral memory of childhood
although time had made him uncertain
if it was his as he lived it, or as he now
chose to remember it after all that happened.
One by one they departed him, first a sister,
then mother and finally father, but he
had grown adept at losing people.
That ability was one of his few familial triumphs.
He never thought to count his birth parents
among the losses until he discovered them
after they were in the grave, but you aren't
deserted by those you never knew, are you?
Than a second father, whose ghost
in the guise of Family Services, took
the sister he had known for all of two months.
And on it went, loss upon loss, disassociated
from a family of which he was perhaps not a part.
And finally, the brother, one that did not die
but declared him dead as an impediment to greed.
But he hadn't died, he had been freed, a balloon
finally released from its moorings, finally able
to take to the sky and look down and back
on a family that was now just ancient history.

PAUL LAMB

LATE NEWS

We are old men now, Kelly and I. Age has found us, despite our evasions and denials. Stairs are steeper. Walks are slower. Tasks are left for when the grandsons visit. Gravity tugs at every slack muscle, every extra pound, every bit of loose flesh. In defiance, or perhaps stubbornness, we remain as active as we can, though each day seems to present new limits. Sometimes, all that feels left to us is watching our son, Clarkson, and our twin grandsons live their own younger lives.

Kelly and I have made a good life together. Through our years, he's helped me embrace my emotions. I've tried to help him control his turbulence. Yes, we've had adversity. Any serious relationship does. Yet we've always found ways to return to normal, to ease back into old routines or find our footing in new ones. It's alarming, therefore, that at such a settled time we would receive this late news.

Our grandson Little Curt—my namesake, who is in high school now and prefers LC or just Curt—asked us all to do one of those genetic tests for a project in his biology class. His brother, David, declined, scoffing that since he's his twin, what would he learn that LC didn't? David has always been a little bossy to his brother, but they both seem to need that kind of dynamic.

LC knows we adopted his dad, so his tests wouldn't discover any genetic link to Kelly or me. He's met his father's biological mother a few times, though I don't know if she took the test for him too. On their mother Jordan's side, the twins have a grandmother and an uncle, and presumably a grandfather, though he is never discussed. Years ago, Clarkson had tracked down his biological father using a similar genetic test, but that never went anywhere, apart from making Clarkson and me grow closer. In all, these genetic tests that LC had us take weren't supposed to produce any surprises.

Except they did. And now I sit beside Kelly in our silent front room, as I have many times in our lives, and wait for him to escape the darkness we hoped he'd eluded long ago but that is trying to take him once again.

I came home late from clinic this afternoon—I volunteer twice a week to keep my hand in—and found the house quiet. Normally, Kelly has something bubbling on the stove, some delightful meal that strengthens the pull of gravity but nourishes his soul because he loves to prepare food for me. Not today. I had supposed he was out, perhaps at Clarkson's house on the other side of the park or getting some last-minute item for dinner, but I was mistaken. He was sitting on the couch in the front room with the lights off, his tablet in his lap, waiting for me. That was my surmise because I recognized immediately that his darkness had returned and had taken him quickly and deeply.

Kelly is the literary one between us. I had once thought his reference to his depression as a dark, stalking beast was overly dramatic, but through the years I've come to use it too because it helps us focus our fight. Kelly has battled major depressive disorder all his life. He suffered horrific physical and emotional abuse from his father as a child, withstanding brutalities that he still won't tell me much about. He'd been in therapy much of our married life, tried a host of medications to seek respite from his torment. Some experimental treatments. And, to an extent, it has worked. He's learned coping skills, gained perspective, crossed a great deal of distance, maybe even altered his brain chemistry, and come to love himself. I know this for the monumental victory it is, despite his conviction that he will never truly win. "The monster lets me think I'm in control," he's told me when I comment on his months without an episode. "But we all know it will be back." I don't like hearing him talk this way, partly because I fear he's right.

Kelly's monster has returned as foretold. When I stepped into the dark front room and saw his shape on the couch, he held out his tablet. "Go ahead," he said, and by this I understood I was to read the email open on it.

We never read each other's emails. Many of mine over the years were patient-related, so I couldn't share them, and most of his, Kelly insisted, were mundane and boring. He might read one to me over breakfast, an account of some mischief got up by one of the twins or his success in getting one of his stories published. But we've respected each other's boundaries, knowing that's how a good marriage works and knowing we each really have nothing to hide.

I dropped my bag and sat beside him. Then I began reading what had sent him into his spiral.

The writer began by saying Kelly did not know him and that what he had to say would likely be shocking. Then he got to the point. Based on the genetic test Kelly had recently taken, and one the writer himself had taken before, the two of them appear to be half-brothers. They appear to share a biological father who was not the man Kelly had known.

Kelly had three older sisters growing up. Only one is still alive, his nearest in age and the one I would have least expected, given her lifestyle. He had no brothers. Yet this man was claiming, with apparently sound basis, to be his half-brother.

I immediately recalled how Kelly would joke that his sisters got their blond hair from a bottle, though he admitted they were natural towheads when they were younger. His own hair was dark brown, though it's thin and wispy and gray now, and he wore it in a shaggy mess as a young man, which was one of the things that had first attracted the nurturing part of myself to him.

Yet he was evidently more different from his sisters than he knew.

"It explains some things," Kelly deadpans as I lift my eyes from the screen, having read once what I will likely read many times again. He continues to stare at his lap, and I realize that he is struggling to remain where he is, to talk with me, rather than retreat to our bed with the sheet pulled over his head.

I see that this episode is more far reaching and potentially far more dangerous than all he's survived in our years together. This goes much deeper than where the abuse of his father and the neglect of his mother had ever led him.

"I can understand better now why he beat me so much," Kelly says to the dark room. "Why he crushed out his cigarettes in my skin. Why he told me I was worthless. Why he could never use my name. Why . . ." He retreats into silence.

There is no prompt I can give, for what would I be prompting? That he continue listing the abuses of the man who raised him? That he relive a past he's been escaping all his life? But I know he needs to talk. My mother had become Kelly's confessor in her later years. He told her things I will never know, things she's taken to her grave. And she told me, when she understood her time with Kelly was ending, that all I had to do was listen. That was what Kelly needed. I have tried.

I am a doctor, though. My job has always been to heal. My initial naivete about mental illness had led to several unhelpful confrontations with Kelly before I understood my limits. "YOU CAN'T FIX ME!" he'd screamed once, and that was all I needed. His depression will never yield to reason, not fully, not finally. Over the years we've grown good at recognizing his triggers and how to avoid them if we can or deal with them if we must. Except no one could have foreseen this.

He begins again with a mirthless laugh. "It turns out I was never his son. I ate food from his table. I lived in his house. I drained his wallet. And yet I wasn't his son. I was an intruder. Worse. I was a daily reminder that his wife had found love with another man and had a child he would have to raise, nonetheless. And he resented this. Resented me." A long, silent pause. "It's all so obvious now."

Kelly speaks into the gloaming. The late afternoon light is fading from the front window. The tablet has turned itself off, sparing us its sickly glow. I dare not turn on a lamp. If my job is to listen, I don't want to change anything that might upset our equipoise and prevent him from speaking further. That he's said as much as he already has is out of character for his episodes.

I've never commented, not aloud, not to Kelly, about the abuse of his father or the neglect of his mother. I cannot know it, and I cannot tell him anything he doesn't already know far better. I have my judgments, certainly. I have things I could say about them, things I *did* whisper to my parents when they were alive. They had loved Kelly as a second son, had become the parents he'd needed as a child. And they stood as powerless as I am before his monster. Yet we all listened, in our ways, and that was a kind of power.

And now I hurry to keep pace with his thoughts. The father he had known was not his father, and some other man was. To his father, Kelly had personified a double transgression: his mother had cheated on him, and she had brought its spawn into his family to be raised.

"For years I'd wish I had been adopted away from them, Curt. That being raised by *any other family* would have been better. I knew my father hated me, so why wouldn't he give me up? Except now I see that, in a sense, I was adopted all along."

He's confessed this wish before. And each time, he tells me as though he is revealing for the first time something he's kept secret from me. I know how deeply it affects him.

In this light, I had come to understand that his urgent need to adopt Clarkson had been his attempt to right a wrong, to do properly what had been done so terribly with him. He wanted to prove that every child is worthy of love by showing it was true with our son. And if every child is worthy, then he had been too. Kelly wasn't the mistake in the equation. He wasn't at fault. He hadn't caused the problem.

Yet, I can see how he understands it this way now. If the man he had known as his father had never been that, then he, Kelly, was the outlier. He could be seen as the thing that upset the custom or the social norm or whatever it is that keeps savage people civilized.

"Imagine looking at a child each day, knowing that his face, his very existence, is a reminder you've been cuckolded, found so unworthy in some fundamental way that your wife fled to the arms of another man. I was that reminder, and I never knew it."

That doesn't excuse the abuse the man heaped on Kelly. It barely *explains* it. Kelly was an innocent in this. If the man had grievances, as perhaps he had, they should never have been directed at the child.

"It's unfair, you know. Learning this rationale for my irrational father. I want to continue hating him for the man I knew him to be. I want him to remain a monster just for who he was, not because he had a reason to be. But now that's changed, and I don't know what to do with my hate."

My early troubles with Clarkson seem like nothing compared to Kelly's revelation. We'd adopted our son more through Kelly's desire than mine. I had feared I couldn't fully love a child who was not biologically mine, and then I lived my fear. Not with fists or berating shouts or cigarette burns but through withheld emotion, and Clarkson knew it. But our son's great need to be loved had led to a confrontation that ultimately broke down my foolish reserve and made me the good father he needed, and that I needed to become. Not so with Kelly and his father.

Yet Kelly continues to talk. This is good. A lifetime of revelation is dawning from this late news, but maybe he's finally far enough from his past to give it a reasoned perspective. He's lived in peace and love far longer than he had in abuse and hate. The balance has tipped, and maybe he's crafted enough self-respect and strength to face it with calm.

"But did he know? The man who wasn't my father. Did he know I wasn't his biological son? The issue of his loins? Maybe my mother managed to keep her secret. I guess if that's true, then his brutality seems even more savage. He beat his kid simply because he was the horrible person I always thought he was, not because the kid was."

Kelly assured me years ago that he'd processed the torments of his childhood, that he'd dealt with them and locked them away and buttoned them up. Of course, he hadn't. I knew this just as I knew he told me so to set *my* mind at ease. Even healed wounds leave scars.

Yet if a wound is reopened, it can present the chance to address the deeper infection.

"And what does this suggest about my dear mother, Curt? Was she so shamed by her adultery that she couldn't love the outcome either? Was I a daily reminder of her sin? Was that why she looked away when my father beat me? Did she let him beat her child so he wouldn't beat her? Maybe she wanted to be punished for her transgression, and it was through me that she could have it. That's nice, isn't it?"

Healing takes effort. Kelly will carry this new pain and torment for the rest of his days. The rest of *our* days because I carry Kelly in my heart. It's a silly, romantic notion, especially for a clinician, but Kelly had opened a door in my heart that needed to be opened, and I've spent my lifetime being grateful for this. So if explaining my love for him in a silly, romantic way is how I can do it, I will.

He is quiet for a long time, following thoughts to ends I can't see. I sit beside him in the silence, waiting for an indication of where he's gone. The streetlamp outside has come on, throwing sallow light into the room.

"It's reasonable to think that I'm too mature, that I've put sufficient distance between me and my parents, to be disturbed by this late news. But have you ever known me to be a mature person, Curt?"

I laugh at this, but I'm not sure why. To agree? To contradict? To assuage my anxiety? To keep him talking? He does talk, but only after several moments of reflective silence.

"I have become a stranger to myself." He shakes his head, whether in disbelief or dismay or shame, I don't know.

But soon he speaks again.

"There are many ways to look at this, but not all of them need to be ugly."

This is something I thought to say too, but he needs to formulate the understanding himself.

"I wonder now if maybe my mother found some tenderness in the arms of this other man. Found moments of joy outside of her bleak marriage. Maybe it was *because* her husband was a monster that she chose to give me a different father." He pauses for a few moments then smiles. "I could probably live inside that belief."

I doubt that was her plan, for why would she have subsequently been the enabler she clearly was? We know nothing more about this other man or the nature of their liaison than what a single genetic report and one cryptic email tell us. Kelly is too clever to fall for his own desperate whitewash. Yet if it will keep him out of his pit for now, let him make livable sense out of the revelation, maybe he's allowing himself to.

He's given me his hand. We sit in the quiet twilight, side by side, holding each other. We've done this countless times, and I know Kelly seeks the comfort and surety it gives him. I will always do this for him.

"I wonder what he was like. This other man? I suppose I should call him my father, but I'm not there yet. Still, I see more clearly now why Clarkson had chased after his biological father all those years ago. Remember that? He and I need to talk."

Yes, our son's own desperate attempt to make sense of his many fathers.

And now here is Kelly, in a similar position. There is no chance for the man who raised Kelly to redeem himself, and it's unlikely that his biological father will step in. Yet maybe Kelly can find solace, can create solace for himself, by painting a hopeful picture of who this man might have been.

"I wonder if he knew about me."

His voice has more life in it.

"If he knew he had a son with my mother. Maybe he was someone who hung around the fringes of my family. I may have known him. An ersatz uncle or a family friend who was kind to me. I wonder how I behaved around him. Was I a polite boy? Did he love me? Or wanted to but couldn't?"

Kelly has no photos from his childhood. He left those behind along with everything else the last time he walked out of his parents' house. So he can't scrutinize snapshots to find some stray face that maybe shares his eyes or the curve of his smile or the unruly brown hair he had. He has nothing now but his speculations. And perhaps that's where it should remain. Sunny and hopeful because maybe this mystery father never knew he had this son. Or maybe he was relieved that he could dodge responsibility for him. Maybe his liaison with Kelly's mother wasn't an act of love or tenderness. Maybe he wasn't a good man either. Maybe it's good Kelly cannot know more.

Except he can know some of it. If that's what he wants. I don't know if he will choose to engage with his new half-brother and begin a discovery of his lineage and lost heritage or if he will want to dismiss this, forget this, repress this too. We *do* have a good life together. We've raised a son who has given us grandsons. Kelly has what he needs in the family he has now. He can find solace in that. And I say this not out of jealousy but out of life-long love for my husband. He is safe where he is, and if that is where he chooses to remain, we will protect his heart.

Yet if he chooses to reach outside of his security, to begin to learn more about this other family he never knew he had, he will find me directly behind him, supporting his tentative beginnings, wherever they lead. This is also what love means.

SUE B WALKER

UNFINISHED JOURNEY

—And she types this waning May morning, 2023, bent over her MacBook Pro. The scent of Café Du Monde coffee and chicory tickles her nose. She pecks: "Time is Relative."

—And what is meant by "Relative?" Depends on the frame of reference, n'est-ce pas? It disappears in a whiff like that from Papa's cigar. Yes, it is relative, and so what if Amalia Nathansohn, Freud's mama, called him "Golden Siggie," it's not the nasal reflex neurosis addressed here,

—and she conjures Albert, *Der Depperte*, Einstein who the maid called, "The Dopey One,"

—and Thomas, "Old Possum," Eliot saying: "What might have been and what has been / Point to one end, which is always present,"

—and Edvard, "Bizzarro" Munch, standing at the bottom of Ekberg Hill where sister, Johanna Sophie, yells in the madhouse nearby,

—and where cries of animals could be heard from a proximate slaughterhouse,

—and the woman tapping on her computer whispers: "Relative?"

> She might write: "Chiromancy,"
> look at her right hand, examine the heart line,
> the headline, lifeline, the fate line
> that fails to convey
> the shriek, the scream, the cries,

—and a wanton woman in the backwoods of Tuscaloosa, Alabama, is giving birth, there where the Black Warrior River blathers and keeps its own annals of time,

—and the typist believes she hears her holler, hears her wail, screech, bawl, blither and cry, "Oh shit!"

—and her baby came then, a second daughter, yclept "Mary" after the mother of Jesus, for three years previous that self-same woman had given birth to another daughter in The City Care Forgot, in New Orleans, Louisiana, but as for Mary, she was given away, an unwanted thing,

—and she never knew that whelping woman, for the newborn had no memories then, no words to describe what was happening,

—and she never knew the names of the couple who took her and kept her for a year before someone reported that Mary—or whatever the child was called then, did not belong to those who had her,

—and the mother was summoned to court where she confessed the base-begotten child was hers, but refused to tell the papa's name,

—and the Judge said the couple had no right to the kid, so he had sent her to Foster Care,

—and from there, loving parents adopted her, and named her Annie,

—and she was nicknamed "Plummy" by her nanny, and Grandma held the child on her knee, reading James Whitcomb Riley, the Hoosier Poet, who wrote: "Little Orphant Annie's come to our house to stay."

—and Little Annie, at three, did not know she was the "orphant,"

—and it was only when she was six, playing Monopoly with three sisters who lived down the street,

—and she had houses and hotels on Boardwalk and Park Place,

—and Eloise, landing on Boardwalk, screeched: "You think you're so smart, well, I'll just tell you, "You're Adopted,"

—and Annie who had never heard the word, knew from the way it was said, tone and tenor, it was something bad,

—and she asked her mother, what does it mean, "Adopted,"

—and her mother said she had picked her child out, and told her daughter, how she loved her,

—and Annie, who was called by her middle name, "Sue," pictured her mother at the supermarket, as she pressed avocados to see which was the perfect one,

—and then time past became time present, and on this day in May, the typist writes: RELATIVE,

—and remembers the night so long ago when her true-mother came to see if her daughter was asleep,

—and bent
—and kissed her on the cheek.

IV
STEPS

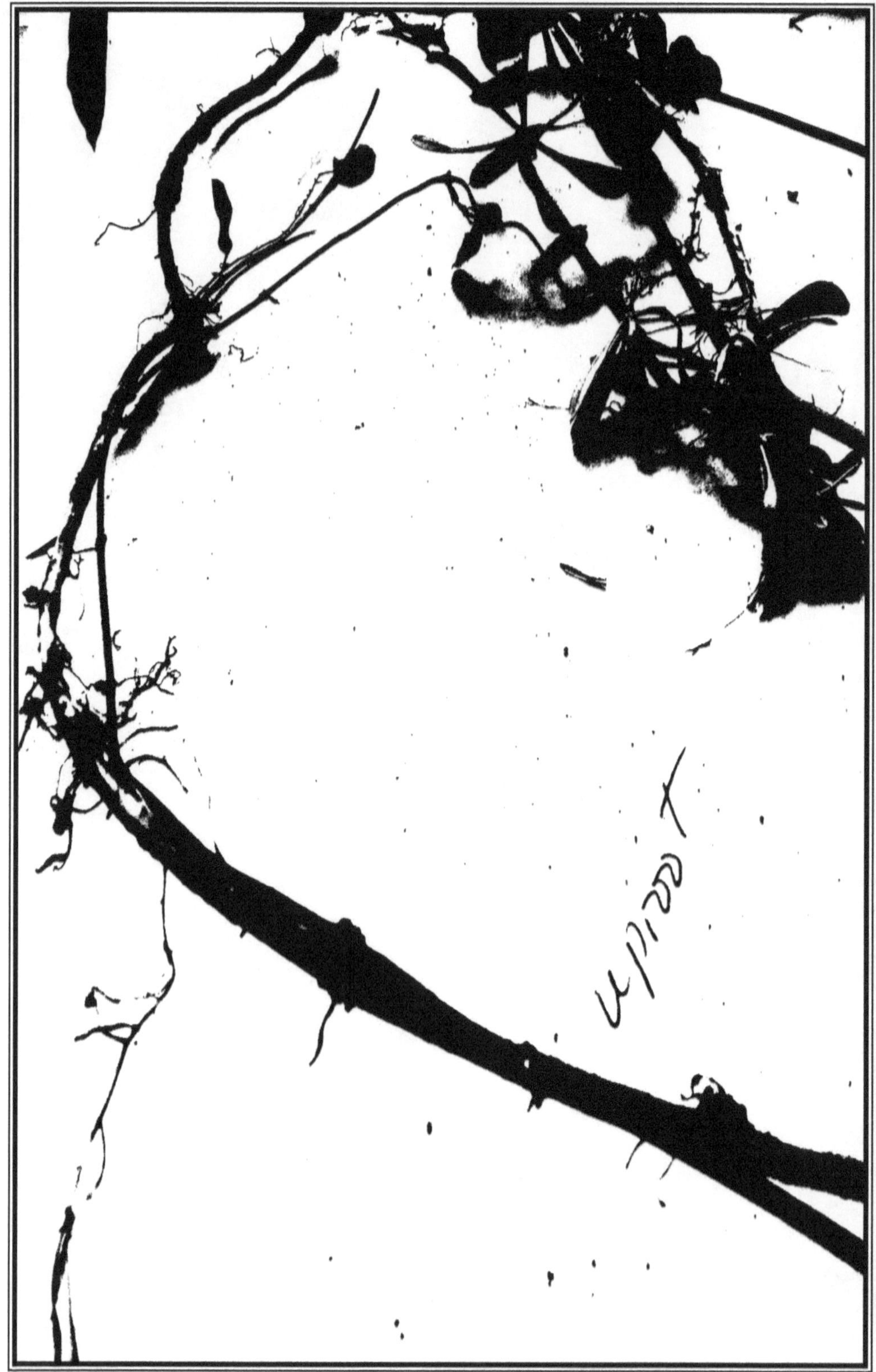

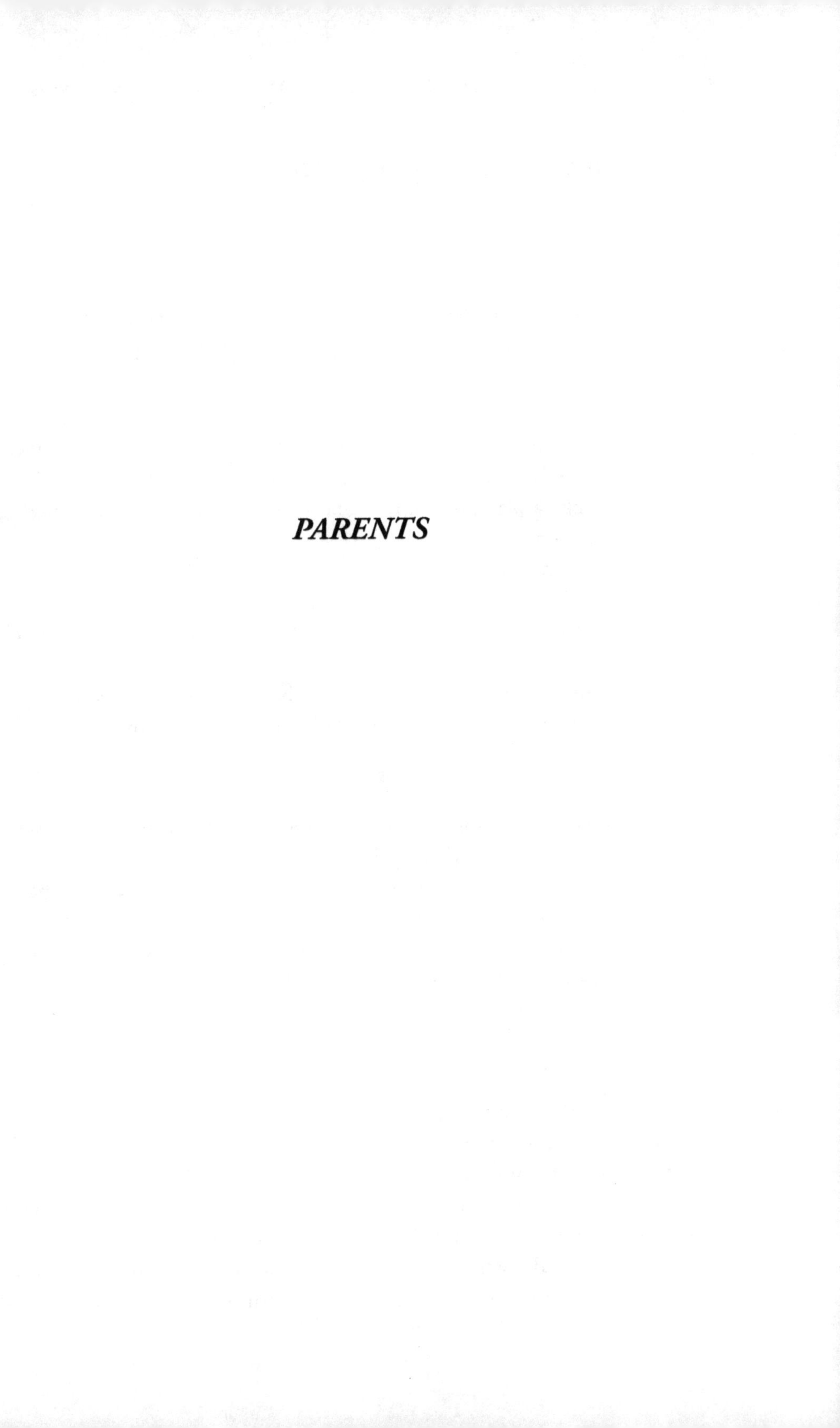

PARENTS

MARY-FRANCES SCHNEIDER

THE ENGAGEMENT: A YES, THREE MAYBES, AND ONE OVER MY DEAD BODY

A corner table on the 96th floor of the Hancock building, the harvest moon dotting the lake's blackness with shimmering specks of silver. He slides into the table like a player stealing second base, a black velvet bag dangling between two fingers.

"Will you?" he asks.

"I will," she answers.

When the elevator opens, he turns to her, babbling, giddy, "Let's tell the kids."

She squints. "Maybe in a month," then hedges, "Or possibly, six."

"Tomorrow morning," he chirps, elation fogging empathy.

❧

Her middle-school son, still young enough to cry, dives into the sofa. "I'm Danny in the sixth-grade play. I'm not moving."

"No one is moving." She sits on the sofa's edge and rubs her son's back.

Her college kid, the engineering genius, so like his late father, paces the living room, delineating the pros and cons of this proposed family iteration. She stands, taking his hands into her own. They breathe together into the stillness of her love for him.

❧

His girls. The oldest daughter, first.

He presses the doorbell and spots an eye in the peephole.

He sighs, "She probably guessed why we're here."

The daughter's husband lets the couple in, calling up the staircase to his wife, who has bolted to their bedroom, hands covering her ears.

But, for her, the winds of a tornado are so irresistible that she stomps back down the stairs, eyes blazing, her hand gripping the railing as if she might rip it off.

The engaged couple trembles. They clutch each other's hands. The father clears his throat.

The oldest daughter screams. "I won't hear what you have to say—never—so get out."

The father stands his ground, frazzled, sweat on his brow and upper lip. He squeezes the hand of his bride-to-be tighter, possibly for courage or perhaps inspiration, or maybe he wants her to be the one to tell his daughter what the daughter says she does not want to hear and vows she will not hear even if she does hear it.

The father chokes it out, "We're getting married."

The daughter releases a growl of rage. She stomps back up the stairs and employs the only weapon available. She slams her bedroom door. Fury building, she repeats the slamming again and again—the noise ricocheting down the stairway.

Sitting on the sofa, her husband breathes deeply, his hands folded in his lap. Eventually, he mutters, "Well, you know how she can be."

The room is silent. No one speaks.

Until the oldest daughter cries the finale, "Get out."

And they get out.

❧❀☙

They drive to the home of his youngest daughter, a recently married dark-haired beauty who eerily resembles her deceased mother. The younger one sits like a cross-legged Buddha on her living room floor, editing the final draft of a graduate school application, her cell phone balanced on her knee.

She already knows. She wipes tears off her wet cheeks with the sleeve of her sweatshirt.

The fiancée kneels next to her. "Can I help?"

Their eyes meet, browns and blues lingering, mingling, registering hope.

"Yes," the younger one whispers, "I believe you can."

DOROTHY OLIVER PIROVANO

THREE PLUS FOUR

I didn't want to say out loud that part of my motivation to write a series of articles on single fathers and their problems was to meet men. I wasn't exactly devoid of dates but being a single mother of five- and nine-year-old boys put me in a special—or not so special—category with men who had not had the pleasure of having children.

There was the "She's nice, but kids . . . " reaction.

There was the "She's nice, but I'm not up for a package deal . . . " reaction.

Then there was the "Kids—get me outta here . . . " reaction, which was actually the most common one.

It made sense, then, that finding men who had kids would put me in a dating pool of kindred spirits. Single fathers likely experienced those same reactions.

Pitching my editor was easy. Finding divorced fathers who were raising their children proved to be surprisingly easy, too. Brazenly walking up to men in the parking lot at my youngest son's day care center led me to several.

Widowers were another category. I knew one—an older guy with teenagers. Not date bait to be sure. A guy whose little boy was also at the day care center agreed, so I had two. But I needed at least one more to give depth to the article, preferably someone who might be having challenges dealing with the loss of a wife and being two parents rolled into one.

I was complaining to my mother about my dilemma when she popped up with her best friend's daughter's brother-in-law, who she was pretty sure was widowed and had little kids. I'd known her best friend and her daughter for years and though we hadn't kept up, I made the call to see if she'd connect me.

Not in a million years would he do this, she said. Larry was about the most unlikely person on earth to agree to an interview with a newspaper reporter on any topic, much less how he was coping with his kids, she said. He's a quiet, very private person and never talks about this—even to her, and they were very, very close. Hesitantly, she said she'd call and give him my number.

The next day, Larry called.

He listened quietly, paused and, to my amazement—and probably his—agreed to the interview as long as he could be anonymous in the story. His office, mine, a restaurant, library, his house—none were private enough for a meeting, he said. We agreed that he'd come to my duplex a few miles from where he lived around eight o'clock, after my boys were asleep. It was unconventional but I needed that third interview and, after all, he was vouched for.

I sat cross-legged on the couch in my living room, posed simple questions and listened as his world opened up. He paused thoughtfully before answering, talking about being dad/mom for the past two years—learning to cook (meat loaf was his specialty), expecting his three kids to help keep things more or less on the right side of clean, building a car with his son for a pinewood derby, being the only man at PTA meetings or classroom outings, buying dresses for his older daughter that she would actually wear, finding a babysitter he could trust, being frustrated when the kids would fight or vie for his attention, finding words to explain why their mother died, wanting to be the one to raise his kids and never, ever farm them out to relatives who were more than willing to take them. After several cups of coffee and six hours of conversation, he went home to his eight-, seven- and two-and-a-half-year-olds.

I called a few days later to let him know when the stories would run. He called back and asked if I liked Chinese food. Why not? Mom agreed to babysit. He picked me up the following Saturday.

Rattling on was my nature. What he lacked in chatter he made up for in kind, gentlemanly ways. Humor was his nature. I think I was born to laugh and was a willing audience. Hours slipped by.

My eager mother, who would have married me off to pretty much anybody just to have me married again, was on me in a flash. "Well? Did you like him?"

"Yeah. He's a really nice guy. But I don't think it will go anywhere."

Her disappointment was palpable.

"Mom," I said firmly, "I need three more kids like I need a hole in the head."

Indeed.

Getting together a week later was not really a date as much as a convenience of sorts. At dinner we found out we had one thing in common: we were both far behind in getting ready for Christmas. He called to ask if we'd bought a tree yet—no—and offered to pick us up in his station wagon to go find one. It was nine days till Christmas and the offer was not to be refused.

His kids, each possessing his dark hair and big curious eyes, peered out of the station wagon windows as I approached with my two towheads. We struck out at a far-away tree farm only to find perfect ones in a lot down the street from my house. He set up our tree before heading down the road, their tree firmly tied to the roof of the car, a little wave from the youngest as he pulled away.

The lotion Larry brought in a perfectly wrapped package when he stopped by on his way to his parents' house on Christmas Eve was especially thoughtful; I was alone that night, feeling sorry for myself with the boys visiting their father. I had nothing for him, our having known each other for only two-and-a-half weeks but remembered the hand-cast metal belt buckles I bought at a hippie craft fair months before, sitting upstairs in my dresser drawer. Excusing myself for a minute, I grabbed the one engraved with a man's head, wrapped it quickly and presented it to him. He seemed pleased.

Slow-forward four-and-a-half years to 1977—past weekly, then twice weekly, then weekend-long dates; past introductions to family and friends, including surviving a dinner with his late wife's five "best friends since grade school" who surrounded him with love after her death; past piling the kids into that station wagon to go vacationing and pretending that sleeping seven in a hotel room with two double beds and enough floor space for three boys in sleeping bags was something many people do; past the romantic dinner at a restaurant he couldn't really afford when a promise and a ring were offered and tearfully accepted; past a June wedding with our 13, 12, 11, 10 and 7-year olds standing on either side of us at the altar as we started our lives together.

We had high hopes that merging these five kids would work. By the time we married, they knew each other well since they were together so often and seemed to get along just fine. They built forts, rode bikes to the park, planned adventures, collected things. The boys played Dungeons and Dragons incessantly, and if anyone was going to be left out it was the youngest. She'd just search me out and join in whatever I was doing.

Happily ever after? Not quite.

The day after he proposed, I told my boys that Larry and I were going to get married. We were driving to a Christmas Eve family dinner at his parents' house. Four of his five siblings and their families would be there to hear our big announcement. I could see my ten-year-old smiling happily in the back seat as I excitedly shared our good news. The thirteen-year-old was silent.

"I thought maybe you and Dad would get married," he finally said, eyes fixed on the floor. Not what I expected, to be sure.

"But honey," I said, "your dad is already married. You know that."

"I know," he said softly. I should have taken his downcast eyes more seriously.

Larry told his three before we arrived and they were all standing together, waiting for us. Well, he said, giving them a nudge to say something as we approached. The seven-year-old hugged me and held on. Her big sister asked if I was going to be cooking for them and when I said yes, seemed satisfied that this could be a good thing. His oldest, the boy who was just a year younger than my son, smiled shyly but said nothing, not unusual for him.

With just six months between our engagement and the wedding, buying a new house, putting ours up for sale, figuring out what to take, and managing all the details of a wedding—we were consumed. The ceremony was perfect, his brother, my sister and the kids as our attendants. We were touched when my son, the one who had seemed so doubtful, stepped forward as we were leaving the altar and shook Larry's hand. Ours were the only kids at the reception and our friends danced them around the floor, brought them soft drinks in champagne glasses and took dozens of pictures of their smiling faces.

Two days after the wedding we moved into our new home in the suburbs of Chicago. It seemed huge—plenty of room for our Brady Bunch. Living room, large dining room and kitchen, extra-long couch and assorted chairs for watching TV in the family room, multiple bathrooms, an unfinished basement where they could roller skate if they wanted to. There were separate bedrooms for each of the boys; the girls reluctantly shared, and while there were countless disputes between them, I didn't worry, having had a sister and years of countless disputes that faded as we grew up.

I was still working at the newspaper a short commute away. Larry was in residential real estate and could drop in at home to check on things. I was off on weekends when he was at his busiest.

Everyone seemed to be adjusting, making friends, getting ready for the start of school. How did I miss it—the building tension between our thirteen- and twelve-year-old boys, the Alpha Males of their families, finding each other's presence increasingly provoking? There weren't a lot of fights but there were enough. A near fist fight between them at the dinner table over passing the gravy stunned us all, even them.

One big happy family was breaking down.

We hoped structure, rules, would help put everyone on an equal footing. If nothing else, they could unite in their disdain for the rules—turn their anger against us.

The Ten O'clock Rule remains legendary in our family. It held firm no matter the excuse. Breakfast by 10 a.m. or no breakfast. Lunch between noon and 2 p.m., then nothing until dinner, except during the school year when you could have approved after-school snacks. It was that or there would have been an endless parade of someone eating in the kitchen every minute of every day.

And the one thing our newly merged children had in common was eating. I was used to the eye-popping quantities my two boys consumed; add a twelve-year-old boy with his own insatiable appetite and an eleven-year-old girl who could rival her brother, not to mention a seven-year-old who'd learned to snatch as much as she could before her siblings took it all. Larry was no piker, bringing his pre-marriage habits along with him—like downing a half-gallon of milk straight from the carton, not even bothering to sit down.

I'm not sure I ever met our milkman, but I loved the guy nonetheless. Five gallons of milk, three times a week usually did the trick as long as everyone—husband included—followed The Milk Rule: no more than a quart per person per day. The girls and I usually didn't drink our milk allotment so with modest cheating by the others, we'd sometimes make it with enough left over for cooking and, at the end of the week, pudding.

On the rare occasion when there was food left after a meal together, we needed a Who Gets The Leftovers Rule. Larry came up with running a lottery to decide who could have whatever was left (and whatever it was, you could count on everyone saying they wanted it). He would select a number from one to a hundred and each would guess. The closest guess won, resulting in complaints that he or she "always wins."

We had the traditional curfew that allowed them to stay out later once they were in high school—10 p.m. for school nights, 12 a.m. for weekends. If we were in bed, the Curfew Rule was that they had to knock on our bedroom door and let us know they were home. In our naivete, we thought they then went to bed, finding out otherwise when they were grown, teasing us about what they got away with when they were kids. Apparently after knocking, our obedient children would often turn around and tiptoe back down the stairs, exiting the house through the back door, which was far, far away from our bedroom. Who knows when they crept back in.

Teaching them to do their own laundry was a stroke of genius. After group instruction I wrote up directions and taped them up in the laundry room. I taught them how to separate coloreds and whites, set the right temperature on the washer and dryer, and the elements of folding. With five of them competing for limited washer/dryer time you'd think they might collaborate and share a load or even take in one piece of clothing from someone else who was frantic to get it done. Not on your life. They didn't mind having their clothes mingled with those of others if I did the wash, but if they had to touch someone else's garment they found it disgusting.

Expecting them to clean the bathrooms they used was wishful thinking. Same with cleaning their bedrooms. It did happen, usually prompted by threats. At some point I learned it was better to just shut their doors.

The year after we married, I quit working full-time, free-lancing here and there to give me more time at home to tamp things down as tensions escalated. But I couldn't control their aging and the hormones that went with it. Our two oldest sons had plenty and almost did us in. The 13 then 14, 15, 16, 17-year-old seemed to become more cocky, more bullying; the 12 then 13, 14, 15, 16-year-old more angry, more resentful. There were "conversations" as Larry and I tried unsuccessfully to repair things. "Do you want us to get divorced?" I asked them separately. Both said no, but it was unconvincing. And it wasn't just them. With four kids moving through their teens with little more than a year apart there was plenty of surliness, sneers and tears for us to ask ourselves, What were we thinking? Would we and this marriage survive?

Don't get me wrong. There were many—not quite most, but many heart-warming Norman Rockwell moments when they banded together and gave us hope: the bentwood rocking chair they all pitched in to buy us one Christmas; the teamwork to turn over and plant the gardens; the rescues when someone was hurt or needed help; the loving and more often funny cards they bought and gave us, signed by them all..

They referred to us as "The Parents" instead of "Mom and Dad" for Larry was officially Dad to three and "Larry" to two; and I was officially Mom to two and "Dorothy" to the other three. The Parents was neutral when they talked about us to each other or to others. It was surprising how easy it was for Larry and me to love across family lines. We never referred to the kids as his, hers, mine, and especially not as stepson or stepdaughter. They were just ours and if someone else raised it, we'd simply say we didn't think of them as anything other than ours. We understood that the kids' acceptance was coming much more slowly. But then this was our idea, not theirs.

We were all more than ready to see the oldest fly off to a college in a state many miles away. I took a three-day-a-week job to see what would happen. Peace didn't completely descend upon our household as the four remaining at home found plenty to fight over, but they were more in the category of "She's wearing my sweater without asking." or "He's a selfish jerk and I hate him."—forgotten soon after. No one seemed to be going over the deep end when left alone—and if they did, we weren't at home to witness it.

We held our breath when he came back home for the summer after his freshman year. He seemed to be transformed. Nice, even. We walked on eggshells that didn't crack. I had to say something.

"You seem to be so much more okay about things here," I said searching for words that would not open Pandora's box.

"It's only for three months, Mom," he said directly. "I can do anything for three months."

Summer over, he flew back to school. The second oldest also packed up, heading to a college downstate. A year later, the third graduated high school, signed up for a local college, got a job and moved to her own apartment at the ripe old age of eighteen. The fourth graduated a year later and decided on a college in the city, happily moving into the dorm.

That left number five. And that's how it remained for the next couple of years as one after another of her brothers and her sister, instead of moving back home after college, took jobs out of state or moved into apartments of their own.

As our friends mourned when the last of their chicks left the nest, we did our best to contain our elation, giddiness—embracing the concept of being really alone for the first time in the sixteen years since we'd met and twelve years since we married. Our precious youngest child announced she was going to college all the way up in Minnesota, far enough away so that a quick weekend visit would be difficult for her, and we would not only have weekdays, but weekends free to scratch any sudden impulse.

We warned the kids who were in the vicinity to be sure to call before they dropped by so they didn't catch us running around the house in our underwear. That little warning worked. They called—and still do.

We were more than ready to launch our we-can-do-whatever-we-damn-well-please life. But there was always a "but." I found myself putting in much longer hours at my part-time turned full-time job downtown, bringing work home most evenings. And then Larry got really busy with clients and, you know real estate—evenings and weekends, showings and open houses, contracts and closings.

We did manage getaways—visiting the oldest in his new home in Atlanta; or the second oldest at his college and then his move to Colorado; or the third oldest at her apartment and then when she, too, moved to Colorado; or the fourth oldest at his various apartments and when he moved to Atlanta; and taking those five-hour trips up north before the youngest moved downstate and then across the border to Wisconsin.

Then marriages, grandchildren—fourteen of them!—great-grand-children—seven at last count!—and my nightly prayer finally answered when the five moved from tolerating each other to setting aside the feelings that so often threatened to tear us all apart.

What changed? I asked our second oldest, who held onto more anger than the others for the longest time. "Life is a series of phases," he said simply. "We've moved on."

Happily ever after. I treasure it, one day at a time. *

Fifty-one years and five days from our first meeting Larry passed away Dec 13, 2023, from Covid and pneumonia, leaving us with aching hearts and memories that have drawn our family closer together than ever thought possible. He was the love of our lives.

PAUL HOSTOVSKY

SCRABBLE WITH AMBER

Zet isn't a word.
    Yes it is.
And you can't go diagonal.
    Yes I can.

8-year old Amber
    is my girlfriend's daughter.
She isn't my daughter
    yet she is

because we all live together
    in the same house—
Amber, her brother, her mother,
    two cats, a rabbit,

hamster and me—
    trying to make
something of it. Do you have
    an *A*? *Zeta* is the 6th letter

of the Greek alphabet.
    No it's not. And anyway
I don't have an *A*. And you're not
    the boss of me.

THE NEW CRITICISM

My stepdaughter
says I'm boring.
"Everything you say
is boring and like
so seventies." Her mother
says I'm wonderful, though.
"She's being fresh. Don't
listen to her," she says.
But I can't help listening
because I want to be
fresh and not boring,
and I want to say 'like'
like my stepdaughter
because everything
is like something, not
exactly but sort of.
And she's so contemporary
and provocative and like
alive. She knows all the new
neologisms and would
never use *neologism*
in a poem. Like ever.

BOATING KNOTS

My stepson only eats hamburgers
and fries. And chicken nuggets.
Nary a vegetable or piece of fruit. And why
doesn't he get scurvy and die?

He never goes outside. Zero
exposure to the sun. Just stays in his room
playing video games all day. And why
doesn't he get rickets and die?

Just look at his room—he hasn't
cleaned it in over a year. His socks
are so defiled you could stand them up
and watch them defile out the door.

The toxic waste under his bed alone
should have killed him years ago.
Don't misunderstand me, I don't
wish him dead. But if he sailed away

on a long sea journey, say,
stuck on board for months on end
with no land in sight and nothing
to do all day but practice

his boating knots, I wouldn't
miss him. I would wish him
bon voyage and give him a lemon
as a parting gift, for the vitamin C,

if only for his mother's sake.

CINDERS

My stepkids bring out the evil stepmother in me.
That's me slamming the doors and drawers that they
have forgotten to close, me imagining their necks
as I throttle the plastic water bottles that they
have forgotten to recycle, me yelling at them to stop
yelling at each other while me and their mother
are watching this tearjerker, or this news program,
which are both "so depressing," say my stepkids,
"like how can you even watch that shit?" Hey,
watch your language, I say to my stepkids, whom
I blame for the decline of the language, the decline
of the culture, the decline of the whole world, come
to think of it, which will blow itself up—"sure as shit,"
I say to my stepkids, quoting my stepkids—one day soon,
maybe tomorrow, maybe even this very midnight.

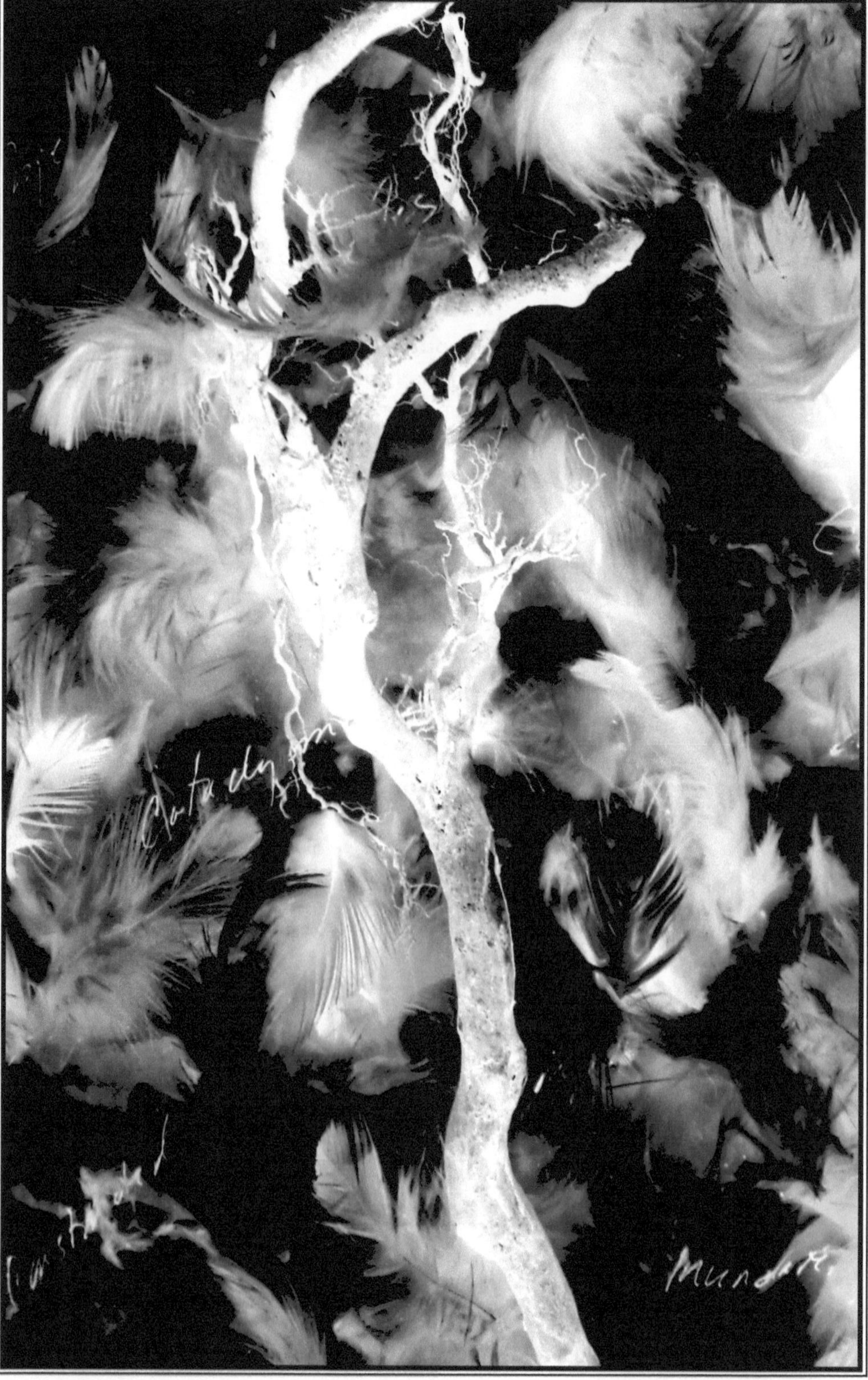

BRIAN DALDORPH

MUD

Matthew's watching some comedy show with a laugh track. A skinny Black kid with an Afro is trying to explain to his dad sitting on the couch why he doesn't want to try out for the football team.

"Those guys are bigger than Mack trucks!"

Loud laughter.

If I don't say something, Matthew will watch TV all evening. I need to tell him to turn it off, go do his homework. I checked his backpack. History homework, math problems, a Richard Wright story for English. If I tell him it's time for homework, he'll tell me that he's taking a break, that he'll go do it later.

That's what he did last night, then stayed up to 3 a.m., refused to get up in the morning. When I tried to shake him up, he snapped: "Why do I have to listen to *you?* You're not my dad."

That's the truth of it: I'm the intruder in this house.

Julia will get home from her late shift at AmTech too tired to get into a homework fight with Matthew.

"*Whatever,*" she'll say. "If you don't want to go to college, Matthew, I can't make you."

Matthew had a rough ride with what happened to his dad, and it's eating at him.

"Wanna go out for ice cream, Matt?"

"No, thanks, Steve. I'm good. Can you shut the door on your way out?"

But I don't leave. I sit down with Matthew on the couch and start watching this comedy show that's about as funny as mud.

HELGA KIDDER

STEPDAUGHTER

As outside polar air shivers into night,
you remember how she came into your life,
a precocious eleven-year-old girl,
red-headed, freckle-faced, and bright.

You remember how she came into your life
when you jumped into new marriage.
Her red hair and freckled face inspired you
to sew skirts and knit sweaters for her.

After you jumped into a new marriage,
you loved her as if she were your own child,
sewed skirts and knitted sweaters for her.
Then two years later her step-sister arrived.

You loved her as if she were your own child
with mild manners and easy-going smile.
Then two years later her step-sister arrived,
had to be nursed, diapered, and cuddled.

Her mild manners and easy-going smile
now placed on a shelf like a souvenir
as you had to nurse and change diapers,
asked her to baby-sit when going out.

Now placed on a shelf like a souvenir,
a precocious fourteen-year-old girl
asked to baby-sit while we went out,
as outside polar air shivered the night.

MORROW DOWDLE

STEPFATHER

Not mine, though I'd always hoped for one—
my husband's the closest I will ever get.
We ride in his pickup—a creature, like him,

rough and blunt—panels caked with dust,
upholstery cracked, vents stuttering warmth.
In our silence, disinfectant sloshes in the truck's bed.

We've gotten used to mopping messes
unrelated to us except by marriage. Today,
it's the house of a desperate relative.

We don't have to enter with our borrowed key
to grasp how bad it will be. Hours bleaching
blood from sheets, scouring toilets and tubs,

scrubbing cat vomit from carpet.
We're thorough, though we know
the work will be unseen, undone.

We wonder, again, how we've gotten here.
Maybe if we'd noticed how twisted
the limbs of this tree—

but with our own roots, were we prepared
for much different? If pressed, we might admit
we do this for no one but ourselves,

martyrs to our vows. They keep us around
because we keep their dirty secrets.
Sometimes we even clean them up.

ANGELA PAGE

TWICE A STEP MOM, ONCE A STEP DAUGHTER

I was twenty-nine when I married, Kurt, a Dane from Copenhagen, who had triplets from his first marriage. I was terrified at dealing with three ten-year-olds. To complicate matters these cute blonde and blue-eyed kids spoke only Danish so Kurt acted as translator.

When the triplets were eight, the family court split them up during the divorce. My husband Kurt fought for full custody of all three and ended up with only one, Clara. Kurt's ex-wife had custody of Elsa and Jan. This arrangement caused a lot of pain over the decades, especially for Jan.

My friends and family thought I was crazy, but I was madly in love with Kurt. I heard step-parenting horror stories and was advised to walk away and fast. I was apprehensive but threw myself into the role accompanied by fears and insecurity. The kids learned English way before I learned Danish.

The day after we were married I sat by myself across the room while the kids were draped around him vying for his attention. I stopped myself from bursting into tears, as I really wanted to cuddle with my new husband.

On the positive side, the kids began to influence me in many ways. I was a young banker but tended to dress matronly to appear older for credibility purposes. After shopping for tween clothes for the triplets, I was inspired to dress more youthfully. I traded dowdy pants, sweaters and blouses for T-shirts, sweatshirts, and jeans. I was up on all the new pop music and trends. They were also sporty and avid bike riders, which inspired me to get with the program. By the third year, I had lost weight, become very fit and looked younger.

I was a pleaser while resenting and wanting to nurture them at the same time. Many times they would overwhelm me. One Saturday when the triplets were fourteen, I counted sixteen kids, roaming around our house. Kurt didn't seem to be interested in setting boundaries or rules for the children.

The triplets were generally well behaved but had an intense rivalry among themselves. Elsa and Jan carried deep resentment about Clara being chosen by their father. They struggled with the divorces, and coping with blended families at both ends. Their mother had re-married and had a child.

We had a chaotic vacation with the triplets to the American West. I then suggested that all future vacations were one kid at a time. We set out a game plan of each of us taking one kid on a vacation. Kurt took Elsa to Stockholm then I traveled with Jan to Amsterdam, at his request, for the Van Gogh exhibition. Then Kurt and I took Elsa to Berlin, then we took Clara to New York.

We tried to encourage their passions. Jan was an accomplished pianist, a kind of child prodigy, from age ten. I cajoled him to enter a national piano competition for young musicians where he won second place. Clara showed great promise as an artist, drawing figures and cartoons. She was offered an opportunity to attend a private high school for the arts. I happily funded it when no one else would. Today, Clara credits me with her becoming a working graphic artist.

I was very concerned about Elsa. As the technically middle child she tended to mope, whine, and appear to have insecurities. I voiced my concern about her fate as she approached her teen years. She showed interest in photography, so we bought her a Nikon and paid for a workshop. Elsa took to it and still dabbles as a hobby.

Once I stopped sixteen-year-old Elsa from running to Athens with a twenty-seven-year-old Greek guy. I dramatically threw my body across the front door and said, "You're not going anywhere!" Kurt agreed with me and there was no trip to Greece.

Now as a mother of a tween girl, Elsa admits I was right and apologized for the mean things she said and thought about me, of which I have no recollection.

Our son Lenny was born when the triplets were fifteen. That same year the triplets' stepfather died of cancer, leaving their mother a widow with a four-year old. A year later, my husband Kurt developed serious pneumonia. We were all shocked to find out Kurt had AIDS-related pneumonia. He never revealed where he acquired HIV, and I stopped asking. His prognosis was poor as this was before the lifesaving drugs.

As Kurt battled multiple AIDS infections, we had to make plans. Our lives turned upside down as priorities changed along with living arrangements, finances, and end-of-life decisions. Though Kurt was weak, he was determined, and succeeded in living until the triplet's eighteenth birthday. He died a few weeks after and was cremated on our son Lenny's third birthday. Life was a shambles, emotionally and financially as Kurt was a bankrupt banker leaving only debts.

Despite the shock and heavy grieving, I tried maintaining a sense of normalcy while looking our for our collective well-being. As there was a large age difference from my bio kid and the step kids, there were different considerations. The triplets were about to graduate high school and enter college while the three-year-old needed routine and a stable mom. I tried hard to keep everyone on track. I found a life insurance policy among my husband's documents and arranged for lump sums to be paid out to all four kids. This helped with their college education expenses.

I think it was the kids, especially the little guy, that saved my ass and kept me from going over the edge. I had to stay grounded to keep the family rolling forward. It was almost two years before I could feel real joy in life.

My role in the everyday lives of my stepchildren ended with the death of my husband. My son Lenny and I moved back to the U.S. while the triplets remained in Denmark. In the first decade, I was determined my son maintain connection with his Danish siblings and family. We visited Denmark frequently, and I paid for the triplets to visit us in the U.S.

I was privy to the triplets' romances, break-ups, studies, career changes, marriages, and even navigating a same sex union. Kurt's death prompted Clara to reveal she was a lesbian, and in her mid-twenties she married a lovely woman. They have two girls, thanks to a sperm bank. Elsa followed, marrying a marvelous stable businessman who adores her and their two children. Jan has two boys with a woman, and they do the "together, living apart" arrangement.

I commend the triplets for building successful lives in the wake of so much drama from the time they were young. I thank them for not subjecting me to any drugs, teen pregnancies, arrests, or serious car accidents, and only three E.R. visits among all four kids.

My time with the triplets often includes long night chats revisiting their father's illness and death. There is a lot of sadness around Kurt choosing to die with me and Lenny and not in Denmark. We also analyze their parents' breakup and the split custody arrangements. Each time we find a new angle as to why Kurt chose Clara and not Jan. Elsa doesn't seem to hold any resentment, being very attached to her mother at that time.

I remind the kids that Kurt was riddled with guilt about the decision of choosing custody of one of them. My stepson Jan has been particularly curious about his father's sexual orientation. He even questioned his own at one point and we discussed it by phone for over an hour when he was in his twenties.

With all the drama and emotional rollercoaster, I became a more experienced parent. I was better equipped when my son Lenny reached his teen and young adult years.

I was only married to their father for seven years, but after thirty-seven years I maintain a strong bond and friendship with my triplet stepchildren and now their own children. In the subsequent almost four decades we have managed to survive, thrive, create new memories and shared experiences.

A decade ago, in my mid-fifties, I married a man twenty years my senior. Joe was in his mid-seventies and was being treated for prostate cancer. He had been widowed like me early and left with small children to raise. We had a strong common experience.

I became a stepmom to his three grown children, and the eldest was only seven years younger than me. I never met Joe's eldest son who lived in Vegas and had a serious addiction problem. I only knew him from middle of the night phone calls where he would like to relive the painful history of his mother's death and Joe's subsequent love life.

Joe's middle-aged daughter seemed to be sweet and caring. However, she was always after a handout from Joe and had trouble maintaining a steady job. He finally cut her money supply off. Then after a flame email exchange they ended their contact.

The youngest son, Adrian, by Joe's second wife, was nearly the same age as my son Lenny. They both worked in the film industry in Los Angeles. So it felt like an interesting blended family dynamic. Joe and I even planned on moving to Los Angeles to be near our sons.

Unfortunately, Joe's prostate cancer advanced after only a year of our being together. He quickly declined, and only then I was allowed to be involved in his medical care. His cancer had metastasized, and he had months to live. I immediately contacted Adrian, who was too busy with work and could not fly from California to New Jersey. He was also annoyed with Joe's condition. "I have no time for this."

Even after he understood the gravity of his father's condition, he still did not plan to visit. It was heartbreaking to listen to them argue by phone. I was devastated for Joe and could not imagine a child ignoring and dismissing a parent who was seriously ill. I knew they had conflicts, but as far as I could tell, he had been a good provider and father. It appeared there were unresolved issues from Joe's divorce twenty years before when Adrian was a teenager.

Adrian was furious I held sole power of attorney, both financial and medical. He went ballistic and shouted, "You've hardly been together with this woman!"

Joe shouted back, "I want to die in love—don't ruin it." He also boasted I had experience in being a caregiver twenty years earlier with my husband Kurt. Never imagined I would have credentials for helping husbands die.

Adrian didn't let up his attacks on Joe and me. It became so stressful I wanted to leave the situation, but it felt inhumane to leave Joe. His condition went downhill quickly. I was now managing his medical care and finances, hiring caregivers, and dealing with his son long distance. Adrian got wind that he and I would be sharing Joe's estate equally. After all the expenses, it wouldn't be a fortune. Adrian complained I was spending too much on home care and should not deplete Joe's dwindling funds.

In reality Adrian was broke, and was looking forward to some inheritance. He asked Joe's doctors and the hospice nurse to find a free facility. It became even more ugly after Joe's death. Adrian invited his mother, Joe's ex-wife, to pick through our furniture for what may have been in their joint home twenty years before.

❧

Long before I became a stepmom I was a stepdaughter from age nineteen. My father married Veronica shortly after my parents' divorce. Veronica is only fourteen years older than me and married my dad in her early thirties. It was a relief that my father had a new wife to rant about his issues. I had been a surrogate wife since age eleven and the recipient of his wrath about the messy divorce with my mother.

Veronica became an advocate as I made my way through college. Without her financial help I would not have been able to finish my degree. My father was a degenerate gambler and lavish spender. At tuition time, it was Veronica who paid his share of the bill per the divorce proceeding. It was probably why years later I paid without hesitation for my stepdaughter Clara's private high school. Stepmoms stepping up for the step kids.

After I received my degree, Veronica, an H.R director, helped me wordsmith my resume and printed copies at her office. My father, a fashionista, picked out and bought me the interview navy suit and shoes.

I lived overseas and on another coast for three decades, so I had sporadic in person visits with Veronica and my dad then. All the while, Veronica stood by my dad and his mental health issues. Both my sister and I were eternally grateful that our stepmom Veronica dealt with our father, who was a handful.

When my father fell ill with cancer in his late eighties, Veronica, became frazzled, developed high blood pressure and knee problems. It was critical that she remain his caregiver as my sister and I had our elderly mother with dementia to deal with.

Veronica developed an evening drinking habit to get through my dad's illness and his sinking into dementia. Chardonnay became her daily coping mechanism along with ordering kitchen items from QVC and HSN.

I helped her when I could by ferrying my dad to doctor appointments and chemo sessions. Veronica was not only essential as my father's caregiver, but his sole financial source. They lived on her pension. If it was not for Veronica, my dad would have been a homeless vet.

After he died in his early nineties, I stayed with Veronica for a month to sort out all the paperwork and get her organized. My sister and I, her stepdaughters, have become Veronica's only family. She's an active eighty-year-old widow living in a large house on five acres. Within the first year of my father's death, Veronica added a multitude of animals, including two old racehorses, two Australian shepherd dogs, seven feral cats, and a sheep named Sabrina, who is supposedly a temporary resident.

Despite the appearance of being affluent in a large, lavishly decorated house on five acres with a barn, Veronica is riddled with debt. This was to some degree the fault of my late father, who insisted on expensive furnishings. They also kept four fridges and two freezers always packed, enough to feed a village.

After forty-five years, stepmom Veronica is a fixture and remains an important part of our lives and family. Not only do we love Veronica, but we are grateful she took care of dad for over four decades. She saved us a lot of grief and drama. So now my sister and I are seniors taking care of seniors.

My step-triplets Clara, Elsa and Jan are eighteen years younger than me, so chances are we'll also be seniors together.

beloved
nurtured
melted
held
healed

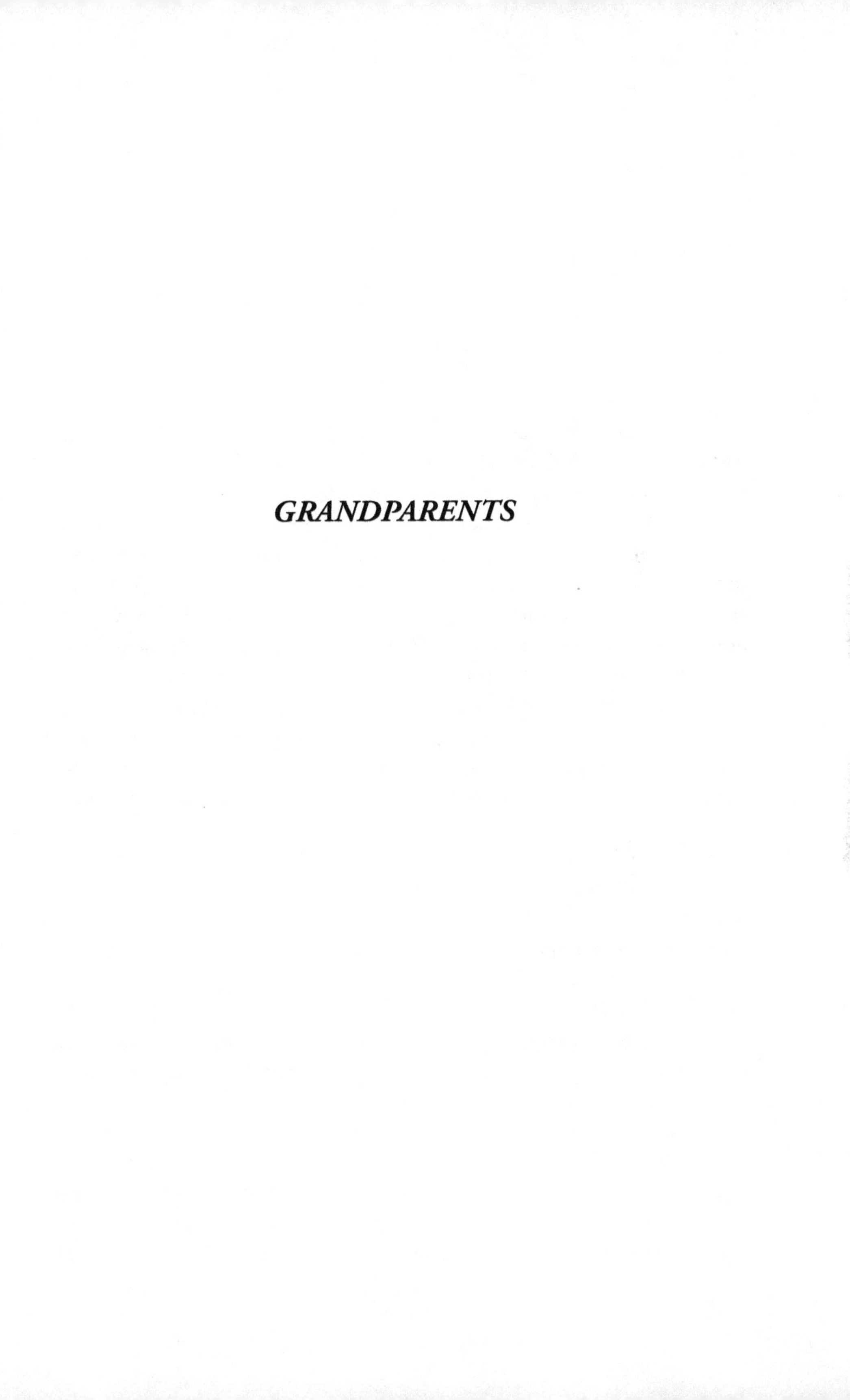

GRANDPARENTS

ED DAVIS

KING OF HAMMERS, QUEEN OF STRINGS

Stepping across the threshold, I trade sunshine for the cool cave darkness of the old garage. Once inside, the smell envelopes me—oil, moldy rope and sweet-sour, aging wood. On my left, I glimpse the dark jumble of scrap lumber, cracked tires and dusty canvas tarp under which lie lumpy, nameless things. At the far end stand the double doors that have not opened to receive an automobile since I've been alive. To the right, Granddad stands at the workbench before windows that overlook the small, sunny garden overflowing with onions, tomatoes and beans. A child's faded brown cowboy boots dangle in one corner of the dusty glass. I'm pretty sure they were mine.

"Eddie-boy," Granddad calls in a liquid voice garbled by the cigar he's chewed to pulp. After glancing past his shoulder, he returns his gaze to whatever project lies before him on the bench here in his kingdom, where he spends most waking hours. What he does out here is his work since he stopped driving the tri-city bus. He's been old and retired all my life.

Tools wait close to hand in half-open drawers. Behind him stands the table saw with its scary teeth and screaming whine that hurt my ears when I was little. Now eleven, I'd bear it more easily, but he hasn't used it in ages. It's been over a decade since he built the adjacent garage apartment and several years since he cut, carved and lathed little swords for me with dull edges and blunt tips. Grandmother would've skinned him alive if any of us kids had had to be rushed to the hospital with a battle wound. Maybe that's why Granddad never let me help him. I remain tool-illiterate to this day, an educational gap I've always regretted.

Across the yard stands the new garage Granddad built, about the time of my birth, 1951, with a cozy apartment above and two divided car stalls below, one for his Chevy, one for the apartment dweller's car. For a year, the apartment housed me, my mom (Granddad's daughter) and my dad, before he got a job driving for Trailways and moved us to Roanoke, Virginia, where I started first grade. Now Mom and I live a couple miles away, in an apartment across from the Mercer County Courthouse, where my dad lived until he got out of jail. He'd been arrested for non-support, at the urging of Grandmother. We haven't seen him since.

Grandmother's worst fears about my father had been realized. A decade earlier, my parents visited with their new baby daughter. Mom was pregnant with me and I'd be born in December of that year. At the end of the visit, Mom returned to Coalwood in southern West Virginia without her daughter, whom she'd left in the care of our grandparents. Grandmother had apparently felt my parents might be competent enough to raise one child but not two. And since my dad was hoping I'd be a boy, my infant sister seemed the obvious choice for my grandparents to raise. In those days, Appalachian families often blended others' children, even non-relatives, into their own families, but usually not when the parents were still living. I like to say that my sister got three good hot meals a day, a backyard swing set and stability, while I got complete freedom. Which, of course, came with a cost.

While the new garage is a tidy, clean, modern concrete block structure, the old one in which I'm standing is from the era of Model T's, crank starters and rumble seats. It houses a man's world, where my grandfather—King of Hammers and Saws—chews cigars, cusses, spits and pees in rusty coffee cans (much too far to walk to the house). When I visit him out here, it's always just me and him—it's best his second wife doesn't know what-all goes on out here. I can't remember ever seeing my big sister in the old garage, but that doesn't mean she never visits.

Grandmother sometimes sends me to fetch Granddad, a task that can take up to an hour. He's always been excruciatingly slow, earning his wife's scorn and ire. She has plenty of that to go around. Long ago, she'd been hired to keep house for him after his first wife, Rhoda, passed away, when Mom was a toddler. After my step-grandmother wed her employer, she inherited Rhoda's eight children, had one of her own, raised my sister and contended with mine and Mom's lengthy stays whenever Dad left the picture. Hers was a very crowded house. She was always in motion: dusting, sweeping, hanging and folding laundry, cutting out biscuits with a water glass, standing before her Hotpoint stove while chicken hissed in her black cast-iron skillet.

The economic dynamo powering the family machine, my step-grandmother could squeeze a dollar till George Washington screamed in surrender. I can still see her sitting in the "breakfast room," pasting

S & H green stamps into booklets to be traded for household necessities and scrutinizing the grocery receipt for errors. At such times, the Queen of Purse Strings was not to be bothered. She wouldn't have been caught dead in that filthy, smelly old garage where the King of Hammers reigned. Like many married couples, my grandparents required some apartness; I never saw affection expressed between them. She referred to Granddad as "him" or "he," as in "Tell him to get up here. He's letting the food get cold." However, he called her by her given name, Mahala, an exotic word to my provincial Appalachian ears. Now I know that, in Hebrew, the name means "tender," ironic for such an iron-fisted woman, whom I can't recall touching me except to deliver discipline with her razor strop, and, once, with a hairbrush.

There was some overlap between my grandparent's domains, but not much. While I'm sure she loathed Granddad's cigar chewing, she allowed him to spit in the can behind the bathroom toilet. The cigar resentment, though, was nothing, compared to her disappointment in my mother. (It would be another twenty-five years before Mom's schizophrenia and "borderline mental retardation" were finally diagnosed by a nursing home doctor.) Grandmother ruled the roost—someone had to—and Granddad, for all his bluster when he became angry, was, like Mom, childlike himself. Sometimes my memory casts him as weak; I wonder if shrewd might be more accurate. He knew what he could and couldn't get by with inside territory conquered long ago by a mate grown ruthless by necessity.

The Christmas I was in first grade, my mother and I returned from Roanoke in defeat. Mom's failure to hold onto her husband ignited Grandmother's short fuse, and my joyful reunion with my sister was cut short when I was drawn by shouting from the kitchen. I got there in time to witness Grandmother furiously slap my weeping mother. Though my grandfather must have been in the house, my memory doesn't include him in the terrible scene. Hours later, awakening beside my sleeping mother, I found my pajama bottoms urine-soaked. I rose in the dark, crept through the hallway and straddled the furnace register, trying futilely to dry myself, reliving the sound of flesh striking flesh. I don't recall what punishment the morning brought, but surely there was hell to pay. Asylum, like freedom, came with a cost in Mahala's strict court.

But my grandmother has no jurisdiction here in the old garage on this sultry summer day. Still, I fidget and stall. I hate to ask Granddad for more, when the supper his wife is preparing right now, plus his company, should be all a grandson needs. But Mom won't forgive me if I come home empty-handed. Ready at last, I approach the man at the bench to make my petition. His face is impassive, eyes lowered. Wordlessly he extracts the old brown billfold from his back pocket. Squinting behind his glasses, he plucks out three worn dollar bills and hands them to me. I pocket them quickly. (The queen's eyes are everywhere.)

My heart settles. Mom will be happy; we'll eat tomorrow and maybe the next day, too. In 1962, $3 bought a loaf of bread, a pound of bologna, two cans of Luck's pinto beans, a quart of milk and a box of Frosted Flakes, enough to tide us over till her $68 monthly welfare check arrives. As an adult, I've always cringed whenever I have to do anything that hints of begging—request a donation, return a product to a store, ask members of my political party to vote for our candidates. I believe what I felt was fear, not shame, asking the man I respected like no other for money. Is it Grandmother's eyes, then, which forever find me betraying her behind her back?

Sixty years on, I know the old garage was the site of psychologically complex family drama, mine and Granddad's transaction just one example of the ways my mother's mental illness forced me to parent her. Granddad knew his second wife resented the wayward daughter who'd failed as wife and mother. But he blessed his grandson anyway there in the dim glow of smudged windows, hulking machinery and his life's detritus, hoarded like treasure. He passed to me something more precious than money, useful as that was in our hard times. Grandmother lectured, needled, slapped and nagged, while keeping everyone sheltered and well-fed. Behind her back, Granddad gave his grown daughter and her son all he could spare, without a single shaming word.

For good or ill, I absorbed them both. Guilt and grace, generosity and greed, judgment and compassion have warred within me all my life. I've been Ebenezer Scrooge and Bob Cratchett in the same day, in the same *hour*. One of my best students told me, early in my college teaching career, that "you smile like John Boy Walton and grade like Genghis Khan." I have expected a great deal from others. Often, I feel like David Copperfield, less the agent than observer of my life. No doubt, that's partly what makes me a writer. Sometimes it feels like I'll be forever telling this story. A good writing friend tells me that's okay, and I'm beginning to accept that.

I slip so easily back to that hot summer day at the beginning of the tumultuous decade wherein I grew taller, began smoking, bought an electric guitar, joined a band, graduated from high school, started college and watched the mother I couldn't save sink deeper and deeper into undiagnosed mental illness. And attended my step-grandmother's funeral, Mahala's untimely death preceding her much older husband's by a dozen years.

That day in August, though, standing among the boxes of wood scraps, rusty nails, washers and bolts, I know that my grandparents rule their respective domains, one of darkness, one of light. They each have their weaknesses and strengths. I've revised, like a good writer must, my memory of Mahala as the wicked step-witch. She fed me, wanted the best for me, worked hard as the head of her family, was a regular church-goer and member of the Order of the Eastern Star, charitable off-shoot of Granddad's Masons. She died trying to feed all of us with our endlessly open mouths. Granddad, gentle and passive to a fault, will, in my memory, always be opening his billfold, extracting three ones, sneaking behind his wife's back to help a perennially needy daughter and her hungry son.

Emerging from the old garage into sunshine and fresh air, I hear the drone of a lawn mower, a neighbor's banging screen door, tinny music from a distant radio. I'm back inside the summer before sixth grade, the royal blood of my surrogate parents running through me: Granddad, my gentle king and conscience; Grandmother Mahala, tender despot, feeder of souls.

Found

TERRI ELDERS

WAITING FOR GOLDILOCKS

I've never thought of myself as a crybaby, though I sob every time I hear "If I Loved You" from *Carousel,* with its allusion to golden chances that we might miss.

And I've whimpered at weddings . . . most memorably at my Grandma Gertie's when she remarried when I was nine years old. My new so-called aunts and uncles and cousins had swiveled their heads around in the pews that autumn afternoon, staring with surprise. I hadn't cared a whit about what these time thieves thought, though. I'd good reason to cry. Grandma would be stepping away!

"I don't mind getting a stepfather," Mama had muttered, "but look at all the rest of them. Mother's picking up so many stepchildren and all their kin. There are only so many hours in a day. She won't be coming around here much anymore."

I'd been horrified. Now I wouldn't be cutting out paper dolls from the Sears catalog with Grandma anymore. And she likely wouldn't have time to make me any new ruffled dresses on her treadle sewing machine. She'd be too busy playing with these new step-grandkids, and sipping cocoa with their parents instead of with Mama and me. I'd counted at least a dozen of these "step" people.

But when tears trickled down my cheeks in the foyer of St. John Romanian Orthodox church a few years ago, everybody in attendance cast a curious glance my way. I mean, who cries at christenings, aside from infants? I felt relieved when baby Kendra obliged with some howls when she was plunged into the baptismal basin, so grateful that she'd diverted attention from me. I fished in my purse for a handkerchief to blot my cheeks dry. My step-granddaughter and I had wailed for different reasons, though. I suspect she just felt cold, while I felt . . . old.

I'd never expected I'd ever become a grandmother of any kind, natural, foster or step, myself, least of all in my seventies. My son, an only child, while still in his teens had told me he didn't anticipate ever becoming a dad.

"Children don't interest me," he'd claimed. "I can't imagine myself feeling attached to one."

"Don't be too sure," I warned. I believed he'd change his mind as he grew older. But I was wrong. A decade later he married a woman who shared his doubts about offspring. The two happily raise cats.

When Steve's dad and I divorced just as our son edged into his twenties, I reconciled myself to a single life, and began to embrace the kind of independence I'd never previously had, having married while still in my teens. I savored several romances, seeing a few men with grown kids whom I sensed seemed appalled at the thought that their dad was dating again, loyal always to their own moms, dead or alive. I'd thought that a totally normal reaction, given my own when Grandma Gertie remarried. I hadn't expected to be welcomed. Nor had I any intention of remarrying!

After her wedding, Grandma spoke warmly of her three new step-children. Mama, however, clearly saw the trio and their own kids as trespassers. I, of course, always followed her lead.

"Why do they go buttering her up on every occasion?" Mama had griped to me as we set the table for the first combined-family Thanksgiving, her face pruning up with resentment. "Just because their own mother died doesn't mean they had to steal mine." I nodded in agreement, scrunching up my own face, as if I'd smelled something noxious.

Clearly Mama had pictured herself thrust into the role of a kind of reverse Cinderella . . . rudely shoved aside to make room for a litter of Grandpa Louie's half-orphans. I soaked up her attitude like a sponge and developed a studied wariness around these alleged relatives I'd suddenly inherited. These new creatures who crowded around Grandma's table, helping themselves to our turkey and pumpkin pie, weren't really family, I'd decided. Instead, I viewed them as opportunistic exploiters, carpetbaggers! After they'd leave at twilight, hugging Grandma farewell, I'd have to restrain myself from counting the family sterling . . . and my comic books. These intruders were not to be trusted.

Nor did I ever intend to insert myself into anybody else's family. So, during the decades after my divorce, I settled into a happy singlehood, traveling the world with the Peace Corps, and then taking jobs in parts of the country I'd never before seen. I didn't mind an occasional dinner out with a gentleman suitor, or a brief fling, but meeting their descendants? No, thank you very much. I'd not become anybody's stepmother . . . not in a million years. I favored the old truisms . . . blood is thicker than water; birds of a feather stick together.

But not having grandkids, now that was a bird of another feather. I'd always kidded myself that I'd adjusted easily to a grandchild-free life. As a therapist, I'd worked for years with infants and toddlers so hadn't missed out on singing lullabies or reading *Curious George*. I reassured myself that I could still enjoy children vicariously. They didn't have to be related to me, after all. I'd raised one of my own. That was enough.

At high school reunions when former classmates shuffled through photos of grandchildren, I'd nod politely and refrain from rolling my eyes while they bragged about how beautiful, brilliant, and perfectly behaved all of their brood had turned out to be. I'd mention my travels and my work and pretend not to see pity fill their eyes when they realized I had changed the subject because I had no grandchildren of my own to boast about.

My son and daughter-in-law had laughed. "Tell them you have grandcats. We'll supply some pictures," they said.

Then, in my sixties, totally spellbound and afraid not to embrace a chance for a new direction in my life, I married a man, Ken Wilson, who claimed enough grandchildren to fill my calendar pages with birthday reminders. That worried me for a bit, but, fortunately, they all lived half a continent away, so we wouldn't be tasked with any onerous babysitting.

Then, gradually, my attitude subtly began to shift. I suffered a few pangs of jealousy when girlfriends alluded to taking their granddaughters to see *The Nutcracker*, or out for banana splits. I began to recall the delight of going to the movies or shopping with Grandma Gertie, who always found time for me . . . even after she remarried.

Nonetheless, I figured that babysitting grandkids probably wouldn't be something I'd really relish. I lead far too busy a life. I've always got weeds to pull or books to read . . . I'd never find time to waste an afternoon baking gingerbread with a child, would I?

I also felt relief that my husband's kids didn't see enough of me to cast me in the role of an evil stepparent. Because of their geographical distance, occasionally we'd see them at a family gathering, a graduation or a wedding. But my husband, who'd never stopped bragging about how much he loved raising his own three sons, now claimed he didn't know how to relate to his grandchildren, especially the toddlers.

"I never know what to say when I see them," Ken complained. "I can play chess with the older ones, but what in the world do you say to a five-year-old?"

I laughed. I worked with little kids. I knew the answer.

"Just invite the child to tell you a story. A five-year-old always has a tale to tell, even if it's only a rehash of 'The Three Bears.' You'll see."

Ken looked doubtful.

"Really," I continued. "It's always worked for me. Just try it."

I noticed that the next time we saw his grandkids, one or two tots blinked up at him with shining eyes. He'd smile for a minute, as if he were about to say something, and then turn away. Still uncomfortable, I'd guess. I never heard him ask them to tell stories. Maybe he was embarrassed. Maybe he worried he'd be thought a silly old fool for wanting to hear a story. Or maybe he simply wasn't interested in hearing about Goldilocks.

Despite early misgivings, I might have welcomed their interest. But though the children called me Grandma Terri, they didn't linger around me for long. I'd guessed they figured me in masquerade, a granny-come-lately, not a real grandma at all. They all had other grandmas who'd been around first, of course. *Fine with me*, I'd reassure myself. *I don't want to intrude.*

Happily, blended families might seem great in theory, I'd concluded, *but in truth, the relationships probably always remain awkward, despite everybody's good intentions.* Even the word *step-grandmother* sounded clumsy to my ear. So did *Grandma Terri*. Both phrases contained far too many rat-a-tat-tatty syllables. The rhythm didn't seem right. Grandma, Nana, even Granny, are harmonious words, cozy, and comforting, reflective of *real* relationships.

Several years passed, and then Kendra came along. Ken's middle son, Rick, had married in his forties, and his wife, Angela, now gave birth thirteen days after my dear husband had succumbed to cancer. This blessed child, Rick declared, would be his namesake. Ken had known she'd be named after him, and in his final days he mentioned more than once that he wished he could last long enough for her to be born. He'd been thrilled that she was on her way.

"I still regret not getting to know my grandkids better," he'd confided in his final weeks. "I hope they understand that I could never figure out how to talk to them. I'm sorry I never asked them for stories."

"I'll make certain Kendra knows that you loved her before she even got here," I promised. "And don't worry. When she gets old enough, I'll ask her to tell a story."

Rick and Angela brought baby Kendra to visit when she was a few weeks old. They drove to our country home in Northeast Washington to pay respects to Ken's memory, as did Ken's other sons. I held her for a while and to my astonishment didn't want to hand her back to her mom, even though the baby made it clear she needed to be fed. To my astonishment, I'd felt that old maternal urge kick into high again. It had been over fifty years since I'd held an infant that somehow seemed to belong to me.

Eight months later I flew to Arizona for Kendra's christening. Rick's own mother was ill, and unable to travel, and Angela's mother lived in a rural village in Moldova in faraway Eastern Europe. I'd figured I'd be a stand-in, but according to Rick, apparently, I was the genuine article, the real thing. No "step" about it. I beamed with pride when he introduced me to the priest in the foyer of the church.

"Here's the grandma," he'd said, throwing an arm around my shoulders.

I couldn't tear my eyes away from this infant. By now, Kendra already had her grandpa's twinkling blue eyes and lopsided smile. It was clear she'd be a Wilson! I was ready to bet she'd display her grandpa's ready wit, too, as soon as she'd learn to talk.

I slowly recognized that this amazing baby could be my own bona fide grandchild. Immediately I started to plot for the years ahead. I began to picture how I'd get to play with her whenever I could get down to Arizona or lure her parents up to Northeast Washington. *Why, I bet she'd love to play with my dogs and cats and watch my neighbor's horses.* As soon as she was old enough, I'd let her accompany me on a walk around our loop. She could hold the leash for Ken's mutt, Natty, and I'd handle the bigger dog, Ken's Akita, Tsunami. As the guests filed to our seats for the baptismal ceremony, I silently vowed that I'd remember Kendra's every birthday, her every Christmas.

That's when my grin turned into a grimace, and I burst into tears. I'd suddenly realized that at my age it was highly unlikely I'd be around to snivel as Kendra graduated from high school. I wouldn't be around to whimper at her wedding. By the time she'd be old enough to have children, an entire century would have elapsed since my own birth date. I'll never make it to become a great-grandma!

I finally pulled myself together. I didn't need to worry about the distant future. I could seize each chance to "grandma" as it came. I could send toys and games and books and cards. I could post photos on my Facebook page. I could display the holiday greetings I'd receive, addressed to "Grandma." I could bore my friends at high school reunions with tales of her antics.

After the christening, one of Ken's old friends approached.

"Were you crying because you missed Ken?"

"Yes," I admitted, crossing my fingers.

It was merely a little fib, a little white lie. I missed my husband. Certainly, I wish he'd been there with me. But in my heart, I knew I cried for all those lost years where I'd never had a chance to sprinkle stardust over grandchildren's lives the way my own grandmothers had over mine.

She's recently turned three, but Kendra better watch out. Stardust will be drifting her way soon. I'm prepared to babysit. So, she'd better be prepared to see *The Nutcracker*, and to eat banana splits. When she gets a little older, I'll rent a video of *Carousel,* and we can sniffle together. I already have *The Last Unicorn* waiting for her next visit.

The last time she visited, Kendra held Natty's leash and took him for a stroll. She helped water my plants and played with the cats. She talks to me on the phone now and has recorded her voice in a "Happy Birthday, Grandma" book for me. I've read to her from her goodnight books. Pretty soon, Kendra will be telling me stories. I can hardly wait!

And though I'm not a crybaby, she shouldn't be surprised if I tear up a little when I give her a welcome hug . . . or more than a little when it's time to kiss her goodbye.

As for great-grandmotherhood . . . guess what? I've made it. A few weeks ago, I got an early morning phone call from Ken's oldest son, Scott. It was about his own daughter, Ken's oldest grandchild. Kiri, barely into her teens when Ken and I married in 2000, had honored us by tending the guestbook at the ceremony.

"I'm phoning to tell you that you're now a great-grandmother," he announced. "Kiri had her little girl, Daisy, just this morning." I noticed Scott didn't say *step-great-grandmother.*

I haven't met Daisy yet in person, but I'm tracking her progress, thanks to Facebook. She looks pretty clever already to me. I see a trace of that Wilson smile. And from a photo her Grandpa Scott posted today, I notice that she's apparently dog-friendly already, as her mother snuggles her in one arm and a puppy in the other. I'm already picturing having the two of them, Kendra, and Daisy, relieve me someday soon of my dog-walking chores altogether.

Now, I've got to figure out how I can get them up here at the same time from the far distant reaches of Arizona and Colorado. It would be great if they could come when *The Nutcracker* makes its annual winter visit to the Spokane stage. Of course, any time of the year is good for a banana split at Barman's old-fashioned soda fountain right here in Colville. And I sure wouldn't mind babysitting a couple of little girls who would play with paper dolls with me.

When I complained about some aches and pains at my annual physical checkup the other day, my doctor told me that I'm not getting any younger. True as that may be, it's clear I need to plan to hang around for at least a few more years.

After all, I've waited far too long to find out what happened to Goldilocks. I wonder which of these Wilson girls, Kendra or Daisy, my granddaughter, or my great-granddaughter, will have the juicier version.

Novelist Alex Haley, the author of *Roots,* understood familial relationships. "Nobody can do for little children what grandparents do. Grandparents sort of sprinkle stardust over the lives of little children," he wrote.

True, but it also works in reverse. Little children can work magic for their grandparents. And for their step-grandparents, as well. As for my doubts about blended families, they've been buried, smothered by an avalanche of stardust. And I haven't shed a tear losing those doubts.

Not long ago, as I flipped through an old family album, I came across some photos taken at Grandma Gertie's funeral. There's Mama, being hugged by her stepbrothers, and holding hands with her stepsister. Now I remember how they'd been there for each other, to comfort one another in their mutual grief. And I also remember, after a reception at Mama's house, after we'd polished off all the punch and cake Mama had labored over, and the entire blended family finally had drifted away, one by one, that Mama sat down at her kitchen table and shared a few confidences with me.

"I gained so much when Mother married Louie," she'd said. "I'd never had a sister before, and the two boys were always so generous with their time and help. We grew so close over the years."

As we cleared away the dishes, I noticed that neither Mama nor I had stopped to count the silverware.

This past Grandmother's Day I got a phone call from Kendra. She's still a bit too young to tell me what happened to Goldilocks . . . but she did tell me all about Dora the Explorer!

I reassured her that one day she, too, can travel all over the world, just like Dora and her Grandma Terri. I reminded her that the dogs and I can hardly wait for her next visit.

"I love you, Grandma," Kendra had said. There was no "if" in that declaration.

When I hung up the phone, I quickly dabbed away a tear. After all, I'm not a crybaby. Just grateful that I'm not letting any golden chances pass me by.

interlace
dispersal
ground
flourish
inherit
disturb
uproot

CHILDREN

SHERRY SHAHAN

FACE BEYOND THE MASK

My stepbrother Kevin S.B. is a drifter with arrests in more than one state. Born in August 1961, he's sixty years old, paunchy, stubby-limbed, and has bad skin. He's a loner with a fondness for young boys.

Early in 2017, he drove his clunky RV from the Pacific Northwest, where he'd lived off the grid, to Southern California. Kevin parked his rig in the driveway of our father's home, Louis P.B. He said he'd be there a couple of weeks before "going on the road with my music."

Truth is, it worried me. I'd grown up in Woodland Hills, a suburb of the San Fernando Valley, a 260-square-mile enclave of Los Angeles. Despite its name, Woodland Hills doesn't have an impressive number of trees or hills. The latest census notes 125,000 residents. Retirement is such a big business that dozens of assisted living facilities are in the area.

I loved the 1950s-style boxy houses with their colonial brick chimneys. Back then, the purchase price was around $10,000. Now, prime real estate. Lisa Kudrow, Maureen McCormick, and Ice Cube attended high school there.

This was my mother's home for sixty-four years. She died a half-dozen years back on the living room couch with the plaid fabric she'd chosen from a stack of swatches at Sears, her favorite go-to department store. A hushed memory of her lounging on the loveseat beneath the window, hooked to an oxygen tank, a balled-up Kleenex in a sleeve, her dark brown eyes deep in a trashy paperback. Memories that make my skin itch.

At eighty-nine, Lou still managed the house and his investments, walked more than five miles a day, and had a robust social life with family and church friends.

Right off, Kevin convinced our father to switch banks and be added as a co-signer on the accounts, thus becoming the sole beneficiary of bank and retirement accounts. I tracked down the institution and eventually spoke to a sympathetic manager. "If Mr. B. agreed to put Kevin on the accounts, then the money is legally and equally his."

Other ominous signs floated around my periphery. Even the air seemed to change. I *knew*.

Kevin continued to take over: Now Successor Trustee of the Estate with Power of Attorney (POA). A judge didn't authorize the POA; it was merely a form printed off the computer and notarized to verify signatures.

Family and friends reported incidents to Adult Protective Services (APS), citing CA Welfare and Institution Code section 15610, regarding undue influence, intimidation, isolation, and more.

From the Los Angeles D.A.'s office:

> *Elder abuse is a rapidly growing criminal problem. As the baby boom generation grays and life expectancy increases, incidents of physical, emotional and financial abuse against elders are expected to grow unless steps are taken. Detection of abuse, neglect and fraud is critical.*

Only one social worker returned my call—leaving a brief message on my answering machine. I phoned every day for two weeks, leaving pleading missives on Lou's behalf. No response.

The problem continued to be proving that Lou was being coerced, intimidated, and controlled. Around that time, he stopped answering his phone. The family suspected the ringer had been turned off. Friends from his church no longer picked him up to go out for lunch, and Kevin didn't allow it.

The circular conversation with myself continued, *Who's going to help us?* It felt like sleepwalking through hell.

That fall, a deep-blue metallic Model X Tesla with dealer plates appeared beside Kevin's rust-corroded RV. The Tesla is worth about $90,000, and registered in Kevin's name. Lou supposedly "gifted" it to him.

After being held a hostage for months, we feared Lou was being shaped by his perpetrator's actions, powerless to change even a small portion of events. When the occasional phone call got through, Kevin or his son listened in on an extension. We heard them coach Lou's end of the conversation.

"I have to make sure no one lies about me," Kevin said.

Lou's bouts of vomiting and diarrhea due to a long-term esophageal hernia became more frequent. Kevin said he'd read about the hernia online. "I know better than the doctors." He admitted to withholding Lou's medication. "It's pure poison." (Kevin often used the word as both a noun and a verb.)

One severe round of vomiting lasted several days. Kevin didn't seek medical help until Lou collapsed in the bathroom. Concerned neighbors (John and Joan, for anonymity) followed the ambulance to Kaiser Permanente, a hospital only a few miles away.

While in the emergency room, the neighbors witnessed Kevin leaning over his father's bed, shouting in his face, "You know you're going to die, don't you!"

Kaiser brought in hospice. Hospice brought in morphine. Lou was sent home to die. However, he began to recover under the care of visiting nurses and hospice. He took his stomach meds and ate small, regularly scheduled meals. But as soon as Kevin dismissed the outside aide, Lou's health quickly deteriorated. It became a vicious cycle.

A concerned friend mentioned Elder Munchausen Syndrome by Proxy, a mental health condition in which a caregiver makes up or causes an illness or injury to a person under his care. While it's most commonly identified in the treatment of children, it has also been reported in vulnerable, dependent older adults.

Deciding what to do next continued to be an inner struggle. I filed additional reports with APS and encouraged others to do the same—referencing isolation, neglect, and financial abuse. I met with a clinical social worker at Kaiser Permanente Hospital and after that updated her by phone.

I told a desk officer at Topanga Community Police Station what I'd found about Kevin's arrest history on a public online site: DUI (2009) and Forceful Eviction (2012). In 2014, he'd been arrested in Utah for First Degree Felony, "Sexual Assault on a Child" (eleven-year-old boy), and Third Degree Felony, "Tampering with a Witness."

The officer turned off his vest camera, saying, "Someone should go out there and beat the crap out of him (Kevin)." A detective at the same station investigated Financial Elder Abuse, Re: Tesla. However, criminal coercion couldn't be confirmed because the car dealer manager said Lou seemed to be "enthusiastic about the purchase."

The two felony cases were scheduled for jury trial in St. George, Utah Superior Court in 2016, postponed to 2017, then to 2018. Kevin knew how to play the system, filing motion after motion to cause delays. Family and friends came to view Kevin as a career con man—reckless and bold. Most of us, it's just to say, believe he's a psychopath.

Ten months after Kevin moved into my parents' home, I visited Lou escorted by John and Joan for safety and to have witnesses. My mother's beloved Meyer lemon tree was lifeless. Her clay pots, cracked, earthy roots exposed. No bees or butterflies. The shade on the porch was deep and cold, intense in an eerie way.

Inside, the air conditioner swirled dust, dog hair, and sour body odor. I was intimate with water spots on the popcorn-textured ceiling, and the crawl space below the raised floor, where mold ate wood. I could almost smell the polished scent of our "good silverware" stored in a velvet-lined case.

A rented hospital bed had been set up in the dining room, an odd arrangement since it hemmed Lou in by a hefty maple buffet on one side and a large oak cabinet with DVDs of classic musicals on the other—his favorites: *Singing in the Rain* and *The Sound of Music.*

I kissed Lou on the forehead and sat beside him on the bed. There were too many pillows. "You seem trapped. How do you get to the bathroom?"

Kevin's short, thick neck flushed. "I take him."

"Really?" I'd once arrived unannounced at noon. Kevin was asleep in the RV; his son crashed in my mother's bedroom. Lou had been doing Sudoku in bed since 8 a.m., filling in squares with neat numbers, believing puzzles would keep his brain alive. He hadn't eaten breakfast or taken his meds.

"Would you like to go out to breakfast tomorrow?" I asked.

Lou reached for my hand. "What time should I be ready?"

Kevin just about lost his mind, his facial tic kicking in, saying I didn't understand Lou's hernia or dietary restrictions. However, I'd been monitoring expiration dates on food in the refrigerator for years. Still, I played along. "I'm sure oatmeal will be fine."

Kevin's fists balled. "Only if my son goes with you."

"I'll see if the pastor is available."

Kevin agreed reluctantly and followed us out, wagging an f-u finger in my face.

The following day, I parked across the street and waited for the pastor. The hotel coffee hadn't even kicked in when Kevin lunged at my car in a sweat-soaked T-shirt, smartphone aimed at me, presumably on video.

He shouted in his shrill, nasal pitch, "If you step on this property, I'm calling 911!"

It struck me then how the once vibrant neighborhood had shut down. Kevin's antics were being tracked from behind closed doors and windows with heavy drapes.

"I'm warning you not to come on *my* property!" he wailed.

Not *his* property. My parents' home. The house I grew up in. I'd spent hours sitting on the edge of the porcelain bathtub while my mother drew on perfect cat eyes and put on coral lipstick. Now, Lou's home, who remained inside, unaware that I'd come for him.

The pastor parked near the driveway, and then my nature—the one that drives me to respect my parents, their life experiences, and their sense of fairness—pushed me to cross the street and step onto the curb.

Kevin punched 911 into his phone.

A pair of police officers rolled up, and Kevin waved a fistful of papers. "I have power of attorney, and it upsets my father to see her!"

The officers talked to Kevin and me separately, hearing us out and deciding it was a civil (family dispute) matter, not criminal (trespassing). Kevin took a dramatic breath, dropped to his knees, and thanked God. Half an hour earlier, he'd genuflected while calling me a "black bitch."

An officer urged me in private to get an attorney.

The pastor drove off.

Poor Lou, abandoned, believing I'd forgotten our breakfast date—such profound sadness for both of us.

From Adult Protective Services:

> *If you are concerned that someone you care about may be the victim of abuse, don't be silent. Here are some signs that could indicate elder abuse:*
> * *Caregiver isolates elder*
> * *Harassment, coercion, intimidation, humiliation*
> * *Lack of basic amenities*
> * *Cluttered, filthy living environment*
> * *Unexplained or uncharacteristic in behavior*
> * *Unpaid bills, new credit cards and/or increased cash withdrawals*

My attorney wrote a letter stating, among other things, that a Power of Attorney "does not permit you (sic) to act in Louis' capacity if he is present and continues to have capacity with his own affairs."

With letter in hand, I drove to Woodland Hills the following week.

Kevin called 911 again, pacing in the driveway and pounding a water bottle. He looked a little desperate, a lot hung-over. I sat on the patio under the branches of my mother's orange tree, planted so she could bag fruit for friends.

Under different circumstances, I would have described the yard as peaceful. Now, I counted trees and shrubs dead from lack of water. Brittle shrubs had been misted with green spray paint.

I heard my mother's voice. *Does any part of us remain here?*

Memories, I told her, not entirely present, not knowing how mad or sad to be.

One of the two responding officers read my attorney's letter and went inside for a "welfare check." When Lou heard I was there, he asked to see me. I sat on the edge of the hospital bed, recording our conversation, proof that I was incapable of concocting such madness.

"Do you want to see me when I come down?" I asked him.

His exact words: "I want to see you the next time you come and anytime after that and as often as you can come."

The officers told Kevin that allowing me in the house in the future would be in his best interest. Kevin looked at them like he'd been offered a rat sandwich.

A few weeks later, I arrived unannounced on a Sunday morning. The Tesla was gone. Lou answered the door in stonewashed jeans, a Hawaiian shirt, and Day-Glo sneakers. The air conditioner pumped icy gusts. A light flickered overhead like a misplaced sunset.

I wondered, *Do houses settle in on themselves when abused? Maybe it's the breath of vibrant occupants that holds them up?*

Lou's eyes were less blue-gray, nearly colorless. He seemed so weak, almost wounded. "You got here just in time."

"We're going to the hospital," I said.

"Can you look for my phone?"

I paused outside the first bedroom in the hallway—my old room. The lace curtains had been replaced with cheap aluminum blinds. When I moved out, the space became Lou's domain for Seduko and *Wheel of Fortune.*

What struck me most was a used adult diaper on the floor. Lou wasn't incontinent, just inconvenient. His flip-phone remained AWOL. He'd misplaced his VA-issued hearing aids.

Lou was admitted to the E.R. at Kaiser Permanente in part for severe dehydration. He began to feel better after receiving two large bags of normal saline and various other medications.

I stood in the square, fluorescent-lit room in a way that allowed me to mouth words to the doctor without Lou knowing: *Elder Abuse. A.P.S. case.* The doctor nodded, understanding, and ordered liver, kidney, and stomach scans. Maybe someone would finally help us.

Lou kept repeating, "We should call Kevin and let him know where we are."

I tried to distract him with amusing stories.

The room was adjacent to the nurse's station, everyone in motion. Even with people running from one crisis to the next, I caught part of a phone conversation. A nurse asked me to step into the lobby. I knew we'd been found.

Predictably, Kevin barged in, brandishing the Power of Attorney.

The doctor-ordered tests were never completed. I wonder if the medical report says "Released Against Medical Advice."

Shortly after that, Kevin filed a Temporary Restraining Order (TRO): Louis B. vs. Sherry Shahan. Kevin signed Lou's name, employing the POA. In his manic handwriting, "Sherry Shahan waited outside until caretaker went briefly to the store and entered the home of Louis B. . . . She convinced him to go to the hospital without leaving a note or calling Kevin . . ." And on it went in frenzied manic scrawl, all kinds of bizarre accusations.

Kevin sent a text as Proof of Service: *I am assured by the court that this text, and my efforts to contact you through various police departments and adult protective services will be sufficient to have the restraining order made permanent. . . . Goodbye. Thank God at last, we are free!* (By California State law a TRO *must* be served in person.)

I was sucked into an alternate universe where psychosis ruled all sense of reason. I became consumed with justice while others begged me to let it go. I waited. *For what?* The life-chronicler in me, the stubborn self, seeking fairness and justice, kept fighting back.

❧❧❧

One evening Lou visited his next-door neighbors, ashamed and embarrassed, as if he didn't know how to move through life alone. A twenty-minute recorded video shows him sitting on their couch, looking as wrecked as the rest of us felt. He talked about "my son's crazy behavior" and "wanting to see Sherry."

An hour or so later, Kevin pounded up their stairs, screaming and beating against their front door. "I'm going on the road with my music! Is that what you want, Dad? Who will take care of you then?" He struck the door with such force the neighbors feared it would break down.

Kevin accused them of "kidnapping my father."

The responding police officer wrote on the back of his card, "Susp-Kevin B. No crime. No kidnap. Advised vic to file R/O" (Incident number 4493.)

Lou told the officer that his son was unstable, violent, and unhinged. Yet, he returned to his home of the last four decades. There is no loneliness like that of an aging person. We all felt it.

≳❀≲

Lou died alone in the house on an amber fall afternoon. He wasn't sick, just worn out.

He'd lost thirty or forty pounds in Kevin's care.

That same day, around that same time, Kevin and his son were seen walking down the curved street with purpose, perhaps heading to their favorite restaurant Something's Fishy for half-priced sushi.

Family and friends learned of Lou's passing from a neighbor who saw a body bag being loaded into an SUV. She said Kevin seemed excited, almost giddy, before collapsing into crocodile tears.

Kevin remained in the house rent-free for more than a year, claiming to be preparing it for sale as per his duties as Trustee. An attorney for the reverse mortgage company filed a petition to begin foreclosure.

Our father had withdrawn hundreds of thousands of dollars, all against his son's threats, "Do you want me to leave you? Do you want to be stuck in a smelly old people's home?" The funds were deposited into their mutually held bank accounts.

From the L.A. District Attorney's office: "One in five seniors has been the victim of financial fraud. Con artists use a variety of ways to get the hard-earned savings of seniors."

For me, so much is wrapped up in loss and sadness. It's as if everything I believed in—justice, fairness, duty, and compassion—had been clawed away, leaving a hole in my core. I understand so little of what happened, and most days wish my mind would just turn off.

ERIC GREINKE

THE WOOD WORK
for Murry Harralson

I resisted him like a knot
resists a crosscut saw.
I didn't want a step-father.
I missed my real father
like a tree bereft of branches.
I never called him father. He didn't
like me any more than I liked him.
He was an ex-Marine,
a strong, silent man of few words.
We co-existed through my adolescence,
but as adults, we warmed to each other.
I hung out with him in his garage
where he carved & burned wood.
We'd have a beer & a late night hot dog,
& he'd tell me about the world war.
Tears came to his blue eyes
when he spoke of Guadalcanal.
In his late sixties, he got into cats.
He built ramps so they could climb
up into the rafters of the garage.
His favorite cat was a feral stray
who had to be tamed. She scratched
& bit him many times before
he became her trusted feline love.
In his mid-seventies he was struck by
congestive heart failure. He
could only sleep while sitting up.
They gave him six months to live.
During that time, he opened to music.

I would sit on his bed & sing to him.
On the day he died, I played him asleep.
It was the last thing he heard.
As his son, I inherited his carving tools.
I also got his uncompleted carvings.
Over the years, I finished some of them.
Others were thrown away, but I kept
the tools, just in case I might find
some wood badly in need of a shape.

FELICIA ROSE

STEPMOM

Before she became
Stepmom, Carol sat
me on an easy chair
by the window
of her top-floor apartment
and strummed *Bridge
Over Troubled Water*
as rain cascaded
down fire escapes.

How I clung
to her ponytail
while she cantered
on all fours
round slippery tile.

And when she fed
the old wooden coffee grinder
whatever I chose:
walnuts, nutmeg, leftover
kugel, the grounds became
my first word
for awe.

The morning she dove
into Lake George to salvage
the boat engine, I gamboled
near the edge of the island.
Later, we two motored
into town, the prow hoisted
above the waves.

No wonder that photo
at the zoo shows
her squatting to my
three-year-old height
and my squatting
beside her.
Who wouldn't want
to be her likeness?

So before she gave
up smoking, I joined
her by puffing on twigs.
What mattered was to be
gathered on the deck
of our new rural home
in overcoats and nighties
with snow settling
on tousled hair.

And to see
the crystal vase
amassing one champagne
cork, then two,
then scores: the flourishing
of *after* years.

Of travels
to the Amish Country:
mulled apple cider
and shoofly pie.
And Stepmom asking:
May we have that grape-
shaped marzipan
for my daughter?

The daughter who flipped
the brisket on the boat
barbeque into the bay.
We'll enjoy canned beans,
(Step) Mom announced.
She turned towels
into napkins. Poured wine
and praised
Dionysus. Transforming
another meal
and moment
into manna.

IV
EXES & IN-LAWS

RACHAEL JONES

MY FATHER'S WIFE

We were talking about strip clubs when the marriage came up. It was a sunny day out, and my boyfriend, Stephen, and I were, as usual, lounging on the porch drinking coffee. He said he wouldn't go to the strip clubs in the Keys on his upcoming vacation if I didn't want him to go, but that of course his father would be going. I snorted, "That's different; your dad isn't married."

"Yes, he is." Stephen said quickly.

"What?" Stephen and I had been together for almost a year, and I didn't know his dad was married. "You have a stepmother?"

Stephen repositioned his arm, "Not a stepmother. My father has a wife." He told me that his father had met a woman in Spain years ago, and they had fallen in love and gotten married in Vegas without telling anyone, "That's my dad for you," he said.

I went inside to get more coffee. What did I know about steps and halfs and in-laws? Nothing—that was what. My parents had been married for thirty years and my grandparents, sixty years. Both sets of my grandparents were best friends, the four of them riding to church dinners and trips to Applebee's together. I burned my hand on the glass coffee pot and cursed as I ran it under the cold water. This would make our upcoming trip to a family wedding more interesting. Stephen had already told me that I would be staying with him at his father's house in Cape Cod, and I wondered if this Spanish wife would be there too.

As it turned out, the Spanish wife was not there. Stephen's twin brother, Arnold said, "God, I never see her. I don't trust her, and I don't know what the deal is. She's always out of the country." I winced at the use of the Lord's name being said like that, but I too thought the whole thing was interesting. Who was this mysterious stepmother of my boyfriend's, and would she one day become my step-mother-in-law?

If Stephen had any thoughts on the matter, he did not express them to me. That was how Stephen was—quiet and easy to get along with. We fought sometimes, but he never picked fights with me. We talked about my minor emotional problems, but he didn't offer up any of his own experiences. I would ask about his parents' divorce from time to time, knowing he wouldn't want to talk about it. I just wanted to know why it had happened; I wanted to know if one day I was doomed to be a divorcee. But he held his ground: "They disagreed with each other, so they got a divorce. I remember it, but that doesn't mean I want to talk about it." We went on that way for a while, dancing around that discomfort, until there was a mild infidelity on his part. Stephen didn't sleep with the girl, but he came very close. She left in a fit of rage and sent me a Facebook message to alert me a couple of days later. She was an ex-girlfriend of his, and said, "I think he has commitment issues."

That night, Stephen poured it all out and I let him. He told me he was jealous of my family with its lack of halfs and steps and in-laws. He told me that his father had hit his mother, and that both of his parents had had a series of affairs leading to both of them getting horrific STDs. He wept and I wept, and we held each other. It didn't help that I had been recovering from a nasty round with Covid when the girl had messaged me. For the next two or three nights I would lie lifeless in his arms falling into a dreamless sleep yet waking up exhausted. I always woke up with the mysterious stepmother on my mind.

Stephen and I beat the odds for that type of situation, I suppose. I did not leave him. He did not beg or grovel, and I did not question why I didn't feel the need to leave him. Some women, I'm told, question everything and wonder if they are good enough. I did not do that either. I simply forgave Stephen, and Stephen came out of the whole thing a changed man.

I don't know if Stephen's mother ever found out about the affair, but his father did. I told his brother, and his brother told his father. The affair or half-affair happened in September, and Stephen's father was set to come and stay with us the weekend after Thanksgiving. "Will his wife come too?" I asked Stephen.

Stephen shook his head and asked, "What is your fascination with her?" She truly was, at this point, still a mythical creature in my mind. You have to understand that Stephen's mother was a force of nature, and Stephen's father was a high functioning alcoholic. So though I very much envisioned Stephen as my husband, I didn't necessarily look forward to the in-laws I would have.

Stephen's dad was short; Stephen and Arnold were both short, and I came from a very tall family. Stephen was just a few inches taller than me, and his dad was shorter than him so when we hugged it always felt strange to me. But nonetheless his dad always insisted on hugging me hello and goodbye. Everyone in his family did as if it were some sort of admission, "you may not feel like you belong here, but everyone belongs here at least for some period of time." That Friday after Thanksgiving was no different on his father's part. He hugged me, and when Stephen got home from work we went out drinking. The next day we also went out drinking.

I was twenty-eight at this time, and I loved drinking. Having grown up in a religious home, it was new and exciting to me—there were so many flavors to be explored, and the buzz made me feel less coordinated but in a way that I absolutely loved. I drank three German beers at the first place, and two Miller Lites at the second place, and then a variety of fruity beers at the third place on the hippy side of town.

I was tipsy and laughing when I returned to Stephen's house with his father. His father could out drink a fish, and he was drunk. Stephen—well, it was hard to tell with Stephen. The three of us stood around in the kitchen, Stephen's father still nursing a neat whiskey poured from one of the bottles Stephen kept in the cabinet. His father told me that he loved this woman— the stepmother who was not a stepmother. He said that she let him do what he wanted without too much fuss, and that this seemed like the right thing for him. He said she loved and supported him—that she knew what his drinking days were and that she would drive him to the bars on those days. "She's beautiful," he sighed, "she keeps her body up."

Some people, hearing me tell this story will think that it's crass on his father's part, to be with a woman for her looks, but I guess I saw something different that night. I think I saw a dirty old man who was mostly happy and mostly in love—and that, well, that was enough to sustain him for the rest of his days.

Stephen asked me to marry him the following spring. Our relationship wasn't perfect, but we were mostly free from the problems that had plagued our parents, and we loved each other more than either of us could imagine loving another single person. It seemed like the right time. Still, I burdened Stephen with questions about his father's wife, "Will she come to the wedding?"

"Not if we don't want her to," Stephen said which meant that he didn't want her to.

That was when I went behind Stephen's back. I was grumpy from trying my hardest to lose weight for the wedding; caloric restriction did not agree with my temper. I was tired of not knowing this stepmother who was not really a stepmother, so I wrote her a letter.

> *I know it seems strange to send a letter in this day and age, but I did not know your phone number. I suppose I could have found your phone number through an internet search, but I don't know your last name. I don't know if you took his when you married or if you kept yours. I wouldn't blame you either way—as I have thought of doing both. That's why I am writing—Stephen has asked me to marry him, and I said yes. I know you probably think you are doing the right thing by removing yourself from the boys' lives. My instinct would be the same in your shoes, but please come to our wedding. Don't do it for Stephen or his father (though I know you likely would do anything for him), but do it for me. I need someone like you there on that day.*

That was part of how the letter read. I closed with my contact information and invited her to give me a call on the phone.

She did, and we talked. We talked many times, actually. While I talked to my mother about the guests we would invite, and I talked to Stephen's mother about the table decorations and the lighting—I talked to the stepmother about the things I loved about Stephen and the movies I was watching after work at night. I talked to her about her childhood in Spain. While I argued with my mother about whether or not there would be a champagne toast at our wedding, I talked to the stepmother about what restaurants I would take her to if she came to visit. While I exasperatedly told Stephen's mother for the fiftieth time, no, I did not like the shade of green she wanted to include in the wedding colors, I sent the stepmother TikTok videos related to wedding humor. The stepmother jokingly sent me memes about bridezillas. She was a place of solace at that time I found not even in my best friend.

When she flew into town with Stephen's father the day before the wedding, I wept as I hugged her. Stephen stood to the side awkwardly before giving her a side hug. Arnold, being the grumpier twin, hesitated but did the same.

I wish I could say my family loved the wedding. They did not—there was entirely too much drinking and dancing through the course of the champagne toast and the three slow songs. I wish I could say that Stephen's family loved the wedding. They did not—there was nowhere near enough drinking, dancing, or fancy decorations. Looking back, I don't even know that Stephen and I loved the wedding, but I do know that we loved falling into each other's arms that night as man and wife. Sometimes, all these years later, we will laugh about that night. "Why did we have that dumb wedding?" I will ask, and he will lower his reading glasses and say, "because you wanted to meet my stepmother."

Stephen has been calling his father's wife his stepmother for twenty-five years now. She is eighty-five, and though Stephen's father has passed she still sends us a Christmas card with the word "love" signed right above her name, and Stephen and I don't doubt that truth.

LOUISE KANTRO

THE BLIND DATE

After squeezing gel into his hands, Conrad parted his thick, graying hair. It was his best feature now that he'd gotten a bit of a pot belly and lines around his eyes and mouth. He looked his age, but he liked to think that he was a good-looking forty-seven. He hoped that his hair would be the first thing she would notice. His occupation, while not as good as being a doctor or architect, was nevertheless acceptable. He owned a glass business that had brought in a good living for nineteen years.

Before his divorce, he'd had an upper-middle-class income. Two years ago, after Miriam asked him to move out, he'd scaled back. He hadn't minded all that much then because, after all, he wanted the best for Misty and Jeff, who took the divorce pretty hard. Now that he was finally starting to date, though, he wished he had a nicer apartment.

Always one to be punctual, Conrad arrived a nerve-racking ten minutes early at The Daily Grind. His blind date, Serena, was nearly seven minutes late. Strike one. Also, she was a little plain. Strike two.

But, like him, she wanted to sit outside to enjoy the just-cool-enough summer evening.

As they sipped lattes, she grew on him. She had a sexy voice and her conversation was lively, not too full of small talk, and not presumptuously intimate. A seventh-grade social studies teacher at John Muir Middle School, Serena was well-informed about current affairs. She "got" Conrad's ironic barbs about politics and kept him on his toes by adding zingers of her own.

The more they talked, the more her appearance grew on him. Serena had thick brown hair and lovely green eyes. Her nose was a little too big and chin a bit pointy and, he decided now, she wasn't exactly plain. She was plain in a pretty way. She was about twenty pounds overweight, but it was distributed well. He liked a woman with some curves. After all, he was carrying a bit of a paunch himself.

As his hopes began to rise, he began to worry that something would go wrong.

They were well into the second hour of the date when he saw Miriam. Trotting along beside her was her new husband, Barry.

Miriam nodded at Conrad, her smile awkward. Conrad nodded back. Barry pretended not to see him.

Stopping mid-sentence, Serena turned her head to see what had distracted Conrad.

"Oh, my God," she said.

"What's the matter?"

"That's my two-timing former brother-in-law."

Conrad's head turned hard so he could verify if she was referring to Barry.

Then an awful thought occurred to him. Would Serena decide that the world was just too small? Or would she see their mutual distaste for Barry as one more thing to have in common?

In an odd and surprising moment of clarity, Conrad appreciated the irony of their interrelatedness, and he hoped she would, too. He would take the chance.

"That's my ex-wife with him," he said.

Serena's eyebrows arched, and a smile turned at the corner of her mouth. "Well, well, well. I guess, hmm," she said, pausing to gather her thoughts. Then she held up her coffee mug to make a toast. "This looks like the beginning of a beautiful friendship." She looked right into Conrad's eyes.

Conrad decided right then that it was time to place the past firmly in the past. Friendship was a very promising start, indeed.

ELINOR DAVIS

THE WIFE-IN-LAW

Fran coasted into the parking garage steering with her left hand and fishing in her purse on the passenger seat for the wedding invitation with her right. She couldn't remember the bride's last name.

"I'm here for the Chatsworth, uh, Burkel wedding?" she mumbled to the parking attendant, squinting at the curlicue lettering on the crumpled lavender card. She had never attended a wedding on the UC Berkeley campus and wondered if she needed to show the invitation to prove she was a bona fide guest. The attendant ignored the card Fran thrust through the open window and waved her to the far corner of the garage.

Fran checked her make-up in the visor mirror, drew a deep breath, and forced herself out of the car, through the garage and into the late afternoon sunlight for the trek across campus to the Women's Faculty Club, site of the impending nuptials. She consulted the map that came with the invitation. Looking up to get her bearings, she saw a gush of giddy graduates pouring down the steps of an imposing stone building ahead. One of the dozens of departmental graduation ceremonies held in late May and early June had just concluded. Flanked by proud parents snapping photos or walking backwards shooting videos, the cap-and-gown-clad grads whooped and cavorted. A mortarboard flung Frisbee-fashion narrowly missed Fran's cheek.

She froze, feeling like irrelevant flotsam in the river of blue robes swirling past. As quickly as the disorderly procession had appeared, it receded behind her, newly minted engineers embarking on their grown-up lives, relieved parents celebrating the end of tuition checks. Fran sighed and plodded on down the cobbled path, spotting a bouquet of lavender balloons tied to a tree sporting a hand-lettered sign: "CHATSWORTH–BURKEL WEDDING THIS WAY!" Below the words, an arrow impaling a pink heart pointed toward an old, dark, wood-shingled building surrounded by ground ivy, holly, an effusion of flowering shrubs, spreading oaks and soaring eucalyptus trees. Fran inhaled the invigorating eucalyptus scent that always reminded her of Vicks VapoRub, the healing balm of childhood colds. Buoyed by this mentholated memory, she strode resolutely into the Faculty Club.

Entering unaccompanied, Fran felt acutely single. The only male friend she would have felt comfortable asking to be her escort was now seeing someone whom Fran gauged unreceptive to the idea of lending her new boyfriend to attend a wedding with another woman. And Fran's ex-boyfriend was now married, an automatic disqualification. The bride's twenty-something son, stiffly awkward in his borrowed too-small suit, handed Fran a program and directed her toward the guestbook. As he pointed, his sleeve hiked up revealing a red and black snake tattoo slithering up his forearm.

Fran ventured into the cavernous main hall, scanning the assemblage for a familiar face. Several dozen round tables swathed in lavender drapery bore glass bowls of floating yellow candles and sprays of iris and narcissus erupting from crystal vases. Sixty or seventy people mingled, chatted, and munched on crab cakes and sushi. They sipped pink wine and dipped asparagus spears into saucers of béarnaise. It looked more like an art gallery reception than a wedding. Since this was the third marriage for both the bride and the groom, the main point was to put on a good party, rather than observe any particular wedding conventions.

Fran couldn't help comparing this sumptuous scene with her one and only wedding, a thirty-second affair at a county courthouse, performed by a clerk who looked even younger and more nervous than she and Paul. He couldn't possibly have been a real judge. Just someone empowered by the State of Washington to perform civil marriage ceremonies. Afterward, they went to a Greek restaurant in Seattle for dinner with her sister from Santa Barbara, their witness and only guest, and then home to Fran's studio apartment where her sister slept on the floor next to Fran and Paul's bed. They didn't really mind, since they had already had their "honeymoon," an extended camping trip on the Olympic Peninsula, the primeval rain forest across Puget Sound.

The wedding was sort of an afterthought, something to do while her sister visited, as good a time as any. Fran wanted babies, and while she had no compunctions about living with Paul, she did want to be legally married by the time any children came along. It seemed only prudent. Paul was not entirely convinced about a life-long commitment, but he didn't want to lose Fran, so he agreed. Fran seemed sure enough for both of them. However, the prospect of planning and starring in a full-blown wedding and sit-down dinner horrified her. And she could think of many more practical things to do with their parents' money than blow it on a lavish one-day event. They had talked about a simple wedding on the beach or at a park, but in the end, they just went to the courthouse and that was that.

It made so little impression on them that for years after, neither of them could remember the exact date of their wedding. They knew it was sometime around the Summer solstice. June 19 or 20? Once they called her sister to ask, but she didn't remember, either. So they always celebrated their anniversary on the weekend closest to the solstice. The marriage certificate got misplaced when they moved from Seattle to Berkeley for graduate school. Then Paul lost the Celtic design wedding ring they had bought from a craft booth at a street fair. One dark night driving home from his job in Oakland, his engine over-heated. He didn't know much about cars, but figured metal on his finger would not mix well with a boiling radiator and all that electrical wiring under the hood. So he took off the ring and set it on the roof. By the time the engine cooled and he replaced the radiator cap and resumed the trip home, he'd forgotten about the ring. It lay somewhere along the 580 freeway. "Why didn't you just put it in your pocket?" Fran wailed. He had no answer.

Two babies came along in quick succession (she had believed the old wives' tale that breastfeeding prevents pregnancy). Paul's PhD went on hold in favor of gainful employment and Fran became a stay-at-home mom. Daycare for two kids under two years old cost more than she made at her catalog copywriting job, which she was tired of anyway. She started freelance editing students' papers at home, much as her mother had taken in ironing to make ends meet.

Immersed in babies and then co-op nursery school, she barely noticed Paul's comings and goings to and from his two jobs. She left grocery lists and phone messages for him magneted to the refrigerator. She was usually in the girls' room when he left in the morning and asleep when he got home at night. Her body belonged to the babies and this just seemed to be the inevitable, natural order of things. Hours of holding and breastfeeding squirmy infants more than satisfied her need for human touch. Exhaustion drained her of desire. Whenever the girls were asleep, she wanted nothing more than to sleep herself. Sex with Paul became a distant memory. Besides, she was terrified of getting pregnant again. She loved her children more than life, but knew she would lose her mind if she had another one before these two left for college.

Then one Thanksgiving weekend when the girls were three and four, Paul announced that he wanted to separate. There was no other woman. He was just worn down, fed up, burnt out. He needed to finish his dissertation and get on with his list of life goals. Fran wondered why raising his own children was not one of his goals. Apparently, she and the kids were an inconvenient obstruction on his career path. He moved his clothes and books to a rented room; she got the kids, the furniture, and a flat she could not afford. After a few months, he bought a do-it-yourself divorce kit and filed the paperwork. She alternately seethed with resentment and floundered in despair. In a recurrent dream that seemed to sum up her life as a single parent, she swam in slo-mo through an endless sea of sticky, dark molasses with a rope clamped in her teeth that towed a little raft bearing her children and all their toys.

After years of intermittent therapy and reflection, Fran came to see herself not as a passive victim of male selfishness, but as an equal partner in the disintegration of her marriage, an unindicted co-conspirator. Her proudest achievement was that she had managed to function as a responsible co-parent with Paul, despite her anger and sadness. Somehow, both girls had survived their teens without getting arrested, pregnant, or dependent on illegal substances. They loved both parents and rarely complained about all the shuttling back and forth. At least they had each other for support and company. As for herself, Fran found living with children more lonely and isolating than living alone.

❦

A harp solo wafted over the Faculty Club, punctuating the genteel chatter of the burgeoning crowd. Fran wondered how many people who had not returned the RSVP card had decided to show up anyway. Several tables away, an orange chiffon clad arm shot up and waved broadly as if flagging down a Manhattan cab. Below the arm, a familiar face mouthed the words "Great to see you!" Not sure if she was the intended target, Fran looked around, then realized the woman was Paul's sister Doreen and she waved back, unable to move through the crush of bodies.

From somewhere to her left, a male voice boomed, "Hey, Fran, you haven't changed a bit!" Paul's childhood friends Sherman and Carol, now thirty years married, each holding crab cakes and a wine glass, edged toward her. She and Paul had rented a flat from them when the girls were little, but she hadn't seen them since her divorce. Fran forced a smile, "Hi, guys, I'm sure that's not true, but it's nice of you to say." Her years as their tenant and upstairs neighbor had not been happy ones—their big fenced back yard, which Fran had thought would be a perfect playground for her toddlers, proved unfit for human use. Rather than walk and pick up after their aging poodle and boisterous German shepherd, Sherman and Carol just opened their back door and let the dogs turn the yard into a canine toilet. In order to give her children an outdoor play experience, Fran had to trudge eight blocks to a park pushing a stroller and wearing the younger girl in a backpack. Carol once remarked that the dogs were "fertilizing the garden," revealing a city-girl's ignorance of agricultural chemistry. The flies, dead grass, and shriveled shrubs should have been a clue.

Fran thought she recognized several other older versions of people she had once known in her role as a wife. As she realized after the divorce, most of them were actually Paul's friends, he being the more gregarious. They had vanished from her life after Paul moved out, but apparently had continued to exist in a parallel universe of couples who have the energy for a social life. For years while her girls were growing up, most of the adults she knew outside of work were parents of her daughters' friends and their interactions revolved around play dates, class field trips, and birthday parties. Once the kids finished high school, she had lost touch with most of them.

As Fran plucked a chicken kabob off a silver platter carried by an androgynous student caterer in white shirt, black slacks, and pony tail, her elbow smacked into the chest of a man squashed up beside her.

"Oh, sorry!"

The balding, fiftyish fellow wearing round wire-rim glasses shrugged and grinned. "Food looks great, huh? Are you a friend of the bride or the groom?"

"I'm the groom's *first* wife." She unconsciously emphasized *first*, lest she be mistaken for Paul's second ex-wife, the shrew. Fran took a perverse pride in being the "nice" ex-wife.

The man's eyes widened, nearly filling his glasses frames. Looking momentarily perplexed, his expression seemed to ask, *Why did they invite you? Why would you come?* "Well, how nice of you to come. I'm the bride's—Joanie's—brother, Marty, from Portland."

Good save, Fran thought. *Welcome to Berkeley.* "It's good to meet you . . . Joanie looks beautiful," she said. They smiled politely, then drifted off toward opposite sides of the room.

Joanie did look beautiful, circulating among her guests in a beige lace, vaguely Victorian gown. Petite and animated, she was bubbly without being saccharine, with a quick wit and ready laugh. Peppy, chirpy, friendly. Fran had found her impossible to dislike as they got to know each other over nine years of holiday dinners and family birthdays. In fact, Fran had spent last Christmas at the home of Joanie's daughter and Jewish son-in-law (his first full-blown Christmas with all the trimmings and he was in severe culture shock). Guests included Joanie's mother, first and second husbands, and the son-in-law's divorced parents with their current spouses. Paul brought his son from his second marriage and Fran brought their daughters, Iranian son-in-law and granddaughter. Joanie's cooing, smiley new grandson provided the entertainment and central focus of attention. A veritable pageant of serial monogamy, a paean to the power of grandchildren to bring broken families together and transcend religious and cultural differences. The ultimate blended family. Much as the older adults might wish for different circumstances, they were all there because they wanted to be with their children. Putting up with their exes was better than moping at home alone.

Fran popped the chicken chunk into her mouth without looking at it. A moment too late, she felt something hard and sharp against the roof of her mouth, but she had already swallowed—the tip of a wooden shish kabob skewer seemed to be lodged in her throat, down beyond her tongue's reach. *Damn.* Should she try to force it down by eating more, or push it out by coughing? What if it punctured her esophagus and she started bleeding all over the Women's Faculty Club?

Fran made for the hallway restroom as nonchalantly as she could manage. Neither gulps of water nor coughing seemed to have any effect. The sensation persisted of something stuck in her throat, poking at her larynx. It was not painful, really, just uncomfortable. She wondered whether she should go to a hospital emergency room to have it extracted. People she knew had already seen her here. If she left now, before the ceremony, what would they think? (*Poor Fran. She shouldn't have forced herself to come.*) But if she stayed and this turned into some melodramatic medical crisis, she would cause an embarrassing scene. Slicking down her cowlick in the restroom mirror, Fran decided that as long as she could breathe, swallow, and was not in pain, there was no emergency.

She fetched another glass of wine from the bar and looked around for her older daughter, Claire. Fran found Claire stooped on the floor by the

"RESERVED—WEDDING PARTY" table, trying to persuade three-year-old daughter Jaleh to put her shoes back on. Remembering similar struggles when her own girls were small, Fran relished her subversive grandmother role. She could give Jaleh occasional candy, let her bounce on the couch, skip brushing her teeth, knowing that the parents would enforce the rules the rest of the time. The world would not end if the baby ran around barefoot or colored on Grandma's calendar with felt pens. Far worse things could, and did, happen every day.

Jaleh insisted the shoes were "too hard." New, patent leather, bought for this occasion, they were probably stiff and uncomfortable. Claire should have let her wear them around the house to break them in, Fran thought, but held her tongue. No good could come from pointing this out now. She wanted to tell Claire, in a purely conversational, non-alarming way, about the shish kabob skewer in her throat, so that if she started choking or bleeding or lost consciousness, Claire would know what to tell the paramedics. It seemed a sensible precaution. After much negotiation and cookie bribery, Jaleh agreed to try the shoes again and Fran told Claire about the skewer.

"Oh god, should I drive you to the hospital?"

"No, no, I'm fine. It's just like a toothpick, really—people must swallow them all the time. It doesn't hurt. I don't want to spoil the wedding. I just wanted you to know, in case . . . "

Claire regarded her mother's mild Midwestern countenance, flat as the Kansas prairie. "Are you *sure?*"

Fran was sure and now that she had told Claire, she felt much better.

The harp chords crescendoed to a climax and an elfin Unitarian cleric with wavy white hair and wayward eyebrows stepped up to the microphone.

"Welcome, dear friends and family of Joanie and Paul. I hope you're enjoying this lovely evening as much as I am. Please find seats and get comfortable, because before the main event, so to speak, the bride and groom would like to share the story of their journey together in the form of some of their favorite music and poetry, performed by some talented friends."

A combo of clarinet, sax, and snare drum, with Paul himself at the piano, launched into a medley of twentieth century show tunes and pop favorites illustrating Paul and Joanie's courtship. A male and female vocalist joined in on some of them, like "Blue Moon" and "Till There Was You." It was sappy but charming. The guests swayed and hummed along, transported on a cloud of nostalgia and romance. The singers read poems by Rumi and Gibran, and then Paul and Joanie recited Valentine poems they had written to each other.

Fran's throat tightened and she felt the skewer poking harder. She wondered how much longer this would go on and whether she was incurring permanent esophageal damage by staying.

At last the performances concluded, signaled by a jazzy version of "Here Comes the Bride." Approximately as rehearsed, the wedding party assembled themselves into two parallel rows to form an aisle in the open space next to the piano. Claire and her husband, holding a fidgety Jaleh firmly by the hand, faced each other. Next to them stood Joanie's brother and sister-in-law, Joanie's daughter and son-in-law holding the grandson, Paul's sister and nephew, Paul's son and younger daughter.

Paul rose from the piano bench and stood at the head of the "aisle" before the beaming minister. Joanie's son then escorted her up the gauntlet of about-to-be in-laws and handed her off to Paul. The ceremony itself was mercifully brief. When the minister got to the "Speak now or forever hold your peace" part, Fran had a sudden urge to blurt *How come they get three weddings each and I barely even had one?* She held her breath and clenched her jaws to stifle this unworthy thought. Where did that come from? Multiple marriages implied multiple divorces, or deaths, nothing one would wish for. When she'd had her chance, she wasn't interested. What right did she have to complain now? Did she really think that if only they'd had a real wedding she and Paul would still be married?

Fran remembered an incident on a Memorial Day weekend some years ago, during one of her perennial attempts to de-clutter and organize her household. She had pulled all the boxes out of all the closets, determined to sort through them and throw away or give away as much as she possibly could. At the bottom of a battered cardboard carton she found a manila envelope postmarked from Gompers, Kansas, addressed to her old Seattle apartment in her mother's careful hand. An installment of "Mom's Clipping Service." Thirty-five-year-old *Peanuts* and *Dennis the Menace* cartoons, wedding announcements from her high school classmates, recipes and self-help articles from *Good Housekeeping* magazine.

She knew she should chuck it into the recycling bin without even looking inside, but couldn't resist taking a peek. Out fluttered the expected yellowed cartoons, newspaper clippings and snapshots, but there was something else, a big, stiff cream-colored sheet of faux parchment. It was her long-lost marriage certificate, the only tangible proof left that she had ever been married. She stared at the florid script, ornate maroon border and the date: June 21, 1974. She must have stuck it in this envelope because it was the only one on hand big enough, and then forgotten where she put it after they moved. She had an impulse to call Paul and tell him she'd found their anniversary date. But why would he care now? He'd already been re-married and divorced again. Their date was an irrelevant footnote.

One of the clippings in the envelope was an article about a golden anniversary party for some friends of her parents. Then she noticed that the photos were of her and Paul on their wedding day, taken by her sister. She had forgotten all about them. She and Paul looked so young, so thin, so unprepared for what faced them. He in tan corduroy bell-bottoms and a purple paisley shirt, she in a gauzy peasant blouse with pink embroidery and a long rippling patchwork skirt. He in brown Beatle boots, she in Birkenstock sandals. She wore a garland of daisies atop her waist-length dishwater blonde hair. Paul's chestnut curls grazed his shoulders as they riffled in the breeze of a partly cloudy Seattle afternoon.

A wicked thought seized her. She would send an "anniversary announcement" to the *San Francisco Chronicle*, accompanied by one of the original "wedding photos." "Paul and Francine (nee Cobb) Chatsworth announce their Silver Anniversary Gala. On June 21, they will celebrate twenty-five years together by reaffirming their vows at Grace Cathedral before 1,000 invited guests, followed by a reception and banquet at the Mark Hopkins Hotel. The mayors of San Francisco, Berkeley, and Oakland will be on hand to toast the resplendent couple and thank them for their many civic contributions over the past quarter century." Of course, she did not go through with it. But she mentally clipped and pasted the imaginary announcement into the wedding album she had never made.

≥❦≤

After the ceremonial kiss, the "aisle" regrouped to surround Paul and Joanie, who performed the first waltz as the guests rose from their tables to join the admiring circle. Then the open space quickly filled with bobbing, gyrating guests. Jaleh grabbed Fran's hand and warbled, "Dance, Gramma!" At last free to be a three-year-old, Jaleh (barefoot again) bounced, jumped and twirled while a doting Fran kept up as best she could.

When everyone had worked up a good sweat, the twinkling cleric again took the microphone to start the toasts. Wait persons appeared with trays of champagne flutes, which they distributed throughout the room. On behalf of his mother, wife, and daughter, Joanie's brother Marty stepped up and welcomed Paul into their family, commenting on Paul's musical talents as an asset they would be sure to tap for future events. Then Doreen spoke for the far-flung Chatsworths.

"In case you're wondering, I'm Paul's *older* sister. We Chatsworths are a big, unruly bunch, but I think Joanie has proved she can handle us! Some of us couldn't be here tonight—our brother in prison—just kidding, he's really in Hong Kong on business and couldn't get back in time. We lost our mother last year, but she adored Joanie and really looked forward to this day. I know her spirit is with us. My youngest is taking finals at UCLA and if he doesn't pass, he won't be showing his face here any time soon!

"But a family isn't just legal kin. People can become family by playing a positive role in our lives, however that might happen. When my first husband re-married, his second wife and I hit it off really well. She helped raise my kids and we cooked a lot of turkey dinners together at their house or mine. She started calling me her 'wife-in-law' and I've always considered that title to be an honor. Well, Joanie, now you have a wife-in-law, too!" Doreen pointed at Fran. "Fran's got to be the best sport in the world, coming here to wish you well. You welcomed her girls into your life and we want you to know our family appreciates that. I'm proud to be part of a family that's big enough for the both of you!"

Scattered applause erupted as heads turned toward a stunned and blushing Fran. Many there had not known who she was and they craned to view the "wife-in-law." *Good grief,* Fran thought. She'd hoped to duck out as soon as these toasts were done and now she was the center of attention. She wondered what Joanie was thinking. Joanie smiled and nodded in her direction, so Fran nodded back, cementing their odd bond. Champagne flutes tipped all around and the combo broke into the Beatles' "When I'm 64."

An anxious Claire rushed over to Fran, gave her a hug and whispered, "You OK, Mom? How's your throat?"

"OK, but I think I'll go home soon. It's past my bedtime," Fran croaked.

Paul threw a burly arm around her shoulders, "Thanks for coming, WIL." Fran gave him a quizzical smile. "That stands for Wife-In-Law," he explained.

Now Fran wished she had gotten them a better present. They didn't really need anything, so she'd just put a Pier 1 Gift Certificate inside a card and let them do their own shopping. As the music, dancing, drinking, and chatter continued, Fran slipped out to the restroom and then out a side door into the cool Bay breeze. Inhaling the eucalyptus vapors, she felt the skewer poking at her insides and decided to drive herself to the nearest Emergency Room, lest she meet an ignominious end. She imagined the obituary headline, "Woman skewered by hors d'oeuvre at ex-husband's wedding." She wanted to live to dance at Jaleh's wedding, or civil union, or swearing-in, or whatever.

After a two-hour wait in a crowded ER, she paid the $50 co-payment to the cashier and explained to a very young-looking resident that she had a wooden shish kabob skewer stuck in her throat. He peered down her mouth with a lighted scope, then sent her to radiology. Glancing at her x-ray twenty minutes later, he informed her there was nothing in her throat. She had probably swallowed the broken bit of skewer and it scratched her esophagus on the way down. "You're feeling irritation from the abrasion, not the stick itself."

"But does wood show up on an x-ray?" she asked.

"There would be a little shadow, and some displacement of your throat lining. Believe me, there's nothing in there. Whatever you swallowed should just pass through your intestines without any problem. If your throat hurts, take Tylenol. Of course," he added, a bit too off-handedly, Fran thought, "if you develop severe pain, vomiting, or bleeding, come back in."

Fran nodded, uncertain whether "Thank you" was the appropriate response. She slid wearily off the exam table and drove home where she fell into a fitful sleep featuring random, disjointed dreams. Some may, or may not, have involved lacy wedding gowns and trailing veils, butter-cream frosted five-tiered cakes topped with plastic bride-and-groom figurines, champagne fountains, orchid corsages, or Jordan almonds in little fluted foil cups. She simply did not recall. The thud of the six-pound Sunday *Chronicle* landing under her window the next morning drove any lingering dream fragments from her consciousness. She made no effort to retrieve them, the meaningless firing of neurons and synapses, by-products of her brain repairing itself during sleep. Laying down new memories, discarding old ones. Instead, she used her renovated gray matter to read the entire Sunday paper and complete all four crossword puzzles, the cryptogram and the acrostic in bed while sipping jasmine tea. Her throat felt just fine.

ANNA STEEGMANN

THE MOTHER-IN-LAW

She looked like a chubby, lovely old lady. Her hair was straight, short, and very white, and her skin had the texture of parchment paper, a testament to having spent too many summers at the Jersey shore. She reminded me of a lizard. The small eyes. The wrinkled skin. Zofia moved around, wobbling from side to side with the help of a cane or walker. She lived alone in a house in a small village near Lumberland in Upstate New York. There was not much to the village of Glen Spey: a gas station, two churches, a Byzantine Catholic and a Ukrainian Orthodox church, a cemetery, a camp for terminally ill children, and a recently revitalized Ukrainian Cultural Center. Anyone would feel sorry for an eighty-four-year-old woman living alone in an isolated place covered with snow for many months. Except me, her daughter-in-law.

Zofia lost her husband of fifty-two years in a car accident. She was in the hospital for several months afterward, recuperating from her injuries. Arthritic pain, a new hip, and the extra pounds on a small frame made it difficult and painful to get around. For years, she had not used the beautiful upstairs, airy master bedroom with its shiny parquet floor, large windows, balcony, and panoramic view of the lake. She preferred holding court in the dark family room with the large TV and its seventy-five channels and made the sofa her bed. Upstairs, the sunny living room was preserved like a museum display, with sixties furniture and garish wallpaper. Even when her husband was still alive, they never used the living room, not even on Christmas or Thanksgiving. Life was spent in the dark basement. The couple had different tastes in TV shows and always had two television sets blaring simultaneously.

Initially, Zofia seemed to like me. I was from Germany, where the family had ended up at the end of World War II as displaced persons from the Soviet Union. She had fond memories of her neighbors in the small village on Lake Constance, her husband wheeling and dealing on the black market. Roman had warned me: "My mother is weird, especially around food. She cooks enormous amounts of food, and you'll have to eat a lot, or she'll be very unhappy. She'll try to force us to take home shopping bags full of Ukrainian dishes, and the garlic smell will waft through the entire train."

I wasn't worried. I had a good appetite. Everyone's parents were weird.

I could understand her hoarding food. The pantry held at least twenty-five mason jars of dill pickles, several restaurant-size cans of cooking oil, numerous bags of flour, sugar, and rice, and twenty gallons of bottled water, even though there was a well on the property. There were countless cans of beans and red beets, two refrigerators, and an industrial-size freezer. My parents and grandparents had experienced hunger during World War II. They, too, never felt safe unless they had enormous provisions stockpiled.

Zofia snuck butter, heavy cream, and whole milk into the dishes and claimed she had not used any fat. "Why does it matter to you? A little butter never hurt anyone," she'd say.

"Oh yes, it does. My father died at fifty-one. Heart disease, obesity, and diabetes run in my family. I want to live a healthy life. Besides, my cholesterol is high. I'm at risk for heart problems myself," I would answer.

"Just take Lipitor. Then you can eat all the meat and butter you want and keep your cholesterol low."

Who was I to tell Zofia she was wrong? At eighty-four, she was a showpiece for the advances of modern medicine: a triple bypass, pacemaker, hip replacement, and lower cholesterol than me.

If we arrived at 11 a.m., Zofia had set the table hours before and anxiously awaited our arrival. She did not want to hear about our trip, work, or life in the big city. She was only interested in feeding us. First, we had to have mushroom soup, which was lukewarm because she couldn't bear to wait for the few minutes of delay caused by heating it. The bowls were enormous and easily held three portions. Zofia filled them to the brim and added a gigantic portion of egg noodles. The hot broth gave off a wonderful aroma and tasted divine, but when she offered seconds, we declined. We knew there was more to come. Zofia was disappointed when things were not going according to plan. She never sat down and ate with us. Instead, she hovered by the stove, moved back and forth between the stove and the Formica kitchen table, served us, and watched intensely how much we consumed and whether our faces revealed approval. The next course was often roast pork with a mountain of garlic, onions, mashed potatoes, and no greens. I learned that vegetables and leafy salad were unimportant, insubstantial fare, something one could do without. The most one could hope for was a cucumber salad, lyrically named miseria.

Christmas Eve was especially traumatic. The traditional Ukrainian meal for December 24th included twelve courses but had been downgraded to six. Since the old country lacked refrigeration, only foods that grew in the wintertime and those that could be preserved were served. I liked the Christmas borscht and uschka, small dumplings stuffed with mushrooms. But I absolutely hated the pièce de résistance, Carp Jewish style, horrible tasting fish in aspic, followed by starch, starch, and more starch. I asked if we could divert from the tradition by adding a vegetable dish since all the carb loading made me feel bloated and constipated. No exception could be made, not for me. If Roman asked for a salad, he would get it.

Every visit followed the same pattern. We were fed as soon as we arrived, and then she asked us, "When are you leaving?"

"We just arrived, and you need to know when we're returning? What for?" That's what I assumed, my husband said. Not understanding Ukrainian, I had learned to read their body language and tone of voice. I imagined their conversations. Once in a while, Roman translated the key components.

"Take more meat. Have more potatoes. You're not eating anything."

"Leave me alone, Ma. I've had enough. It's 11 a.m., and I'm not even hungry yet."

"Take some babka. Drink some more orange juice. Have some Linzer tarts."

Zofia hobbled to the sideboard and picked up a gigantic plate with pastries, small tarts filled with rose jam, poppyseed cake, honey cake, and other sweet and yummy delicacies. Just as she was about to place an assortment on the dessert plate for her beloved son, he turned to her with an evil expression. "Stop stuffing me with food, Ma."

Zofia retreated, pouting, obviously hurt. A few minutes later, she made an attempt to reconcile and asked him to bring his dirty laundry so that she could wash and iron his shirts. She had rightfully assumed that I wasn't the kind of wife who was ironing her husband's shirts. "Ma, I'm an adult," he screamed. "I served in the army. I can press my own damn shirts."

It was downhill from then on. She offered babka, a big pot of borscht, holubchi (stuffed cabbage), jars of dill pickles, chicken paprika, and pierogies to take home. The tension in the small kitchen intensified to an unbearable level. Roman's face turned red; his blood pressure rose to a dangerous level.

Zofia, almost hyperventilating, looked as if she was going to have a panic attack. After taking a big breath, she asked us when we wanted to eat dinner.

"Ma, I don't want to think about dinner. I just ate lunch. I am full. I don't ever want to eat again. I have food at home. My fridge is full. I am not starving. Do I look as if I had just been liberated from Auschwitz? I'm ten pounds overweight, for Christ's sake. There are supermarkets and plenty of restaurants in New York City. We even get invited to dinner parties."

His voice changed from angry to ice cold, hard, and mean. I watched in awe as he rose abruptly from the table, almost knocking over his glass of juice, and stormed outside to sit by the lake alone. I was left with his mother in the kitchen. She was distressed, hobbling back and forth, peeking through the window to see where he had gone.

Then she tried to enlist me. "What's wrong with him? He's so ungrateful. Let's pack the food you'll take home." Her face lit up when I told her we'd take the poppyseed cake, babka, and chicken home. Maybe now that I had become an ally in feeding her son, she would like me a little more. Maybe she would even like me for being friendly, remembering her birthday, being a good eater, and making Roman happy. Did her precious son not look much better, happier, even younger than a few years ago?

No time to rejoice. Roman and I were together for seven years before we got married. Zofia must have hoped that I was a fling, a temporary distraction, and that he would settle down with a nice Ukrainian doctor one of these days. As an immigrant, she was immensely proud that both sons had become lawyers. She was unaware or perhaps did not care that he was unhappy in his profession, unhappy in his first marriage. He had taken a liking to cocaine to help him cope with the problems in his life. She might have blamed me for the breakup of his marriage, although his first wife had fallen in love with another man. The couple stayed together for almost ten years, afraid to let their Ukrainian parents know that they wanted to divorce. Unable to comprehend this, I asked him, "What century do you live in?"

Zofia's attitude towards me frequently turned hostile. She might have blamed me, a school counselor, for his new, much less prestigious profession when he left law to become a public school teacher. She could no longer brag about him and his achievements. In her Ukrainian community, no one got divorced. I might have represented the shame this caused her family. People gossiped.

When we visited, Zofia spoke Ukrainian ninety percent of the time, even though she had been in the US since 1949 and could communicate in English. I wished Roman would stand up for me or insist that we speak English. He didn't. This was a source of hurt feelings and bickering between us for years. I observed how Zofia acted with her other daughter-in-law, also named Anna. At least Anna belonged to the right ethnic group and spoke Ukrainian fluently. But she was not good enough for Zofia's precious oldest son, just as I was not good enough for the precious younger son. When Zofia called our home, she hung up immediately, unwilling to talk with me when I told her Roman wasn't home. She never thanked me for the birthday and Christmas cards or the gifts we sent.

During one visit, Zofia placed a plate with apple slices before him. When I wanted to take a slice, she took the plate away and told me in English: "This is for Roman. He likes apples." Roman, who had watched his mother treat me with disdain for years, finally came to my rescue and yelled at her. "You don't treat my wife like that. What's wrong with you?"

Once, she called, crying hysterically. I could not make out what she was saying and felt that someone must have died. I urged Roman to call his mother when he came home from work. His brother had brought his Jack Russell terrier to an animal shelter near Princeton, where he lived. His daughter was in the hospital being treated for anorexia, and he and his wife felt they could no longer care for the dog. Zofia was fond of little Max. She had him for three summers when the family was traveling and was distraught that they didn't ask her to take him. "You have to get the dog from the shelter and bring him to your mother," I said. Roman did not want to, but I pounded away at him until he gave in and called his brother for the shelter's address. His brother urged him to leave the dog in the shelter. Again, I insisted that he should bring the dog to his mother.

"I did not want to get Max, but Anna made me do it," he told his mother. Roman had taken the day off from work, rented a car, and drove to Princeton and then Upstate to deliver the dog. He did not get home until 10 p.m.

Zofia was overjoyed. The next time she called, she did not ask to speak to her son. She said in more or less perfect English, "Thank you for making Roman bring Max to me. And thank you for your birthday cards and your Christmas cards. I know you wrote them. I know you bought the gifts, wrapped them, and sent them. It was always you. Thank you from the bottom of my heart."

And just like that, her tense and often hostile attitude melted. Maybe she would become the kind mother-in-law I had always wanted. Maybe from now on, I would be looking forward to our visits.

DEBORAH STRAW

A REVELATION

Mom, i.e., mom-in-law,
was the smallest, palest old lady I've ever known.
Psychologically, she was in her own world.
What did she love? Ice cream, a yellow cat,
rummage sales, TV quiz shows.
Catholic church rituals.
She had few friends; she had little to say.
She did not initiate.

Despite reading only romance novels,
how to raise children manuals and *Redbook*,
she could answer all the questions on Jeopardy.

After her husband died,
we visited her twice a year.
As soon as we arrived, we would all hug;
she'd tell us to relax.
Then she had nothing to say,
no stories to tell.

For dinner, she made lasagna, over-cooked asparagus,
A sweet one-crusted apple pie.
We ate at 5.
As we traditionally eat at six or seven,
we were not hungry.
But who are kids to question their parents' rituals,
repeated year after year,
all in the name of comfort?

We had little else to do while there:
maybe a rummage sale, a garage sale, grocery shopping.
My husband would change the car's tires in season.
Maybe dinner in a cozy ethnic restaurant,
eating, of course, at 5,
or, if we procrastinated, at 5:30.

We tried to engage her
But we had dissimilar TV preferences,
we read different books,
we did not talk politics.

Finally when we visited her,
we decided to see if she could play Scrabble.
Wordsmiths that we are, we love the game.

We believed it would fill up an hour or two of silence.

She might look forward to an activity during our visit.

We started.

We played each weekend we visited her.

We played once, twice.
And she began winning.

She would think for a long time between moves,
then she would pounce.
She used good words—importune, vague, leopard, waning.
We were surprised, heartened, really.
In the end, she became as sharp as a hawk with unsuspecting prey,
careful and cunning.

She was competitive, gleeful,
holding her tiles tightly
trying to beat her two literary, more educated guests.

She won, she won again, then she won again.
We thought maybe winning
would encourage her to stretch herself in other ways.
It didn't happen, but at least she had Scrabble.

With Scrabble,
she hit her stride.
She found her voice on the tiles of a piece of cardboard,
on a small Formica table,
in a small kitchen in suburban New Jersey
every spring and every fall
for 10 years.

She found her voice.

Lose
Step
Whole

TERRI WATROUS BERRY

DEAR SHANNON

The sun is falling. The lake has turned into a mirror. I am alone. It is what I've sometimes longed for, the solitude for which I often yearned, never believing for a moment it would ever come to pass. Justin is spending his first night away from me, but of course he doesn't know that. Justin doesn't know a goddamn thing anymore.

Oh, where does the soul of a soul mate go? Soul mate. I chuckle at the very word. Combine hearty lust with someone you can trust, a hefty board of blessings, a certain amount of inertia, and everyone oohs and ahhs over your good fortune at having found your *soul mate*. Bodies mate, not souls, and soul mates roll right on into oblivion like everyone else you've ever loved or ever will. Just like every family, for they too pass. Understand. They too pass. . . . Cattails creep closer to the shore, winter crouches unseen in the details. A nice line to leave in this, the last entry of my last journal. I did come here to write, didn't I? But there would be more time, there would always be more time. Now, where was I?

Oh yes, families. Looking back over fifty years I see families waving dumbly from the albums. Yes, I have had my share of families, all permanent thought I, all dissipated in the afterwinds of desertion, whims and death. Life travels in just one gear and it is *DRIVE*. Justin and I were my last family. Just me and Justin, and this cat I suppose. Poor old cat, you've never found a welcome in *my* lap, have you? Get down, Mouser. Justin is the one who wanted you, who took care of you. His Mouser boy, his fine furry friend. Well, he's gone you poor dumb creature—*gone*—and by tomorrow morning I will be too. You'll be a mouser then, won't you? You damn sure better be a mouser then. . . .

I swore I'd never spend a night alone here in this house in the middle of these woods, miles away from any other dwelling, yet here I am. Given my decision though, what is there for me to fear now? The doors I always insisted Justin check remain unlocked. Come in, you anonymous bastards, if you are out there sneaking around in my darkness, come on in! I no longer fear the possibility of you, I am no longer afraid.

Terrified I was as a child. A child risen in a bowl of welcome yet mute with fear in the comfort of my own little bed. Where did that come from? How did my parents manage to convince me of the fairy tale goodness of the world yet of its looming black danger as well? Show me a woman raised in the fifties and I'll show you a Mickey Mouse mess. Eight years younger than me, Justin just didn't get it. Born. And now dead. Justin is dead. I shall retrieve another bottle of our wine. . . .

It is quite night now. Stars peek in at me here in the sunroom. What do you call a sunroom after the sun goes down? Useless. Dark. A darkroom? No, a darkroom has a purpose, a reason to be. Shannon will arrive tomorrow. She wants me to return with her to Chicago. Now, what good would that do her or me? She has a family of her own now, she has Rick and the kids. But Justin is the only father she remembers having. And I her only mother. No, I can't think about that. Shannon is strong. And she still lives in that beautiful bubble of belief the family she's created will last forever. Just as I believed, dear daughter, in blind youth. Evidence to the contrary mocks us always, but neither can we conceive our own mortality. Still, even looking back at families that no longer exist, this one—this one now—will be ours forever. Ha! Get down, Mouser. Oh, alright, I'll feed you. I need another pill anyway. . . .

Let's see, oh yes, Shannon. Whatever good I had to lend my child's life was a long time ago. I wonder what memories of her childhood—of me—she'll carry with her to the end? To Shannon's end, as inconceivable to me as little Joey's was before he drowned, before that scorching summer day lit a flame capable of burning down the family Danny and I built together. No! I won't think about that now. . . .

I prefer to think, for the very last time, about the night my first family began to disappear. I was fifteen, all of life's lovely possibilities budding before me, surprising as my own changing body. That evening I watched *Where The Boys*

Are on a small TV in my room. What fun there was to be had in the wide wonderful world, in just a few short years when I would be old enough! Life was warm and I couldn't wait to embrace it. The future grinned.

When the movie ended I washed my hair and rinsed it in beer, which an article in *Ingenue Magazine* guaranteed would produce a movie star shine. Later on, when I found my father lying on the living room couch, which was odd, I leaned over him, asked if my hair smelled like beer, and explained why. He told me I had wasted a good beer, but he was smiling. The next morning brought my mother's screams and an ambulance and by that night I no longer cared where the boys were, only that my daddy was dead. I don't think I ever told Shannon about that night. So many things I never told you, dear Shannon, things that might help you understand my decision now. Yes, I shall leave this, my journal, for you. . . .

The moon's O face looks surprised, as if hit full force in the stomach of a body it does not possess. My gait weaves. A fine wine. Pretty pills. Justin, my darling, these pills didn't help you much, but beneath this little bottle's cap tonight they sing to me of sweet salvation. This night. This silent night. . . .

Call me weak, Shannon, damn me for my weakness, a coward's way out, your mother is a coward, believe that if it helps, just know it's not because I didn't love you enough. Did I love you enough? Does anyone ever love anyone enough? Enough to last when they are gone? Justin and I used to muse about that when the fact one of us would die first was just an interesting abstraction. *I'll always be with you,* Justin would say, *when I'm gone you will still feel my presence.* I can't feel you, Justin. . . .

He saved my life back then, Shannon. Did you know? Probably not. You don't remember life without Justin. It occurs to me now you lost *three* families before you were old enough to realize you were in them. Grandma's death brought an end to one for both of us. Oh, sure, Uncle Chet's still alive, but only on a Christmas card once a year from Texas. I gained a house when our mother died but lost a brother, unable to accept she left it only to me, to Grandma a matter of who needed it most, but to Chet a matter of negation.

You and I were part of another family by then, part of your father's until he left, too. Funny how you can lose a whole family when just one person doesn't want you anymore. Oh, at first you still belong, at first everyone falls all over themselves making sure you know you will *always* belong. It is surprising, really, how quickly that passes. No matter how many years you've been the dutiful daughter-in-law, smiling sister-in-law, adoring aunt, no matter how many holidays you've spent drying dishes amidst a cacophony of confusion and complaints, it is astounding how fast that passes after Sonny takes a hike. Give it a year. When membership dues come due again, it's *your* card that won't be stamped.

Sorry, Justin. Please don't think I mean that would happen now with your family. They accepted me and Shannon right from the start, and you never understood why I wouldn't get closer to them but this is why. When I married Danny, I believed his family would be mine forever. Danny showed me how short forever can sometimes be. You are not here, Justin, I am not talking to you.

But you know, don't you. You know how you can lose families. You pulled a Danny too, didn't you, when you met me. I was adrift in a sea of sorrow. Joey's death. Danny's desertion a year later. Danny who I've forgiven, who I forgave a long time ago. We all do what we have to just to survive such grief as losing Joey, although I'll never understand him then distancing himself from Shannon.

You rescued us both, Justin, but my gratitude is tempered by what you lost because of it, because of us, real closeness with your kids, your parents lost them too, and your brothers and sisters. Lynn did everything she could to sever those ties after you left her, and Lynn succeeded. Your kids are grown now, the longstanding damage only theirs to assess. But I am sorry, Lynn. Wherever you are tonight, even though you'll never know it, I am truly sorry.

What's this? Confession time? Do I fear retribution in the void to which I soon go? I don't even believe in that shit. Where's that damn cat? He's been out an awful long time. The moon is hanging itself in the distant trees, soon it will drop out of sight. Man in the moon, bad moon rising, full moon, harvest moon, last moon. Better go see about that animal. Raccoons raid us regularly here. Sometimes they have rabies. . . .

He's here with me now, Shannon, curled up at my feet the way he used to curl up at Justin's. More wine anyone? Allow me to pour. Deep red kind wine. Pretty glass of wine, good thing you are here, warm on my lips as these tears. Everything is so vivid tonight, Shannon. The light from the lamp glares upon this page, a little white sea on which my words float, little boats, a fleet of defeat, yearning to be understood, to be heard. But by whom. . . .

Dear Shannon, what more can I tell you? That your heart will break but it will mend again. The mother of your childhood is already gone, along with the rest. Still, there is so much loveliness in life, Shannon, don't waste it, don't get mired down in your grief and waste it. Ha! Do as I say not as I do, huh? I'm just so tired, Shannon. So tired of picking up the pieces, so tired of pieces being lost. Sure, I could go on, but for what? To grieve again? Grief is a long and painful process, my girl, with no discernible end. Would you sentence me to suffer it again to spare you? To spare you. . . .

The bottle is empty. Pink and purple wound the sky where the sun once again will rise. I am very sleepy. Mouser will follow me to our—to my—bed. It's just me and Mouser now.

BRIAN DALDORPH

FATHER-IN-LAW

He wants to die in his own house, that's the last thing he wants: "I've lived here fifty years. Why shouldn't I die here too?"

I try to explain again that at hospice he can get everything he needs, medications to ease his pain and 24/7 medical care.

"*This* is my home. Right here. I don't want to die in hospital. What if some nurse doesn't like me and the last thing I see in the world is her mean face?"

Just that I'm not sure I can do this, help my father-in-law to die the death he wants. I don't know if I have the strength. I must admit that I want him shipped off to hospice where I'll visit him, the good daughter-in-law, leave when it's time to go. I shouldn't call myself the "good daughter-in-law" because I didn't bring him the grandchildren he wanted.

My father-in-law takes my hand and says: "I really appreciate what you're doing for me, Amanda. I really appreciate it."

"That's OK, Bob. You know I love to help."

I don't tell him that I have to do this because his only child, Brent, is married to his law office.

I closed my antique shop to be here, with a sign on the door: "Closed Until Further Notice Due to Illness in the Family." I'll lose half my customers but who cares about that? Just so long as my father-in-law gets his dying wish.

Jesus Christ, here I am wanting my father-in-law to die, just so that I can get this whole thing over with.

MORROW DOWDLE

WHO KEEPS THE PHONE ON ALL NIGHT FOR YOU?

Some people have a parent, a best friend.
A god they neglect then call on in their moment of duress.

You have none of that. You have a mother-in-law.

She matters too much or matters not at all. You say you see light in
everyone,
then act as if her bulb's burned out. She puts in her two cents, and
a bank vault
falls on you. She makes holiday fruitcake, and you want to hurl it
out the window on the highway home. Once, you have.

You reject her apology when she feeds your children Chef
Boyardee, buys them
more plastic crap. You want her to accept the pills by your sink, the women
you once loved. You demand she eat her son's sins, remake him
in your image. You rage when she fails to deliver.

You are a sack that she cannot fill. Not doughnuts on Sunday afternoons.
Not getting you into grad school. Not living rent-free in her house.
Not underwear and socks and tea and chocolate. Not airplane tickets
to come home for Christmas. Not cleaning your dirty dishes and linens.

Yet you trust her the way you trust your car to run, not knowing
when your last oil change was. You trust her the way you trust
the sink compactor to grind the large chunks you shove into it.
She, too, swallows your garbage.

Unlike your mother, she won't walk away. You can try to stem her tide,
but she comes anyway. And comes. Comes for the babies and the marriage
in collapse. Comes for pneumonia and overdose. She carries her children
and your children in her maw. The mythical she-wolf.

She is teaching you the limits of love, which is to say none so far.
It's a foreign taste, when love was an exclusive nightclub, a blind date
who never showed up. When love was one tab of ecstasy that cost
a life's savings. Then disintegrated in the gut.

You see her, or you see through her, imperfect and holy spirit that she is.
If you can find your way, maybe you can find your way to her.
Maybe you can stop refracting her, dissecting her colors.
Let her be whole. Let her be light.

PAULA RUDNICK

MOTHER-IN-LAW

My mother-in-law asked our nanny
if she could borrow her panties.
She was sitting at the breakfast table
when she spied them drying on the rack.
They looked so fresh and clean.
She hadn't put enough inside her suitcase
when she packed it in Palm Beach.

She liked this girl,
who spoke good English,
not like the last one
with the gold tooth and the attitude.
My mother-in-law could buy her own of course,
if her stomach weren't so full of gas
it hurt to try things on.

She told the nanny of her constipation
as she watched her rinse the dishes,
confidentially, like they'd been friends for years.
She used to have such lovely things—
fur-lined coats and diamond pendants,
everything stolen while she was at the club
winning first prize in the cha-cha contest.

Her husband was a handsome man,
a good provider, but he drank too much
which made him say mean things.
She had a closet full of clothes then,
nothing with elastic waists.
Now she has to stay close to the bathroom
on account of the suppositories.

Enjoy life while you can,
she told the nanny
as the girl wiped down the kitchen sink,
and got up from the breakfast table
panties clutched against her ample bosom,
cotton jersey trophy
from her latest competition.

SHOPPING FOR A SON-IN-LAW

Thumping melons in organic produce
or shuffling shoeless in the line at TSA,
I scan for men to be my daughter's husband.
I'm not looking for Adonis,
the kind who needs a mirror's confirmation.
Not somebody Olympic-fit,
my baby's skin too fair for outdoor sports.
Someone with a ready smile.
Her wit can bite, not that she's dark
just that her heart's too kind
to ignore the world's injustice.

She says she's done with dating apps,
pointless virtual encounters
that climax in a coffee date
where checks are split.
Easier to leave one's fate to chance
than waste a weekend swiping right
through seas of Mr. Wrongs.
She'd be annoyed if she found out
I trawl for suitors as I drop zucchini in a plastic bag
or extricate 4 ounces of conditioner
from my rolling carry-on.

Technology has fooled a generation into thinking
they can cut through slog of courtship straight to love
but some things don't outgrow old-fashioned ways,
and while I don't presume to know what's best for her,
the guy in the plaid shirt who's asked the butcher
how to cook a piece of halibut is cute
and doesn't have a wedding ring.
I think I'll tell him it's great baked
with parsley butter in a Pyrex dish
the way I taught my daughter who's a virtuoso in the kitchen
and just happens to be single.

LIZ LYDIC

ALL WE WON'T KNOW

Nathan's mother was stalling returning his call. He'd left three messages this week, and Kitty listened to each several times, in her usual place at the dining room table.

"Can you call me, Mom? Please? I want to talk about this Grandfather trip. I'm at work until 5:30 p.m. my time. Love you."

In one hand, Kitty pressed the sideways triangle on the answering machine to restart the message, while tapping the edge of a plane ticket on the table with the other. She had planned to send it in the mail today to her ex-daughter-in-law, in whose name it was. *Sara Gwendolyn Butler*, mother of Kitty's grandbaby boys; the next generation's first woman to take the Butler name; the wife Kitty's son had left.

"I just don't understand," was all Kitty could say to Nathan a year ago. Nathan sighed a lot, and responded methodically, in four-word sentences. "You don't have to." "I've already explained it." "Things change, you know." Kitty didn't know.

"Where did we go wrong?" she'd asked her husband, Carter James, who simply shook his head. Kitty tried her best friend, who was also her cousin. "Where did I go wrong?" she asked, pushing her pinky into the inside of the phone cord's curlicue coil until it swelled.

Odessa sighed on the other end. "It's not you, baby. These kids are just so . . . " But she'd never completed the sentence.

Once Kitty got the gumption to tell her father about Nathan's divorce, she received her answer. "Don't blame yourself," Buddy Stetson had told her, then patted her hand. "There's a lot we won't know in life."

Now Buddy was in hospice, his formerly hulking body depleted to a skeleton with skin. His main doctor predicted two more weeks of "significant life." When Kitty made the call to her only child to tell him of Buddy's fate, her voice had shaken badly. "I'm okay, baby," she'd told Nathan. "I'll be OK.

I just . . . oh, baby, I'm so glad Daddy knew you before all this." She halfway meant the cancer and halfway meant Nathan's divorce.

At 5:30 p.m. Nathan's time, Kitty reached her son. Nathan offered soothing statements to Kitty, memories from times when everyone was younger, specifics of Buddy's influence on Nathan's life. The words helped Kitty's breath return to normal, but she focused on her main purpose for the call. "You'll be here, of course. I've got the tickets for you all. The boys need to see Buddy one last time. It'll be so good for him."

"Yes, Mom. I'll be there. The boys and I will be there."

"And Sara? Sara can come too, right? Daddy loved—Daddy just loves Sara. Do you remember the Trivial Pursuit night—"

"Mom! Sara? Wait. Did you already call her?" Nathan's voice was tinny, far away.

Kitty twisted her yellow gold wedding ring counterclockwise with her left thumb, until a place on her palm cramped. "Well, no, baby. I figured you could just ask her. Maybe at one of your hand-offs? For the boys? Just let her know the dates, but the ticket is already bought, since I know her birthday and all."

"Mom!"

Kitty sat back at Nathan's sharpness. She rose. The phone cord stretched to its maximum length, as she crossed the kitchen and began rinsing dishes.

"Mom, please turn off the water."

Kitty looked out the kitchen window. The tomatoes needed weeding and the birdfeeder was running low. She'd ask Carter James if some time in the backyard would be nice for them later. She could make iced tea. If he said no, she'd go out there anyway, grabbing the dried vines and pulling them up roughly until her shoulders ached, hoping Carter James would see her work and change his mind about joining her.

"Mom, are you there?"

"Yeah, baby. Sorry." Kitty turned off the water, and began scrubbing the sink with a yellow and green sponge from the windowsill. It was browning, and she'd need to buy a new one. She ought to start a list for the market.

"Mom, you remember I told you about Jamie?"

At the name, Kitty stopped scrubbing, as if she'd been caught doing something wrong. She had no picture of Jamie, but in her mind, Kitty had conjured Nathan's new girlfriend as a young, sharp-haircutted brunette with thick eyeliner, melancholy and rigid. "Right, yes, how's she doing?"

"Mom. She's fine. She's great, actually. Things are going really well." Kitty heard Nathan's voice brighten, and now he sounded closer to his phone receiver than he had before.

"Great, honey!" Kitty's voice was high and too loud. "Send me a picture, will you?"

"Sure, Mom," Nathan said. "Or . . . actually, I'd like to bring her home to meet Grandfather."

Kitty heard Nathan swallow to control tears.

Good he's crying, she thought. *Good he feels something about Daddy.* Her own breath caught.

"Baby, I'm glad things are going nicely between you all. But I'm not really sure how it would go, Jamie and Sara here. I don't know if—"

"No, Mom," Nathan interrupted. "Only Jamie. Sara wouldn't be there."

Kitty's neck ached from the strain of holding the phone receiver between her ear and shoulder. "Ow!" she said.

"Mom! What?"

"It's nothing, baby." Kitty switched the phone to the other side and went back to the dining room table. The plane ticket was to the right of a printout from Dr. Acker, recommending exercises Kitty could do for the pain in her right elbow. Kitty looked at the third picture where a lone peach-colored cartoon arm held a blue ball that was to be rotated inward eight to ten times. "I don't know if I mentioned, but I have some great news on that physical therapy appointment," she said, picking up the flyer.

"Mom! Please. Please, don't avoid this," Nathan said. "Answer the question."

"What was it, baby?" Kitty asked, putting the paper back down. She slid the plane ticket and it caught on something sticky on the table's surface. *Sara Gwendolyn Butler* it said above the flight information.

How pretty she'd looked on her wedding day, Kitty thought. Normally reserved, Sara had handled her guests graciously and kept warm with all of Nathan's cousins, great aunts and uncles, and, of course, with Buddy. She'd held his hand as he shared advice of never going to bed mad and always saying "I love you" when parting, laws Kitty knew drove Buddy and Carol Ann's marriage for those fifty-eight years until Carol Ann's death. Sara had cried, and dabbed her eyes while embracing and thanking Buddy before being led away by Aunt Leanne.

"She's a good woman," Buddy had told Kitty the first time he met Sara;

then at that moment at the wedding; and then once more last week when he'd ask if she was coming to see him in hospice. Kitty had said she'd make sure of it, that she'd come, but didn't know if Sara's heart—already so keen to sensitivity and now further destroyed by abandonment from the men Kitty loved—would allow her to pick up a phone call from her ex-mother-in-law.

"Jesus, Mom. I asked—or actually said—I want Jamie to be there, not Sara, for Grandfather's last . . . to say good-bye to Grandfather."

Kitty pressed her pointer finger on the dining room table to collect crumbs, then flicked them to the floor. "Well, baby, I'm not sure, since Daddy never really knew this Jamie gal."

"Mom, I know. It's . . . she's not a Jamie gal, she's my girlfriend, and we care about each other a lot." He paused, and then sighed and Kitty pulled the receiver away from her ear. "I knew this would happen."

"Baby, I just don't want to upset Daddy, and I know how much he wants to see you and also the boys, and he said Sara, too."

"I get that, Mom. But what about what I want? I want Grandfather—and you, and Dad—to meet Jamie. Jamie is my life now. She never got to meet Grandfather. Sara did."

Kitty looked out the front window. The first time she met Sara, when Nathan had flown her back with him from across country where they attended graduate school together, Kitty had spied from this same place to see her son and his new girlfriend walking up the front driveway, Sara holding Nathan's forearm. Nathan looked down at her and the way their heads dipped toward one another before they pulled back in laughter was certainty to Kitty that her son had found someone who loved him. "She's right," Kitty had told him in a whisper that night while Sara was in the restroom. Nathan had looked at her puzzled. "She's right for you. And she'll do right by you."

Nathan had nodded and taken Kitty's hand to squeeze it. "Right," he'd said. "I'm so lucky."

The day was graying, and Kitty wanted to get to the leaves on the front lawn.

"Mom?"

"Yes, baby?"

"Well?"

Kitty paused and stood, the plane ticket still in her hand. "Okay, Nathan. I understand. I'd like to meet Jamie."

Nathan breathed out and his tone lightened again. "Thanks, Mom. I know it's hard, or that you don't like—"

"No, baby. It's not hard. And please don't tell me what I don't like." Kitty's own tone surprised her. Her elbow ached. "What's Jamie's last name? I'll need to call the airline. Please make it quick, I have things to do."

peplebush

VI
MELTING POTS

HEATHER TOSTESON

BLOODLINES AND BABIES

Diane

He's our first grandchild. Andy and I were so excited when we heard. We'd had our concerns about the marriage, which we did our very best to hide. It happened so fast and there was a child on her side. And Dylan, at twenty-four, was five years younger. Honestly, we expected to learn within months that they were expecting, that that was what had precipitated the visit to Asheville City Hall in September when they had only met in May. But we didn't get that call for a full twelve months. By then, we'd all come into some kind of new balance, or so Andy and I thought. Certainly the start hadn't been smooth.

No one was being invited to the wedding we were told at the time. Sparrow said she thought it was enough change for her daughter Sam just to have Dylan as part of their household. She didn't want to burden her with extra personalities. Andy and I were a little taken aback. We're mild-mannered people, so it made us wonder how Dylan had described us to her. But, like I said, we thought the marriage expedient and we thought Sparrow had a point if they had, as we assumed, another baby on the way only five months after the two of them had met.

So, we invited them all to join us up here at Thanksgiving instead. But Sparrow, who taught fifth grade, said Maryland was too long a drive for a short visit and she didn't have the time for a longer one.

Christmas, we suggested. Dylan's sister would be home from Seattle with her boyfriend, and both Andy's parents and mine would be coming over from their retirement homes. We've always been a close family. Andy and I are both only children, so it has been a joy to us that our parents have enjoyed each other so much that we've all always celebrated holidays together.

But Christmas belonged to Sparrow's family, Dylan told us. Sam had always done this. She counted on it. They couldn't change this—certainly not this year.

So Andy and I drove down to Asheville right after Christmas intending to spend three or four days with them. It was only as we pulled into Asheville that Andy told me that Dylan had called him to say he'd made a reservation for us at a motel in the middle of town. Andy said he hadn't told me because he wanted us to have a good time on the road trip and not to spend it analyzing. "Besides," he said with a smile, "I decided we could treat it as our own romantic get-away."

When we met her at last, Sparrow was polite and hospitable. She was clearly not pregnant, indeed, if anything, looked anorexic. She was wearing her spandex running gear when we arrived. She told us she was off for her run—but that she had made sure we would be well-attended in her absence, nodding at Dylan and a rather rotund and very pretty girl of six who was wearing a long pink dress and a princess tiara. On the counter, Sparrow had set out cups, a plate of ginger snaps, a bowl of orange and apple slices. Green tea was steeping.

She slid by us out the door and, with a wave, pounded off down the steep road like a super hero in hot pursuit, her long curly blonde hair spreading and coiling as she strode.

Dylan, who had been slouching against the wall, straightened and came over and gave us warm hugs. "She'll be more relaxed when she gets back," he murmured. "It's just that she wants everything to go well. She really wants you to like Sam."

"And why wouldn't we?" I asked him.

Dylan stepped back a moment to look at us, this searching expression on his face. Dylan is a wonderful surprise to us. Andy and I are attractive but not striking. Dylan, though, seems to have inherited only our best features, and we are a little awed by these unforeseen possibilities. His sister Allie, two years older, feels periodically peeved. "Beauty is as beauty does," she has warned her less ambitious brother for years. She has just joined a high pressure law practice in Seattle. Marriage, should it ever take place, obviously won't happen before she is made partner. Too distracting.

Dylan's eyes, which are the most forgiving of colors, something like sandstone, softened even more as he smiled and hugged us again. "I'm so glad you made the trip. Next time we'll have you stay with us."

"Everything in its time," Andy said.

I turned to Sam, slipping down to my knees so we would be more on the level. "Now who is this beautiful princess?" I asked her.

"I am a fairy," Sam said, "not a princess." And then a little mischievous smile crossed her face. "What story do you think I come from?"

"Peter Pan?" I asked. "Are you Tinkerbell?"

She shook her head.

"The one who turns pumpkins into coaches in Cinderella?"

"No, the one in Sleeping Beauty who gets even because she didn't get invited to the birthday party."

"Oh," I said. "Were you not invited to a birthday party?"

"No one would dare do that," Sam said seriously. "I've told everyone at school all about my powers."

Were these the powers, I wondered, that had kept us out of the wedding—for it turned out that it was only Dylan's side of the family that wasn't invited. People Sam already knew were welcome—all Sparrow's vast extended family (I believe each parent had been married three times, all the grandparents twice, with children from every union), all her colleagues from the elementary school where she taught, and, since she had grown up in the area and stayed on, friends from elementary school through college. Even Sam's paternal grandmother, one of Sam's nine grandparents (if you count all the steps). We learned this because there were wedding photos in frames on the mantel, a photo album on the coffee table, and Sam, over the next hour, walked us through the whole cast of characters.

"There's me cutting the cake. There's my daddy's mom getting the first slice," Sam said.

"And your daddy?"

"He's with God. That's what my grandma says. My mom says no one can prove any different since God is a matter of belief not science. He is where I get my fire power."

"That sounds pretty impressive," Andy said. "What do you do with it? Explode buildings or provide heat to homeless people?" Andy is an accountant but is the more fanciful of the two of us.

I just kept looking from the album back to Dylan, who shrugged and went into the kitchen and started pouring us tea.

I patted Sam on the head and went in to join him.

"It was the only time in her life Sparrow had her family's full attention," he said. "You have no idea what this meant to her. She and Sam's dad never married. She's the second child of both her parents' second marriages. She wanted Sam and her to have pride of place—just once."

"And you were just a glamorous means to this end? Would a cut-out have served as well?" I asked him bluntly. Both of us took a quick, shocked breath. I can't remember ever speaking to my charming, amenable son so harshly.

"I knew I had to explain it in person," Dylan said.

"You can't." Then I reached out and touched him gently. "And you don't need to. We love you and trust you—and we want you to be happy."

And to be part of our life, I told Andy as we drove away a day and a half later, during which time somehow Sparrow had scheduled the three of them in for a family therapy session and a family yoga class. Dinner was gluten-free and vegan and in a restaurant downtown near our motel. "To save you the drive back and forth," Dylan told us, looking at Sparrow like she was a teleprompter.

"Why?" I asked Andy as we drove home. We had been listening to Maeve Binchy without comment for three hours at that point. "Why is he doing this to us?"

"It will be easier if you think of it as his doing something *for* them, not *against* us. I do believe he thinks nothing can change the love we feel for him or the love he feels for us," Andy said quietly, his eyes on the snow beginning to fall. "Give it all some time. She's like a mama bear with her cub. Her world as she knows it is her lair, it's where she can keep Sam safe."

Truly, I tried. But it's very strange if you have always known yourself as tolerant and welcoming to be treated like a dangerous intruder.

"I predict when they have children of their own, things will change. She'll feel more sure of Dylan, of the relationship, of Sam's well-being," Andy said, putting his wipers and lights on and moving into the slow lane.

I was surprised at the feelings that surged in me as I remembered Sam's fat little hands opening the wedding album, that smug little look on her freckled, pudgy face. Or Sparrow's practiced school teacher murmur of greeting as she rose from the table at the vegan bistro. "Mrs. Lamar, Mr. Lamar, so pleased you could join us." When she sat down again, I expected her to open a file, discuss Dylan's reading level, his social relations with his peers as I sat submissively in a chair a third my size.

Quietly, Andy and Dylan worked something out so Dylan would visit us on his lonesome twice a year. Never on holidays—and only for two nights. We paid. Dylan always spent a good third of the time fielding calls from Sparrow or Sam, always beaming at us after he said good-bye and telling us they said hello or sent their love.

I actually liked watching Dylan on the phone. More accurately, listening to him. He had, I could hear, modeled himself on Andy—that warm calm. I heard it as he listened to concerns about Sam's homework or a broken ice-maker or something one of Sparrow's myriad halfs or steps had said to send her into a trilling fury. "Have her start over from the beginning," Dylan would say about Sam and her homework frustration. "Let her reward herself with what she's already learned." "I have the repair man's number here. I can call if you want." "They were just being thoughtless, Sparrow. They don't realize how sensitive you are. But you have your own home now. Nothing they say or do can take that away."

It made perfect sense to me when Dylan called in May and asked Andy and me if we would help him finance a degree in social work with a focus on clinical counseling. We said yes immediately.

He applied and was admitted to an MSW program designed for working students and arranged things with the restaurant where he waited to take one day off a week. He said Sparrow was relieved he was going to join the professional class, that his future earnings and improved social status would make up for the time it would require. He and Sam were bracketing off father-daughter time on weekend mornings—so Sparrow could sleep in.

He told us this as we all sat in our kitchen over coffee in late July. We were celebrating his twenty-fifth birthday a few weeks late. His grandparents were all coming within the hour, and we were going out to brunch so he could catch an afternoon flight back to Charlotte—in time to have a late dinner with Sparrow and Sam at home in Asheville.

"You haven't even had time to unpack," my mother said a little petulantly at brunch.

"He's a family man now," my father said with a proud, understanding smile.

Dutifully Dylan handed around photos of him with Sparrow in her running lycra clinging to one arm and Sam, now dressed as a ninja, hanging from the other. He didn't show the wedding photos.

"We'll see you all at Christmas this year," Andy's mom said innocently. "We can't wait to meet them, honey." Somehow this whole interchange felt worse than what it had felt like last December when we visited. Dylan, to his credit, blushed.

"It may be a little longer," he said. "I'll come for sure somewhere in there. But the Christmas period is reserved for Sparrow's family."

Two years in a row, we all understood, would make it a tradition. His grandmothers each looked at the photos he'd given them and dutifully handed them to their husbands. The clatter of cutlery on the surrounding tables was brisk.

In the silence which went on so long no one could break it, I realized we had created this little bubble, Andy and I and our parents and our two children. No one had meant to. It was just such a joy for all of us no longer to be so triangulated. There is such a thing as too much attention, as any beloved only child knows. And we came from two generations worth. Perhaps Dylan and Alison had felt smothered by all that adult attention all those years. Maybe they felt exposed rather than embraced by it. Maybe that was why Dylan had agreed to realize Sparrow's vision of what rightful family was—and what his part in it was (tallest, dead center, both backdrop and material support).

To be honest, whenever Dylan called that fall I expected him to tell us that he and Sparrow were divorcing. *Anticipated* his telling us.

Instead he was filled with stories about his friends in the social work class. There were several guys in their early thirties, all with young families, and women making mid or late career changes (he was the youngest in the group by four or five years). He was finding his counseling class, especially the unit on family therapy, fascinating.

"Do you think our family would have met the definition of enmeshed, Mom?" he asked me once.

"You tell me," I said, having a vision of minnows thrashing brilliant silver in a net.

"Sparrow says so."

"And how would you describe her family?"

"She says she doesn't have one, just a jigsaw puzzle with lots of missing pieces."

"I asked what *you* see, Dylan." I sounded like the high school English teacher I am.

"Everything," he said with a loud, genuine laugh. "Chaos, hardening of the boundaries, enmeshment, neglect, over-protectiveness, substance abuse, in-breeding, delinquency, emotional cut-off. It's great. I'm acing all my papers. I've started sharing my riches with my classmates. We're thinking of making them up into a book of case studies: 'What You're Liable to Find in Any Appalachian Hollow.'"

"Sparrow approves?"

"Of course. She wants to out them all for being the neglectful, self-absorbed, fatalistic SOBs they are and ever will be."

I couldn't read his tone at all. I think at that moment I began to be afraid for him in a way I had not been before.

❧❦❧

Sparrow

Sam's as close to a clone of her daddy as any child can be—boy or girl. Round-cheeked, pig-eyed, and bull-headed. Hair so pale it looks like rice noodles. To die for in a uniform—although hers are restricted to brownie uniforms and school T-shirts, ninja costumes and princess gowns. Possessiveness I expect she inherited from both of us. In spades.

All of which goes to say, there's no chance I'm going to be forgetting the lessons I learned when the three of us failed to make a family.

"How can you generalize from there?" Dylan asks me. "You were sixteen when you met, pregnant when you split, two days post-partum when he died. You never married. Never even lived together for more than two months at a stretch."

"Death intervened—but that doesn't mean I didn't see where it was all leading."

"And where *was* that exactly?" Dylan asked. A year ago, he would have asked anxiously. He wasn't at the eye-rolling stage—yet. But coming closer than I liked. "Was he looking around at other women? Spending too much time at work? At his parents? With his buddies? Or were you afraid he was spending too much time at your belly listening for Sam, leaving you on the outside yet again?"

Dylan's tone was actually kind, as were his eyes. They were large, accepting, a strange tawny color that went well with his red hair, which he used to pull back into a ponytail but which now, cut short for grad school, curled boyishly over his still boyish face, emphasizing our age difference. There were dark circles under his eyes, testimony to how much he was trying to cover all the bases—work, school, time with Sam, time with me, preparing for the coming baby.

Dylan was turning his wedding ring (silver and turquoise, I insisted we save gold for our tenth anniversary) round and round his finger, a gesture he would need to relinquish when he became a counselor: it made him seem nervous and indecisive. Which he isn't. He's actually pretty determined. Strategic. He was choosing his words now.

"I am going to do my utmost to make a strong resilient family with you, Sparrow. I'm doing so now. But it needs two of us. Patterns are inherited, adopted, fallen into—but they are all learned, Sparrow. They're not hard wired. They are not biblical curses. Fate. Your mom and dad are both in solid marriages now, so are your grandparents. *They* learned."

"You're wrong," I said. "They just wore out."

He laughed. It was such a simple, genuine sound it made my eyes water. One of the most amazing things about Dylan is that just being myself I can make him laugh. Not at or with me—just because I am who I am and he likes that.

I wish I could say he felt the same for Sam. But he doesn't. Whether that is a can't or a won't, I'm not sure. It is just a fact. One that Sam wakes with every day. We're over a year into this marriage, and it hasn't really changed. It's not like Dylan isn't trying. It's not like Sam is helping. I can *see* that. Whatever it might look like, I'm not blaming anyone—including myself. And if there weren't another baby on the way, I might have just accepted it. Up until now Sam has had no basis of comparison. The constant pausing and reorienting, that deep patience-inducing breath are just what Dylan *is* to Sam. But bring his own baby into the picture and she'll feel the difference. I can swear to it, many times over. If there was one thing I promised myself, it was this was never going to happen to my little girl. She was never going to feel second best.

Dylan's righter than he thinks. I never married Sam Jewell because I *did* feel he loved the Army and his own mama most and that his attention was destined to slipslide to someone in the Army, someone who could look at him with his mama's eyes.

But I always had a *hope*, you know, a hope that we might pull it off. In the letters he sent me from Afghanistan, he was sounding the same way. He was imagining himself as a family man. Of course, he was imagining a son—and I didn't let him know different. I've never regretted that the news never reached him, although I do think, if he'd seen Sam, he'd have been just as proud to have a daughter. It wasn't true of his mother. She came to the apartment the day after I brought Sam home, and she looked at her and just started crying.

"My *boy*," she sobbed. "Where is my beautiful boy?" She's a big woman, Darla Jewell, and she just rocked back and forth on the sofa wanting some man to make it right. Sam got real quiet, so did I, and we rocked in our rocking chair as the sun slipped behind the trees, sending this sad cold glow, like a shawl, over Darla's shoulders.

Darla has come round somewhat since Sam is really all she has left of her husband or son. I take Sam over there once or twice a month, and she and Darla go to the cemetery, and Darla tells her what a brave man her daddy was, how he killed those wicked Taliban and Al Qaeda Muslims to keep her safe, how if he were alive now the two of them would be going hunting or fishing. Then they go back to the house and eat Snickers cheesecake and look through Darla's picture albums and open up the box with the Purple Heart and Bronze Star. Your name would have been Jewell, Darla will tell her—more often now that I've married Dylan and changed our names to his. (I was just so tired of Crabtree. I liked the idea that people here would have to wait a minute or two before they placed me.)

When Sam comes back from her afternoons with Darla are the worst evenings for Dylan. Sam goads him. "What kind of star do you have, Dylan?"

"There are different ways to be brave, Sam," he answers. "One of them is conscientious objection."

"Conceited is having a swelled head," Sam says.

"*Conscience*, Sam. Knowing right from wrong." And then Dylan pauses, kicking himself.

"My dad was right," Sam says, her voice wobbling a little.

Dead right, I think. Sam went into the Army because he couldn't find a job and he wouldn't have graduated high school except for the special football dispensation. But he was a good soldier, a good follower, and, in time, a good leader. He made sergeant. He died pulling two of his men out of enemy fire.

"Bath time," I say as Sam opens her mouth tonight to prod Dylan again. Her dad liked to pick at people too. I'd forgotten.

"I haven't had dessert," she complains.

"Snickers cheesecake doesn't count?" I ask, hugging her firmly as I march her down the hall. I can *hear* Dylan exhale.

I ache inside. My beloved child truly isn't lovable. And then I rage—

at Sam for her six year old's peevishness, her crazy belief that she can do anything and still be loved, at Darla who doesn't give a shit if Sam and Dylan and I connect, at Dylan because he can't see, will never see, what I see in Sam, at me for having gotten us all into this mess. The only one I leave out, because at present he's incapable of speaking in his own defense, is this son who has five months more of amnesty.

"Ouch," Sam cries. "You're rubbing my skin off, Mom." I stop scrubbing off the chocolate on the back of her neck, under her chin. I stand up.

Did we fall into this pattern, like Dylan says? Was it forced upon us? It feels like a rack to me—and I'm strung on it. The only time I feel I'm free is when I'm running. I can't imagine what's going to happen when I stop.

❧

Dylan

I've always adhered to the water theory of life. It seeks the vast. It follows the path of least resistance. It isn't afraid to change forms. Lately, though, I've become more aware of the other ten percent of our make up. How fucking ungiving it is.

My mother didn't take the news lying down. I don't know why she should really, except that she and my dad have never chosen to be a rock when I've been pressed up against a hard place. Honestly, I haven't tested it much. There was the marijuana smoking at senior prom—but no one got busted. And having to repeat a math course my freshman year in college at their expense (and to my sister Allie's scorn). But other than that, they've not had much of a challenge from me. I've always been there at holidays, worked summers to help with college expenses, found a job within a month of graduating. Not, at least, until this marriage. What has hurt most is seeing their hopefulness dissolve.

They had been so positive when I told them about the pregnancy.

"What good news, Dylan. You'll be a great dad. We can't wait to hold the little one in our arms. Our first grandchild," my mom crooned.

"Timing's a little off," my dad agreed, "but stick with the program. You'll be solid as a provider once you get the degree. We'll do whatever is needed to see you through."

Honestly, I don't know how it happened. Sparrow has been on the pill since our first scare. Besides, she been running so much she's not having periods. But something messed up. Maybe it was, like she said, because of the antibiotic she took for that sinus infection at Christmas. The timing isn't good. She's due around our second anniversary. I'll have just started the second year of my program.

I know Sparrow wants me to say I'll drop out for a year, but I'm not going to. I've told her that the first semester, when I'm commuting down to Chapel Hill for two days of classes, I'll do all the daytime babycare on the five days I'm in town—and night feedings after I get off my evening shift at the restaurant. Second semester, when I have the full-time internship, I'll do everything needed when I get home in the evening. We can supplement for anything else.

It's not just that I don't want to waste my parent's money, I want this degree. I want to go out and fix problems for people who have it worse than me. Shell-shocked guys who see a flash of white fabric turning the corner and are on their knees, aiming. Men the age of our fathers with Korsakoff's who keep reliving their first day in Nam rather than the first time they got laid.

Sparrow's voice when I told her was as hard as my mom's. "That takes care of the new one, catch as catch can. But what about Sam?"

I was amazed at what came to mind. "Maybe she'll learn to read." "Maybe she could pick up after herself." "Maybe she will discover some inner resources."

Instead, I said, "Sam's routines aren't going to change. She will still be going to the same school. She'll have her days with her Grandma Jewell. Maybe she'd like to have a few more. Or have play dates with some of her cousins. Who knows, Sparrow, maybe having a baby brother or sister is just what she needs." *They take orders better than parents*, I thought but had the grace (at least that day) not to say.

The truth is the ice we're skating on is thawing fast, cracking like thrown plates.

"Honestly," Sparrow said, "you haven't given her a thought." She looked at her protruding stomach with the all-consuming sorrow of a child. She turns thirty tomorrow. It isn't, hasn't been from the first breath she drew, the world she wanted for herself. And there's not a goddamn thing in the world I can do to change that.

"My parents could come down for a couple of weeks to help," I said. "They could do it more than once. They both have a lot of vacation time. My mom says she can't imagine a better use of it."

"You talked to them about it before mentioning it to me?" Sparrow said.

Oh, at that moment, her eyes were as small as Sam's, but they weren't even mammalian. She twisted her head back and forth like the bird she's named for, but I'd make her for a larger, darker family. Crow.

"I didn't want you disappointed," I said. "I didn't know if they would be open to it." And why should they be? I thought, remembering their only visit here, how Sparrow wouldn't even let them stay in the house. *Her* house.

The truth is, there are times I imagine getting my MSW and applying for a divorce and custody the very next day. For a child whose sex its mother won't even divulge to me. Either way, it's going to be too much competition for Sam.

"Clearly, we're going to need back-up, Sparrow. We need a village, like everyone else," I told her. "Would you rather ask your mom or your step-mom to come help?"

This was a low blow. Sparrow's two sisters from her mom's first marriage were pregnant (older) and divorcing (younger), her full brother had just lost his job and had moved back in with his father (with three kids and a wife with a drinking problem), her full sister in full throttle sibling rivalry had announced her own pregnancy a month after Sparrow and had promptly snapped up promises of assistance from both grandmothers. I could go on, but it would be more of the same. Besides, everyone, quite reasonably, expects reciprocity—and how many kids can I babysit for and still study?

"My parents don't require a lot of attention," I said. "My dad cooks, my mom *likes* to clean. They're excited as can be at the idea of their first grandchild." I shouldn't have said it, of course. And since I did, I should have stopped there, but couldn't, of course.

"And I, Sparrow, am very excited about the idea of *my* first child."

"Which makes me *what*, Dylan. Surrogate? Breed cow?"

"Let it go, Sparrow. For god's sake, let it go. You have this really kind, undemanding family ready to take you in, ready to love you if you'd let it happen, ready to help us be the parents we both want to be. Why do you insist on having all of us living under your own shadow as if it's not you causing it by standing in the way of the sun?"

"Sam," Sparrow said, pushing herself off the sofa. She was dangerously thin, brittle. The obstetrician had told her she needed to put on at least thirty pounds, fifteen for herself and fifteen for the baby. After her first trimester and the extra weight she lost with morning, noon, and night sickness, the obstetrician had upped the needed weight gain to forty. It was *my* baby she was starving.

"Would you mind watching Sam while I go out for a walk? I have to clear my head." Sparrow looked at me, her large blue eyes welling. "I have to get a handle on this."

I stood at the picture window watching her start down the hill, shoulders curling around the load inside her that she couldn't carry and couldn't release. She looked older than my own grandmothers. Like someone in a story Sam would tell—about a beautiful queen changed by a wicked fairy's curse into a frail old witch.

"What do you mean you don't want us to come, Dylan?" My mom's voice echoed with Sparrow's slow steps. "It's our first grandchild. The first *great*-grandchild on both sides. What you're asking is unnatural. We are not giving up so easily, believe me."

I don't know where I went. It was like time slowed, spread out. Every slow step Sparrow took was like a year together. I began to count them. At three I was breathless, damned as Sisyphus.

Sam's hand on my arm brought me out of myself.

"If I went to stay with Grandma Jewell, would you and mom stop fighting? Would there be room for this new baby?" she asked quietly.

There was something in Sam's voice, something clear and sad and generous and yearning and true and tough, really tough, the way we can be at that age before we've decided what will break us. I understood she would do that for us, and for her own, her very own.

"It's going to be a boy," she said. "I heard mom telling Aunt Kathy that Grandma Darla would be mad to hear it. Grandma Darla wanted me to be a boy, you know."

"I don't," I told her, putting my arm around her. "I want you to be exactly who you are, Sam." And, for the first time, I meant it. I could tell she could feel that too—and it surprised her, and she moved into the space that had mysteriously opened up for her.

"Your mom, does she want a girl or a boy?" Then I turned and grinned at Sam. "It doesn't matter. She doesn't have to choose, does she?"

"No, she has me and Alex, right."

"Alex?"

"Yes. It's like Sam. Girls and boys can both use it. That way we don't have to let Mom know we know what's coming—but we can plan."

I smiled. We stood there, the two of us, holding hands, breathing quietly, looking out at the empty street, the daffodils lilting in the spring breeze, the scatter of dogwood petals on the overgrown lawn, feeling the world curving protectively around us, so much space, so much space.

I wondered if something similar was happening to Sparrow out there alone in the big world, remembering what I had said, feeling it stretching her from the inside out, just like our quickening son, and feeling the fragrant and welcoming spring air folding around her body, so small, so wanted, so worn—making it all more than bearable, making it buoyant, home for herself and everything in her.

grief
choose
chosen
relax

SHOSHAUNA SHY

NEW SISTERS

They are the fur slippers sought first
Step out of bed, the bookends to your
Holiday weekends, the buffer from
The wider world's clang and concrete,
This bevy of women raised
With your husband.
Wearing cabled cardigans and full-
Throated laughter, they hold your
Babies, play with your children,
Attend their graduations, beam
Through their weddings, comprise
The bedrock, the infrastructure
For your decades of marriage.

THANKS GIVING

I wanted feasts for my kids
after my own skate-scabbed
years steered by parents
for whom holidays draped
heavy with obligation,
kitchen chores detestable
with their tyranny of preparation—
and so went ignored.

But luck in marriage grants me
pie crusts stenciled with stars;
nephews arm-wrestling; a toddler
crawling lap-to-lap; Rummy 500
where Great-Grandma wins.
There's a niece performing carols
on her violin; a quartet of sisters
tackling dirty dishes; hand-whipped
mashed potatoes, cranberries
sauced with limes; a dressing that
takes more than three days to make.
Here are elders at the table combing
over confessions: a son's abrupt job
loss; an elective Cesarean; a whiskeyed
bankruptcy; an uncle's separation
from his honeymoon bride.
Every Easter the circle widens

as more babies arrive, as middle-agers
spread, and into teens their children
lengthen. And it contracts, too, when
a patriarch dies, fickle in-laws get
outlawed, graduates leave for Memphis.

My husband slices oranges onto
a berry platter; I butter frittata pans,
fold egg whites into batter; recount
that year our teenaged son
managed to devour
two entire pumpkin pies.

ROBIN LANEHURST

HOW TO BE A STEPMOTHER
TO YOUR DEAD BEST FRIEND'S DAUGHTERS

First, I love you.

First, you know how to do this.

First, everything you know about being a mother is wrong.

Sit with this, if you can find a moment. Close the door to the bedroom you will soon share with my husband, even if you are alone in the house, alone with the echoes of our children hurtling down the stairs, stomping about in the attic, screaming and swinging and leaping from branches in the backyard. The echoes make it hard to hear, I know. The echoes remind you of all that you've learned in the past three decades about being a mother. We learned how to be mothers together. We will unlearn how to be mothers together.

Listen: you may not hear my voice saying these words, you may not be able to imagine my voice ever saying words like these, words in this order, words in this tone, words at this volume. This may not be my voice at all, but one you've invented and attributed to my ghost. I understand. I understand how the dead fall silent, how I must allow myself to be reinvented, over and over and over again, used for someone else's purposes. Take a lesson from that— this is what it means to be a stepmother.

Hold on to your belief in life after death, in grace and faith alone, even though my husband and my daughters believe there is no heaven and no God to have sent me there. Hold on to my uncertainty of what came next, my ambiguity between an Episcopalian childhood and a microbiology degree. Keep me in your prayers, whisper the pleas you might have cried had I allowed you at my bedside when I took my final breaths. Forgive me my shame; I wanted to die alone.

Display photos of the two of us on the walls, on the fridge: the one of us laughing in sagging camp chairs, the one of us raising our beers at a concert in the park, the one of us splayed across your couch with all five of our combined children sitting at our feet. We looked more like sisters as time ironed out our differences and wrinkles softened the contrasts in our bone structure and white hairs melted my blonde-brown and your red-brown into the same dull grey.

When one of my daughters calls you and asks about a strange boil on her thigh or a white curl amongst her pubic hair or discharge from her breast, give her the same factual and normalizing answer I would have given, blush the same way I would have blushed. When she stops calling for advice, clench the disappointment and rejection around your heart the same way I would have clenched.

Do not tell my daughters each time you reach for your phone to call me before remembering that I am dead (when the ending of a book makes you cry, when you can't decide which color to paint your living room, when you find the cutest throw pillow at IKEA, when you perfect your sourdough recipe, when you run into a friend about whom we used to gossip). Bear it. Hold your heartbreak close.

When you marry my husband on a hilltop in rural Illinois, hold his hand and say *forever* the same way I said *forever* thirty years ago in the dry desert air of El Paso. Do not invite my daughters.

Do not tell my daughters the way you fell in love with my husband. Do not reveal the way your feelings grew over margaritas, dinners cooked, hands held, tears shed. Love him. It's okay to love him. It's okay to be sick over the way you love him. It's okay to be sick over being the other woman, as if I were still alive.

Do not tell my daughters everything you love about my husband. (How he smells like cigars and mowed grass and baby powder, how his nose wrinkles when he smiles, how he keeps stubbornly tying his last strands of white hair back in a ponytail, how he holds his hands behind his back when he peers at a rock or a leaf or a worm on the sidewalk, how he snaps his fingers when he's happy, how his eyes turn stormy and thick when he's sad, how he leaves little messes around the house like a rodent collecting treasures for the winter.)

Tell the story about the time your ex-husband didn't help with your birthday party, and I yelled at him, defending you in an uncharacteristically direct way. Tell the story of how we became friends, how I warned you I wasn't very good at making friends, and then spent twenty years proving myself wrong.

Do not tell the story about how I cried when my eldest daughter told me she drew a five-hour radius around our city so she could get away from me. Do not tell the stories of all the crash diets I attempted. Do not tell the story of what finally changed my mind about spanking children. Do not tell the story about how I didn't approve of my youngest daughter's engagement. Do not tell the story about the letter I received from my college boyfriend, that I read and then tore into neat squares over the trash can. Do not tell the story about how I lied that our cat peed on the new rug as justification for putting her to sleep.

Remember that these stories don't belong to you, not really. Remember that I don't belong to you, not really.

Prepare for the world to change and change and change again. You will figure it out—who you are to them—and then a baby will be born. Then your son will have a baby. Then other babies will be born. Then, you are no longer just stepmother—you are grandmother. You do not have the privilege of taking your time to figure out what that means. You do not have me to talk to about what that means. We were supposed to become grandmothers together—now you are grandmother to my grandchildren. That has been stolen from me and stolen from my daughters and stolen from their sons. Carry that burden alone. Do not let on that it is a burden.

Allow your flaws to breathe, out in the open, like wounds that need oxygen to regenerate broken skin. You have become a new mother again, you must regenerate.

Do not be opaque. Opacity is a threat. Let them see inside of you. Let them see through you.

Give all the grandchildren the same Christmas presents. My daughters will notice. They will remember how I was such a good gift giver, how I personalized everything, how every gift under the tree was perfect (until that last Christmas, three months before I died, when I gave everyone gift cards because my brain was mush, because I was about to be hospitalized and never discharged again, and they all noticed, they knew something was different and something was wrong but they never thought it meant death, just that Mom suddenly didn't care about their Christmas lists, and so that last Christmas they were angry at me, which set the bar lower for you—was that a gift to you, as well? could I have known that was a gift to you, as well?)—they will think you love them less because you don't spend as much care and time to individualize the gifts. Do not let that change your mind. Let them think you love them less. It would be worse if you showed any kind of favoritism over your son's children. It would be worse to point out that they are no one's daughters.

Don't feel ashamed when you fail to comprehend the complex constellation of love and envy and resentment and disconnection and friendship and joy between my daughters and my husband and my ghost. I know you thought you understood, I know you thought it would be easy to integrate into our solar system, to nudge moons and planets ever so slightly, but after death there is no gravity, and tiny shifts cause large ripples, and it's not the same as it was. My influence is heavy, but transparent; you never know when you'll bump into me.

Decide for yourself what to do with the holes I've left behind: which to fill in with soil or cement, which edges you will skirt to avoid scuffing your shoes, which to climb into and make into a home for yourself.

Let my daughters love you. They do love you. They find you easy to love. They love you and they wish you didn't exist. Accept their love and accept their rejection. They want your heart. They owe you nothing. They do not know what to do with your heart. They owe you less than nothing. Give it to them anyway.

Give my eldest your trust and respect. Treat her as your equal, even when you know full well she is not. Do not take her independence personally; do not take her distance as rejection. Offer her book recommendations instead of advice. Do not argue with her about her politics. She can be uncomfortable with closeness—you must invite her in, you must hold her in your arms two more seconds than you think are necessary. Do not assume she knows how much you love her. Do not assume she thinks you even like her at all. Assume she thinks you hate being around her, you find her annoying, a know-it-all, snobby, standoffish, argumentative, rigid. Of course, she is those things. Of course, you must never tell her this. Give her what she wants the most—your approval, your belief in her rightness, your value in her intelligence, your acceptance. Tell her things that will make her cry, if only so she can fold herself into your arms, tether her heart to yours for a moment, turn off her own engine and idle in peace before the engine of her mind clicks on again and she scampers away.

Give my youngest daughter your praise and approval. Allow her to be better than you. Allow her to be better than you at everything. She will make her own choices, loudly, boldly—you cannot tell her she is wrong, you cannot tell her she is making a mistake, you must help her pick up the pieces when the consequences arrive exactly as you predicted, you must maintain her innocence and lambast her enemies. When she is harsh, you must be soft. When she is rough, you must be sensitive. When she is loud, you must be quiet.

Remember that none of this has anything to do with you. Remember that all of this has everything to do with you. This is calculus you will never comprehend. You teach middle school math. This is above your pay grade.

If you follow my recipe for the pork marinade, add an extra half cup of orange juice. If you follow my recipe for the tomato sauce, add the sugar a teaspoon at a time to taste. If you double my mudslides recipe, add a few extra squeezes of chocolate syrup. If you follow my recipe for queso, add an onion. If you follow my recipe for beef and potato burritos, buy tortillas from that place on Cherokee Street. If you follow my recipe for dump cake, use crushed pineapple instead of diced.

Do not frame things to yourself or to anyone else as, "This is what my best friend would have wanted." You have no way of really knowing what I would have wanted in this situation. You may have some idea of what I would have wanted in this situation. My daughters are desperate to know what I would have wanted. Unless it will comfort them to know, unless you truly know the answer will bring them comfort, will make things smoother between you, will make things less complicated, do not tell them. Keep my secrets in death the way you kept them in life.

Do not forget who you are. Do not hide who you are. Run your home the way you've always run it. Run your home the way you did when no one was watching, when I was the only one with whom you discussed morning habits and journal entries and chore calendars and spring planting and Christmas shopping and deep cleaning and to-do lists. My husband won't notice any of it, he won't ever know all of the things he never had to notice. My daughters will notice all of it—how you store your rice and what kind of dish detergent you use and how often you rearrange the bookshelves and where you keep your spare change and the size of your coffee pot and what kind of soda you keep stocked in the fridge and whether you write your to-do lists in a notebook or on sticky notes or the backs of receipts or a magnetic notepad on the fridge.

Accept that your questions are unanswerable. Accept that your questions are only answerable by one person—your dead best friend.

Try angling your bed against the north window of your bedroom. Try arranging the candlesticks on the dining table in a different order. Try painting your living room blue. Try painting your living room yellow. Try painting your living room green. Try the carpet from the entryway in the kitchen. Try painting your front door purple. Try planting daffodils along the sidewalk. Try planting wildflowers for the butterflies. Try hanging a hummingbird feeder in your kitchen window. None of it will make your house into their home. Try anyway.

When you are planting seeds in your garden, dig your fingers deep into the wet earth, and imaging you are touching my fingers, reaching up. You know I was not buried in your garden—you know I was not buried at all—but this is the closest you will ever feel to me, touching the broken-down pieces of dead things that are feeding new life.

release
grief
grief
release

ACKNOWLEDGMENTS

A small portion of Deborah Barrett's "The First Meeting" first appeared in her poem of the same name in her chapbook *The Desert Speaks to the Dreamer* (Finishing Line Press, 2019).

Paul Hostovsky previously published "Scrabble with Amber" in *Hurt Into Beauty* (Future Cycle Press, 2012); "The New Criticism" in *Is That What That Is* (Future Cycle Press, 2017); and "Cinders" in *Late for the Gratitude Meeting* (Kelsay Books, 2019).

Peter Schmitt's "Lonely Hearts" originally appeared in *Goodbye, Apostrophe* (Regal House Publishing).

Heather Tosteson first published "Bloodlines & Babies" in her collection *Germs of Truth* (Wising Up Press, 2013).

Images by Heather Tosteson.

Wanted

CONTRIBUTORS

Lenore Balliro has published her poetry in a number of literary journals, including previous Wising Up anthologies, *Atlanta Review, the minnesota review, The Comstock Review, Patterson Review,* and others. She is a former recipient of the Rhode Island State Council on the Arts Award for Poetry and the Gloucester (MA) Writers' Center Award for flash fiction.

Deborah Barrett (Burch-Lavis) is a professor of the practice of writing at Rice University in Houston. She teaches graduate courses in creative writing and literature and has been chosen as a contributor at several writing conferences, including five times at Bread Loaf. She has published creative nonfiction essays and a chapbook of poetry, *The Desert Speaks to the Dreamer (2019).*

Terri Watrous Berry is a Michigan septuagenarian whose work has appeared nationally in anthologies, journals, magazines and newspapers, and whose prose has received awards from venues as diverse as The Hemingway Days Festival and the Des Plaines/Park Ridge NOW Feminist Writers Competition, as well as from The Amelia Islander Literary Competition and The Tallahassee Writers Association.

Janie Braverman is a poet, memoirist, and collage maker. Her work, including excerpts from her experimental memoir manuscript, has appeared in *Persimmon Tree, Diary Poems, The RavensPerch, Medical Literary Messenger, Poetry in Public* (Iowa City UNESCO City of Literature), *The Baltimore Review, Steam Ticket, Desert Voices, Pinyon, Poetica, Colorado Lawyer,* and elsewhere. She lives in Colorado.

Courtney J. Cornelius is a writer, journalist and editor based in Northern Virginia. Her prose has appeared in *The Washington Post's* "Life Is Short—Autobiography as Haiku" column and the literary magazine *Borrowed Solace;.* She is a regular contributor of feature articles for *Hopkinton Independent* newspaper. Courtney most enjoys exploring human emotion and behavior through creative nonfiction.

Brian Daldorph teaches at the University of Kansas and Dare Center for people experiencing homelessness. His most recent books are *Kansas Poems* (Meadowlark Press, 2021) and *Words Is a Powerful Thing: Twenty Years Teaching Creative Writing at Douglas County Jail* (University of Kansas Press, 2021). He edits *Coal City Review.*

Ed Davis has published stories, essays, and poems in journals such as: *The Write Launch, The Plenitudes, Hawaii Pacific Review* and *Slippery Elm.* His latest novel, *The Psalms of Israel Jones* (West Virginia University Press, 2014), won the Hackney Award for an unpublished novel in 2010. His full-length poetry collection is *Time of the Light* (Main Street Rag Press, 2013).

Elinor Davis was born in Iowa and led a peripatetic early life. After finishing a sociology degree and realizing she had no marketable skills, she became a nurse, just in case writing short stories didn't pay the bills. Based in Northern California, she is a healthcare writer/editor. Her fiction and nonfiction have appeared in numerous U.S. and international publications.

Morrow Dowdle has poetry published in numerous journals and nominated for the Pushcart Prize and Best of the Net. They edit poetry for *Sunspot Literary Journal* and run "Weave & Spin," a performance series featuring traditionally marginalized voices. They teach creative writing to incarcerated folk and facilitate workshops on healing trauma with poetry. They live in Hillsborough, NC.

Tarri Driver studied art and psychology before earning a master's degree in education. She then worked with young people for a decade as a board-certified, registered art therapist and licensed professional counselor. Since leaving the mental health field, she has written and illustrated two children's books. This is her first published work for adults.

Terri Elders, LCSW, a lifelong writer and editor, has contributed to nearly 150 anthologies, including three previous Wising Up Anthologies: *Surprised by Joy, Goodness,* and *Flip Sides.* After working all over the world with the Peace Corps, and then retiring with her late husband to Northeast Washington State, ten years ago Terri returned to her native Southern California.

Sherryl Engstrom of Lake Geneva, WI, is a writing coach and retired adjunct professor. She has an essay in the *Jane Addams Peace Collection* at Swarthmore College and a story in *The Willow Review* at College of Lake County, IL. Her current project is a play based on her parents' WW II correspondence. This is her third piece for Wising Up Press.

Louis Faber's work has previously appeared in *Cantos, Big Wing Review, Pensive, Arena Magazine* (Australia), *Atlanta Review, Flora Fiction, Alchemy Spoon* (U.K.), *Driech* (Scotland), *Exquisite Corpse, Rattle, Orchards Poetry Journal, Midnight Mind, Pearl, Midstream, European Judaism, The South Carolina Review* and *Worcester Review*, among many others, and has been nominated for a Pushcart Prize.

Eric Greinke has been active on the international literary scene since the early seventies. He is the author of several books. His poems and essays have been published in hundreds of magazines including *The American Journal of Poetry, Gargoyle, The New York Quarterly, Poetry Pacific* and *Rosebud*. He is a contributing writer for the *Schuylkill Valley Journal* of Philadelphia.

Paul Hostovsky's poems have won a Pushcart Prize, two Best of the Net Awards, the FutureCycle Poetry Book Prize, *The Comstock Review's* Muriel Craft Bailey Award, and five poetry chapbook contests. He has been featured on Poetry Daily, Verse Daily, The Writer's Almanac, and the Best American Poetry blog. His latest book of poems is *Pitching for the Apostates* (Kelsay, 2023).

Rachael Jones is a public health professional from East Tennessee where she champions food safety and indoor air quality, and enjoys spending her free time in nature with her fiancé. This is her first publication, and she looks forward to spending more time writing in the future.

Louise Kantro, retired teacher and cat-lover, plays bridge and volunteers as a CASA (Court Appointed Special Advocate for foster children). She has published poetry and prose in such journals as *Quercus Review, Cloudbank, the new renaissance, The Chariton Review, South Loop Review, Monterey Poetry Review,* and *Caesura*. Her latest project is scanning family photos that span more than a century.

Diane Kendig's latest books are *Woman with a Fan* and *Prison Terms,* and she co-edited the anthology, *In the Company of Russell Atkins.* Her poems appear in *New Verse News, Hobo Camp,* and *The Broken City,* among others. Kendig led a prison writing workshop for eighteen years, and now curates the Cuyahoga County Public Library's weblog, *Read + Write.*

Katie Kent lives in the UK with her wife, cat, and dog. Her fiction has been published in *Youth Imagination, Breath and Shadow* and *Northern Gravy,* and a number of anthologies. She won second place in *Writing Magazine*'s 2022 "Love Story" and 2023 "Age" competitions. Her non-fiction is published in *You & Me Magazine, Ailment,* and *OC87 Recovery Diaries.*

Helga Kidder lives in the Tennessee hills with her husband. Her poems have recently been accepted by *Persimmon Tree, Orbis, Poetry South* and others. She has five collections of poetry, *Learning Curve, Loving the Dead* (winner of the Blue Light Press Book Award 2020), *Blackberry Winter, Luckier than the Stars,* and *Wild Plums.*

Paul Lamb lives near Kansas City but escapes to his Ozark cabin whenever he gets the chance. His stories have appeared in dozens of literary magazines, and his two novels, *One-Match Fire* and *Parent Imperfect* are published by Blue Cedar Press. He rarely strays far from his laptop.

Robin Lanehurst writes from Portland, OR where she lives with her wife and their preschooler. Her work has appeared in *Psychology Today, Counseling Today, Motherwell, Literary Mama,* and *PDX Parent.* She was a finalist for the 2023 Fishtrap Fellowship and the 2021 Pen Parentis Fellowship for New Parents. A teaching artist for Portland's Writers in the Schools program, she is a graduate of The Attic Institute's Creative Nonfiction Studio.

Zoë Losada is a college counselor living and working in South Florida. Although her writing mostly consists of recommendation letters for seniors applying to college and emails to students, parents, and colleagues, she enjoyed contributing to several Wising Up Press anthologies. She has lived in Venezuela, Costa Rica, and Italy and is married with two grown children and a grandson.

Liz Lydic is a mom, writer, and local government employee in the Los Angeles area. She also does theater stuff.

Michele Markarian is a fiction writer and playwright living in Cambridge, MA. Her work has appeared in numerous places, including *Bridge Eight, The Furious Gazelle, Daily Science Fiction, Roi Faineant and Yuzu Press*, and in six anthologies by Wising Up Press. A collection of her plays, *The Unborn Children of America and Other Family Procedures*, is available on Amazon.

Felicia Mitchell is author of *A Mother Speaks, A Daughter Listens: Journeying Together Through Dementia* (Wising Up Press). Other poetry collections include *Waltzing with Horses* (Press 53). Poems recently anthologized are in *The Southern Poetry Anthology, Volume IX: Virginia* (Texas Tech Press) and *Writing the Land: Virginia* (NatureCulture). Mitchell, retired from teaching, makes her home in the Virginia mountains.

Angela Page is a writer, producer, and author. Her films are featured on the Shorts TV channel, and Indiepix. Published books include *Matched in Heaven, Suddenly Single Sylvia* and *There's a Dead Girl in My Yard*. Her essays have appeared in the *HuffPost, Next Avenue, Business Insider* and *The Independent*. She divides her time between South Florida and Los Angeles.

Dorothy Oliver Pirovano began chronicling her family life as a columnist, writer and editor at a suburban Chicago daily newspaper, accumulating hundreds of bylines before moving to a career in public relations. Retirement led to memoir writing, capturing the humor and chaos of her past and present. Her memoirs were published in the *Goodness* and *The Kindness of Strangers* Wising Up Press anthologies.

Felicia Rose has published in various anthologies and journals including *The Westchester Review, The Lavender Review, The Dandelion Review, Mr. Beller's Neighborhood, Mother Earth News, Poetica Magazine, The Sun, The Helicon West Anthology,* and *Soul, Sand & Sky: Stories and Poems of the Great Outdoors*. She lives in an uncool neighborhood in Brooklyn.

Paula Rudnick is a former TV producer. Her poems have been published in *Halfway Down the Stairs, LA Jewish Journal* and *Kosmos Quarterly,* as well as in anthologies by Darkhouse Books, Truth Serum Press and Constellations. Her first solo collection, *Now is Not a Good Time*, was released in 2022. Paula has two grown daughters and lives in Los Angeles.

Peter Schmitt is the author of six collections of poems, most recently *Goodbye, Apostrophe* (Regal House). He also edited, and wrote the introduction for his late father's *Pan Am Ferry Tales: A World War II Aviation Memoir* (McFarland).

Mary-Frances Schneider, PhD, a clinical psychologist focused on family life and writing as a therapeutic intervention, has been published in *American Psychologist, Counseling Psychology*, and *Journal of Individual Psychology*. She authored the *Children's Apperceptive Storytelling Test* and two award-winning screenplays: *Saving Grace* and *The Summer She Turned Zero*. She produces *Telling Stories@Oil Lamp Theater*. Her blended family lives in Chicago.

Sherry Shahan is a teal-haired septuagenarian who writes in a laid-back California beach town. Her short stories and personal essays live in *ZYZZYVA, Exposition Review, Memoir Magazine, Confrontation, Progenitor, Hippocampus* and elsewhere. She holds an MFA from Vermont College of Fine Arts and is currently nominated for The Pushcart Prize in Poetry.

Shoshauna Shy has poetry included in anthologies by Marion Street Press, Random House, Midmarch Arts Press, Grayson Books, Ragged Sky, and Dos Gatos Press. She is the author of five collections, and the two most recent ones titled *What the Postcard Didn't Say* and *The Splash of Easy Laughter* won Outstanding Achievement Poetry Awards from the Wisconsin Library Association.

Anna Steegmann, a native of Germany, is a bilingual writer based in New York City. She has taught writing at the City College of New York, published essays, poetry, short stories, and journalistic articles, and is a staff writer for the *New York City Jazz Record*.

Deborah Straw is a writer and retired English instructor at several area colleges. Her two book titles are *Natural Wonders of the Florida Keys* and *The Healthy Pet Manual: A Guide to the Prevention and Treatment of Cancer.* Straw lives in Burlington, VT with her husband, a dog, and a cat.

Sue Brannan Walker is professor emerita at the University of South Alabama (Mobile) where she taught for thirty-five years. She is the editor/publisher of Negative Capability Press. She will be admitted to the 2025 Alabama Writers Hall of Fame and has been inducted into the 2024 College of Education, University of Alabama Hall of Fame. She has published numerous critical articles, poetry, and essays and twenty plus books.

Tiffany Washington is a high school English teacher, mother of four, lesbian, poet, and writer. Her works have appeared in a number of print and online publications, including *Rumble fish Quarterly*, *The Raven Review*, *Torrid Literature Journal*, *Night Picnic*, and most recently *CT Literary Anthology*.

EDITORS/PUBLISHERS

HEATHER TOSTESON is the author of seven books of fiction, poetry and non-fiction, including most recently the novel *The Philosophical Transactions of Maria van Leeuwenhoek, Antoni's Dochter*. She has worked in health communications with a focus on communication across disciplines, racism, social trust, and how belief systems develop and change. She has an MFA (UNC-Greensboro) and PhD in English and Creative Writing (Ohio University).

CHARLES BROCKETT has a PhD from UNC-Chapel Hill and is a recipient of several Fulbright and National Endowment for the Humanities awards. A retired political science professor, he has written two well-received books on Central America and numerous social science journal articles and book chapters. With Heather Tosteson, he is co-founder of Universal Table and Wising Up Press and co-editor of the Wising Up Anthologies.

Visit our website and learn about our other publications,
our readers guides, and calls for submissions.

www.universaltable.org
wisingup@universaltable.org

P.O. Box 2122
Decatur, GA 30031-2122